Praise for Book #1 of the *True Game* Series:

"At this point in time, I tend to blanch when, as in Sheri Tepper's *King's Blood Four*, something called a Gamesmaster turns up in the second paragraph. . . . However, in this case I bring this up only to encourage perseverance for readers who may have the same reaction; Tepper trancends her gamesmanship to create a solid fantasy world. . . ."

—Baird Searles
Isaac Asimov's SF Magazine

Praise for Book #2 of the *True Game* Series:

"Adjectives such as second-rate and soporific may sometimes be applied to SF sequels, but not in the case of this effort by burgeoning talent Tepper. A worthy successor to *King's Blood Four*, *Necromancer Nine* offers a full complement of psi-endowed heroes and villains in a plot that solidly stands alone. . . . This deft mix of SF and fantasy promises a very satisfying series."

—*Publishers Weekly*

Other fantasy titles available from
Ace Science Fiction and Fantasy:

The Malacia Tapestry, *Brian Aldiss*
The Face in the Frost, *John Bellairs*
The Phoenix and the Mirror, *Avram Davidson*
The King in Yellow, *Robert W. Chambers*
The Borribles Go for Broke, *Michael de Larrabeiti*
A Lost Tale, *Dale Estey*
The Broken Citadel, *Joyce Ballou Gregorian*
Songs From the Drowned Lands, *Eileen Kernaghan*
The "Fafhrd and Gray Mouser" Series, *Fritz Leiber*
The Door in the Hedge, *Robin McKinley*
Jirel of Joiry, *C. L. Moore*
The "Witch World" Series, *Andre Norton*
The Tomoe Gozen Saga, *Jessica Amanda Salmonson*
King's Blood Four, *Sheri S. Tepper*
The Devil in a Forest, *Gene Wolfe*
Daughter of Witches, *Patricia C. Wrede*
Changeling, *Roger Zelazny*

and much more!

WIZARD'S ELEVEN

SHERI S. TEPPER

ACE FANTASY BOOKS
NEW YORK

WIZARD'S ELEVEN

An Ace Fantasy Book / published by arrangement with the
author and her agent, Gloria Safier

PRINTING HISTORY
Ace Original / February 1984

ISBN: 0–441–90208–1

Ace Fantasy Books are published by The Berkley Publishing Group,
200 Madison Avenue, New York, New York 10016
PRINTED IN THE UNITED STATES OF AMERICA

THE ORDER OF DESCENT BY LINEAGE

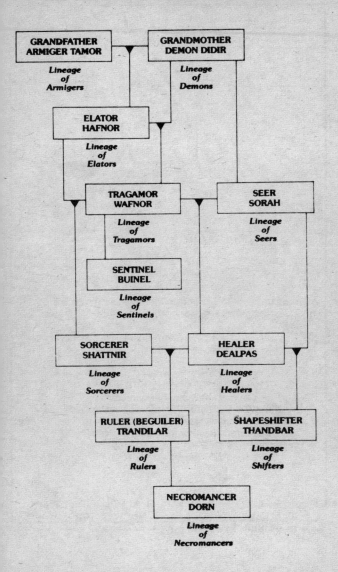

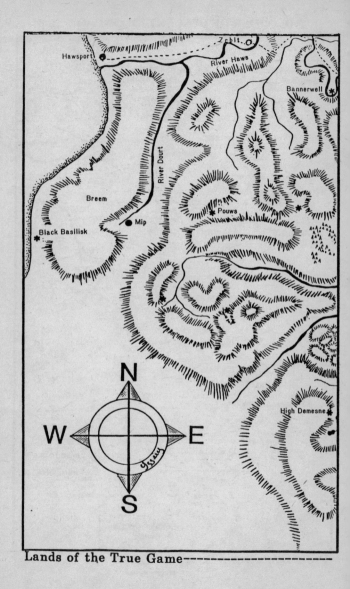

Lands of the True Game‒‒‒‒‒‒‒‒‒‒‒‒‒‒

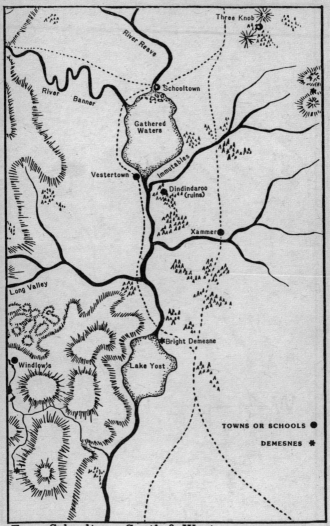

From Schooltown South & West

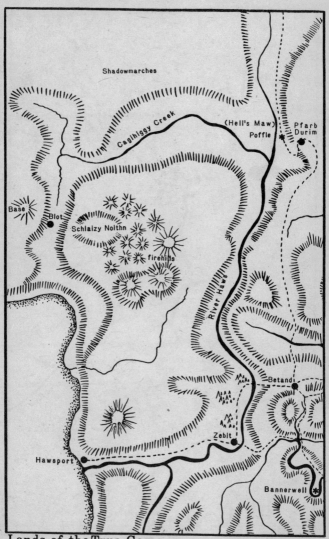

Shadowmarches

Caghiggy Creek

(Hell's Maw)
Poffle

Pfarb
Durim

Base

Blot

Schlaizy Nolthn

firehills

River Haw

Betand

Zebit

Hawsport

Bannerwell

Lands of the True Game

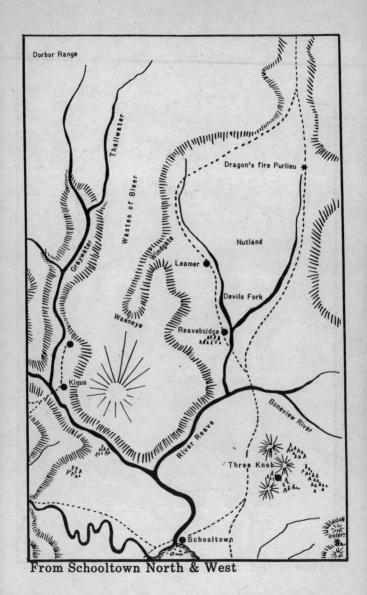

From Schooltown North & West

A FEW HELPFUL NOTES

The Gamesmen of Barish

1. Dorn, Necromancer Talent: Deadraising
2. Trandilar, Ruler Talent: Beguilement
3. Shattnir, Sorcerer Talent: Power Holding
4. Wafnor, Tragamor Talent: Moving
5. Didir, Demon Talent: Mind Reading
6. Dealpas, Healer Talent: Healing
7. Tamor, Armiger Talent: Flying
8. Hafnor, Elator Talent: Traveling
9. Buinel, Sentinel Talent: Firestarting
10. Sorah, Seer Talent: Seeing the Future
11. Thandbar, Shifter Talent: Shapechanging

In addition, the Immutables were reckoned to have Talent Twelve, and Peter was found to have Talent Thirteen. The Talent of Wizards is never specified. "Strange are the Talents of Wizards."

Notes on the Fauna
of the World of the True Game

The animals, birds, and water creatures originally native to the world of the True Game lack a backbone and have evolved from a vaguely starfish-shaped creature. The basic skeleton is in the form of a jointed pentacle, or star, often elongated, with the limbs and head at the points of the star. Despite this very different evolutionary pattern, the bioengineers among the magicians succeeded in meshing the genetic material of the new world and that from which they came. Among the creatures now native to the world of the True Game are:

Bunwits: Any of a variety of herbivorous animals with long hind legs and flat, surprised-looking faces under erect, triangular ears. Like all animals native to the world, bunwits are tailless. They eat young grasses and the leaves of webwillows.

Flitchhawks: Swift, high-flying birds which prey mostly upon bunwits of the smaller varieties. Noted for their keen eyes.

Fustigars: Pack-hunting predators, some varieties of which have been extensively inbred and domesticated.

Gnarlibars: A huge animal which lives in the high wastes below the Dorbor Range. It feeds upon anything it can catch, including old or ailing krylobos. The gnarlibar has a ground-shaking roar which has earned it the name of "avalanche animal." Gnarlibars always pack in fours, two females and two males; females always bear twins, one male and one female. A set of Gnarlibars is called a "leat" or crossroads, because of their invariable habit of attacking from four directions at once. It is thought that the gnarlibar is the descendant of a prehistoric race of animals so prodigious in size as to be considered mythical.

Grole: A long, blind, legless animal with multiple rows of teeth which lives by burrowing into soil, stone, or other inorganic materials, utilizing the light metals in its metabolism. The teeth are of adamant and can be used as grinding tools. The so-called "sausage groles" are not related to rockeater groles but are smaller creatures of similar configuration which eat only organic materials, notably the meat of the ground nut.

Krylobos: A giant, flightless bird with well-developed wing fingers, capable of very high running speeds. The krylobos dance contests are among the most exciting of spectacles for adventurous zoologists, as the birds are extremely agile and powerful.

Pombis: Carnivores distinguished by clawed feet and the ability to climb tall trees or nest in virtually inaccessible locations. Pombis are irritable and have a reputation for unprovoked belligerence.

Thrispat: A small omnivore which bears its young alive, lives in trees or upon precipitous mountain slopes, and mimics the calls of other animals and the human voice. Small thrispats are favorite pets in the jungle cities where breeders vie in extending the vocabularies of their animals. A good thrispat can speak up to a hundred words and phrases with some indication of understanding their meaning. Thrispats are particularly fond of ripe thrilps, whence the name.

Warnets: A stinging, flying insect of minuscule size and legendary bad temper, which lives in hordes. Called "saber-tail" by some. It is said that krylobos will take warnet nests and drop them into the nests of gnarlibars during territorial disputes.

Native Peoples

At least two peoples are known to occupy the lands around the area of the True Game.

Shadowpeople: Small, carnivorous (omnivorous when necessary) nocturnal people delighting in music and song. They are extremely fond of festivals, dance contests, song contests and the like and have been seen to assemble by hundreds within sound of the annual contests at the Minchery in Leamer. While Shadowpeople eat bunwits of any size, it is notable that they do not attack krylobós and are not attacked by pombis, gnarlibars, or warnets.

Eesties: A people said by some to be aloof and withdrawn, by others to be friendly and helpful. Seen most often as solitary individuals. Native language unknown. Habits unknown. In appearance, star-shaped, moving as Armigers do or rolling upon the extremities.

WIZARD'S
ELEVEN

1

Wizard's Eleven

Mavin Manyshaped, my mother, had told me that when a Shapeshifter is not Shifting—that is, when he is not involved in a Game—it is considered polite for the Shifter to wear real clothing and act, insofar as is possible, like any normal Demon or Necromancer or Tragamor. I like to humor Mavin when I can. The proper dress of a Shifter includes a beast-head helm and a fur cloak, so I had had a pombi-head helm made up, all lolloping red tongue and glittering eyes, with huge jowls and ears—fake, of course. A real pombi head would have weighed like lead. My fur mantle was real enough, however, and welcome for warmth on the chill day which found me midway between the Bright Demesne and the town of Xammer. I was mounted on a tall black horse I had picked for myself from Himaggery's stables, and Chance sulked along behind on something less ostentatious. We were on our way to visit Silkhands the Healer, not at her invitation and not because of any idea of mine.

Chance was sulking because he had recently learned of a large exotic beast said to live in the far Northern Lands, and he wanted me to Shift into one so that he might ride me through the town of Thisp near the Bright Demesne. It seemed there was a widow there . . .

1

I had said no, no, too undignified, and wasn't Chance the one who had always urged me to be inconspicuous? To which he had made a bad-tempered reply to do with ungrateful brats.

"If she had seen you mounted on a gnarlibar, Chance, she would never have let you in her house again. She would have felt you too proud, too puissant for a plumpish widow."

" 'Twould not be too warlike for that one, Peter. She's widow of an Armiger and daughter of another. Great high ones, too, from the telling of it."

"But she has no Talent, Chance."

"Well. That's as may be. Boys don't know everything." And he went back to his sulks.

Whoops, Peter, I said to myself. Chance is in love and you have been uncooperative. Thinking upon the bouncy widow, I could imagine what Talents she might have which Chance would value. I sighed. My own history, brief though it was, was mainly of love unrequited. I resolved to make it up to him. Somehow. Later. Certainly not before I found out what a gnarlibar might look like. This rumination was interrupted by more muttering from Chance to the effect that he couldn't see why we were going to Xammer anyhow, there being nothing whatever in Xammer of any interest.

"Silkhands is there, Chance." I didn't mention the blues which were the ostensible reason for my trip.

"Well, except for her there's nothing."

Right enough. Except for her there was probably little, but between the blues and old Windlow the Seer, I had reason for going.

The Bright Demesne had been like a nest of warnets since Mavin, Himaggery, and I had returned from the place of the magicians in the north. Those two and Mertyn had great deeds aflight, and all the coming and going in pursuit of them was dizzying. They had been horrified to learn of the bodies of great Gamesmen stacked in their thousands in the icy caverns of the north and had resolved to reunite those bodies with the personalities which had once occupied them, personalities now scattered among the lands and Demesnes in the form of blues, tiny Gamespieces used in the School Houses in the instruction of students. Mavin had appointed herself in charge of locating all the blues and bringing them to the Bright Demesne, though how she planned to reunite them with the bodies was unknown unless she was depending upon the last of the magicians, Quench, to make it possible. In any case, uncertainty was not standing in the way of action. Pursuivants were dashing about, Elators were flicking in and out like whipcracks; the place was fairly screaming with arrivals and departures.

Coincident with all this was a quiet search for my enemy, Huld. We were all eager to find him, accounting him a great danger loose in the world and ourselves unable to rest in safety until he was in some deep dungeon or safely dead.

And, of course, there was still much conjecture and looking into the matter of that mysterious Council which was rumored to be managing or mismanaging our affairs from some far, hidden place of power. Anyone not otherwise occupied was trying to solve that enigma. Meantime, I traveled about, collected blues, spent little time at the Bright Demesne. Standing about under the eyes of an eccentric mother, a father who kept looking at me like a gander who has hatched a flitchhawk chick, *and* of my thalan, Mertyn, who persisted in treating me like a schoolboy, made me short-tempered and openly rebellious in a few short days. I said as much to the three of them, but I don't think they heard me. They considered me a treasure beyond price until it came time to listen to me, and then I might as well have been a froglet going *oh-ab, oh-ab, oh-ab* in the ditches. I would like to have been involved at the center of things, but—well. It would have done no good to talk to Mavin about it. She was a tricksy one, my mother, and though I would have trusted her implicitly with my life, I could not trust her at all with my sanity. Matchless in times of trouble, as a day-to-day companion she had remarkable quirks. Himaggery and Mertyn were preoccupied. Chance was courting the widow in Thisp. There were no other young people at the Bright Demesne—all locked up in School Houses. What was there to do?

Given the state of my pockets, I had decided to go swimming. During my travels in Schlaizy Noithn, I had learned to do without clothing most of the time, growing pockets in my hide for the things I really wanted to carry about. When one can grow fangs and claws at will, it is remarkable how few things one really needs. Well, pockets in one's skin sound all very well, but they accumulate flurb just as ordinary pockets do, and accumulated flurb itches. A good cure for this is to empty the pockets, turn them inside out and go swimming in one of the hot pools with the mists winding back and forth overhead and the wind breathing fragrance from the orchards. All very calm and pastoral and sweetly melancholy.

Well, enough of that was enough of that in short order. I sat on the grassy bank with the contents of my pockets spread out, sorting through them as one does, deciding what to do with a strange coin or an odd-shaped stone. While I was at it, I dumped out the little leather pouch which held the Gamesmen of Barish.

There had been thirty-two of the little figures when I had found them. Only eleven had been "real." The others were merely copies and carvings made by some excellent craftsman in a long ago time in order to fill out a set of Gamespieces. The ones which were only carvings were in my room. The eleven real ones were becoming as familiar to me as the lines in my own hand.

There was Dorn, the Necromancer, death's-head mask in one hand, dark visaged and lean. I could almost hear his voice, insinuating, dry, full of cold humor, an actorish voice. There was voluptuous Trandilar, Great Ruler, silver-blonde and sensual, lips endlessly pursed in erotic suggestion. There was Didir, face half hidden beneath the Demon's helm, one hand extended in concentration, the feel of her like a knife blade worn thin as paper, able to cut to inmost thoughts and Read the minds of others.

There was stocky Wafnor the Tragamor, clear-eyed and smiling, his very shape expressing the strength with which he could Move things—mountains, if necessary. He had done that once for me. There was Shattnir, androgynous, cold, menacing, challenging, the most competitive of them all, the spikes of her Sorcerer's crown alive with power. Beside her lay the robed form of Dealpas the Healer, tragic face hidden, consumed with suffering, her they called "Broken leaf." And, last of those I knew well, Tamor the Armiger, Towering Tamor, poised upon the balls of his feet as though about to take flight, Grandfather Tamor, strong and dependable, quick in judgment, instant in action. I knew these seven, knew the feel of their minds in mine, the sound of their voices, the touch of their bodies as each of them remembered their own bodies. I could, if I concentrated, almost summon the patterns of them into my head without touching the images.

There were four others I had not held. Sorah, the Seer, face shadowed behind the moth-wing mask, future-knower, visionary. There was fussy Buinel, the Sentinel, Fire-maker, much concerned with protocol and propriety, full of worry, holding his flaming shield aloft. There was Hafnor, the Elator, wings on his heels, quicksilver, able to flick from one place to another in an instant. And, lastly, there was Thandbar the Shifter whose talent was the same as my own, tricksy Thandbar in his beast-head helm and mantle of pelts. They lay there, the eleven, upon the grass.

And one more.

One not disguised by paint as the Gamesmen were. One icy blue. Windlow. I had not taken him often into my hand, and there was reason for that, but I took him then beside the warm pools and held him in my palm out of loneliness and boredom and the desire to be with a friend. He came into my head like good wine and we had a long time of peacefulness during which I sat with my legs in the water and thought of nothing at all.

Then it was as though someone said "Ah" in a surprised tone of voice. My mind went dreamy and distant, with images running through it, dissolving one into another. My body sat up straight and began to breathe very fast; then it was over, and I heard Windlow saying inside my head, "Ah, Peter, I have had a Vision! Did you see it? Could you catch it?"

And I was saying, to myself, as it were, "A vision, Windlow? Just now? I couldn't see anything. Just colors."

"It is difficult to know," he said. "Your head does not feel as mine did. It doesn't work in the same way at all. How strange to remember that one once thought quite differently! It is like living in a new House and remembering the old one. Fascinating, the difference. I could wander about in here for years—ah. The vision. I saw you and Silkhands. And a place, far to the north, called—'Wind's eye.' Important. Where is Silk-hands?"

"You and Himaggery sent her to Xammer." This was true.

It had happened well over a year before, after the great battle at Bannerwell. Though Silkhands had long known that her sister and brother, Dazzle and Borold, were kin unworthy of her sorrow, when the end came at Bannerwell which sent Dazzle into long imprisonment and Borold to his death—for he had died there at the walls, posturing for Dazzle's approval to the very end—it had been more than Silkhands could bear. She had cried to Himaggery and to old Windlow (this was long before Windlow had been captured by the traders and taken away) and they had sent her off to Xammer to be Gamesmistress at Vorbold's House. She had gone to seek peace and, I had told her at the time, perpetual boredom. I had given her a brotherly kiss and told her she would be sorry she had left me. Well. Who knows. Perhaps she had been.

"Ah. Then she is still in Xammer. Nothing has changed with Silkhands since I—passed into this state of being."

It was a nice phrase. I knew he had started to say, "Since I died," and had decided against it. After all, one cannot consider oneself truly dead while one can still think and speak and have visions, even if one must use someone else's head to do it with. "She is still there, Windlow, so far as I know. You're sure Silkhands was in your vision?"

"I think you should go to her, boy. I think that would be a very good idea. North. Somewhere. Not somewhere you have been before, I think. A giant? Perhaps. A bridge. Ah, I've lost it. Well, you must go. And you must take me along . . . and the Gamesmen of Barish."

I asked him a question then, one I had wanted to ask for a very long time. "Windlow, why are they called that? You called them that, Himaggery called them that. But neither of you had seen them before I found them."

There was a long and uncomfortable silence inside me. Almost I would have said that Windlow would have preferred that I not ask that question. Silly. Nonetheless, when he answered me, he was not open and forthcoming. "I must have read of them, lad. In some old book or other. That must be it."

I did not press him. I felt his discomfort, and laid the blue back into the pouch with the others, let him go back to his sleep, if it was sleep. Sometimes in the dark hours I was terrified at the thought of the blues in my pocket, waiting, waiting, living only through me when I took them into my hand, going back to that indefinable nothingness between times. It did not bear thinking of.

Now, since I had never told anyone about having Windlow's blue, I could not now go to them and say that Windlow directed me to visit Silkhands. A fiction was necessary. I made it as true as possible. I reminded them of the School House at Xammer, of the blues which were undoubtedly there, of the fact that Silkhands was there and that I longed to see her. At which point they gave one another meaningful glances and adopted a kindly but jocular tone of voice. Besides, said I, Himaggery always had messages to send to the Immutables, so I would take the messages. I could even go on to a few of the Schooltowns farther north, combining all needs in a single journey. What good sense! How clever of me! I would leave in the morning and might I take my own pick from the stable, please, Himaggery, because I have grown another hands-width.

To all of which they said yes, yes, for the sake of peace, yes, take Chance with you and stay in touch in case we find Quench.

Which explains why Chance and I were on the frosted road to Xammer on a fall morning full of blown leaves and the smoke of cold. We had been several hours upon the road, not long enough to be tired, almost long enough to lose stiffness and ride easy. The ease was disturbed by Chance's whisper.

" 'Ware, Peter. Look at those riders ahead."

I had seen them, more or less subconsciously. Now I looked more closely to see what had attracted Chance's attention. There was an Armiger, the rust red of his helm and the black of his cloak seeming somehow dusty, even at that distance. The man rode slouched in an awkward way, crabwise upon his mount. Beside him I saw a slouch hat over a high, wide collar, a wide-skirted coat, the whole cut with pockets and pockets. A Pursuivant. Those who worked with Himaggery had given up that archaic dress in favor of something more comfortable. Beside the Pursuivant rode a Witch in tawdry finery, and next to her an Invigilator, lean in form-fitting leathers painted with cat stripes. What was it about them? Of course. The crabwise slouch of the Armiger permitted him to stare back at us as he rode.

"Watching us?" I asked Chance. "How long?"

"Since we came up to 'em, lad. And they wasn't far ahead. Could have started out from the hill outside the gate, just enough advance of us to make it look accidental like."

"Why?"

"Why?" He snorted under his breath. "Why is sky blue and grass green. Why is Himaggery full of plots. Why is Mertyn bothered about a Shifter boy with more Talent than sense. 'Tisn't me they're bothered over."

"Me?" I considered that. Ever since I had left Schooltown I had been pursued by one group or another, on behalf of Huld the Demon, on behalf of Prionde the High King, on behalf of the magicians. Well, the magicians were probably all dead but one, so far as I knew, but both Huld and Prionde were alive in the world. Unless I had attracted another opponent I knew nothing of.

If someone had put the group together to win a Game against me—the me I appeared to be—then they had selected well enough. Both the Pursuivant and the Invigilator had Reading, though not at any great distance. Both the Armiger and the Invigilator could Fly. Both the Invigilator and the Witch could store some power. In addition, the Pursuivant would be able to flick from place to place—not far and not as quickly as an Elator would have done, but unpredictably— and he would have limited Seeing. Add to this the Witch's ability as a Firestarter (her Talent of Beguilement didn't worry me) and they were a formidable Game Set.

I wondered how much they knew about me. If Huld had sent them, they knew too much. If Prionde had sent them, they might not know enough to cause me trouble. And if someone else? Well, that was an interesting thought.

" 'Their aim, what Game?' " I quoted softly for Chance's ears alone.

"No Game this close to Himaggery, boy. Later on, it'll be either kill or take, wouldn't it? Why Game else?"

"I wonder what I should do," I mused, mostly to myself, but Chance snorted.

"You went to School, boy, not me. Fifteen years of it you

had, more or less, and much good it did you if you didn't learn anything. What's the rule in a case like this?''

"The rule is take out the Pursuivant," I replied. "But no point chopping away at them if they're only innocent travelers. I'd like to be sure."

"Wait to hear them call Game and you'll wait too long." He shut his mouth firmly and glared at me. He did that when he was worried.

"There's other ways," I said. Under cover of the heavy fur mantle, I reached into the pouch which held the Gamesmen. I needed Didir. She came into my fingers and I felt the sharp dryness of her pour up my arm and into me. Lately she had dropped the formality of "speaking" in my head in favor of just Reading what she found there. I let her Read what I saw. A moment went by.

Then, "I will Read the Witch," she whispered in my brain. "Small mind, large ego, no Talent for Reading to betray us. Just ride along while I reach her. . . ."

So I rode along, pointing out this bit of scenery and that interesting bird for all the world like a curious merchant with nothing more on his mind than his next meal and the day's profits. Covertly I examined the Witch in the group ahead. Shifters have an advantage, after all. They, and I, can sharpen vision to read the pimples on a chilled buttock a league away. I had no trouble seeing the Witch, therefore, and I did not like what I saw. She was sallow, with bulging eyes surrounded by heavy painted lines of black. Her mouth was small and succulent as a poison fruit, and her hair radiated from her head in a vast frizzy mass through which she moved her fingers from time to time, the finger-long nails painted black as her eyes. The clinging silks she wore revealed a waistless pudginess. Overall was a Beguilement which denied the eyes and told the watcher that she was desirable, wonderful, marvelous.

"Pretty Witch," I said to Chance.

"Beautiful," he sighed.

Oh, my. She was using it upon both of us, not knowing my immunity to it. Or, perhaps knowing my immunity but testing it? The possible ramifications were endless.

"She's a Witch, Chance," I said sternly. "A perfect horror. Black fingernails as long as your arm, frog eyes, hair like a briar patch and a figure like a pillow.''

His mouth dropped open a little, but he was well schooled to the ways of Gamesmen. "I'll keep it in mind, Peter," he said with considerable dignity. "Be sure I'll keep it in mind."

"But if you act like you know," I added sweetly, "she'll know I told you. Better pretend you think she's gorgeous."

He gave me a hurt look. "I'm not a fool, boy. Had that figured out for myself." And he went back to staring at her with his mouth open. If I had not known about the widow back in Thisp, I would have sworn he was smitten.

It wasn't long before Didir spoke to me again. "They seek to take you, Peter, as agents for some other. The Witch does not know for whom. The Invigilator has something dangerous in his pocket, however, something to make you helpless. Be careful." And she was gone once more. The Gamesmen did not stay in my head. I wondered, not for the first time, if this was courtesy or discomfort. Did they refuse to invade me out of kindness or because my brain was unpleasant for them? As conjecture, it served to keep me humble.

"The rule is to take the Pursuivant out, Chance, but we will break the rule, I think. Since we are warned, let them move first. I'll see what the Demesne feels like. I think the Witch intends to move soon. Can you carry on a flirtation at this distance?"

"Game is announced, is it?" He mumbled something I couldn't hear, then, "Well, if she makes a beckon at me, I can manage to stir my bones in motion." And nodded, satisfied with himself. Old rogue. He was right. Game was announced.

In a formal Game, Great Game, the announcement had to be done in accordance with the rules of Great Game, by Heralds calling the reasons and causes, the consequences and outcomes. In Great Game everyone knew who was Gaming, for what reasons, and what quarter might be given. Then there were Games of Two which were almost as formal. Game would be called by one and responded to by another before their friends and compatriots. Then there was secret Game, covert Game, but even there (if one played according to the rules) Game had to be announced. The announcement, however, could be part of the Game. If the opponent were a Demon, the announcement might be merely thought of. If the opponent were a Rancelman, then the announcement might be hidden. If the opponent were a Seer, then deciding upon the Game was considered announcement enough. A true Seer, it was reasoned, would See it in his future. The variations were endless. In this case the Armiger had called attention to himself and the Witch had thought of the Game. Announcement enough. The only question in my mind was whether the group ahead knew that I could do what Didir had just done. Oh well, tra-la. Game is announced. On with it.

We continued our journey, the group ahead moving only slightly slower than we so that we gained upon them as the leagues went by. The Witch was closer and closer yet, and Chance looked in her direction ever more frequently. We were not within Reading distance by the Pursuivant and Invigilator yet, and I wanted the first encounter over before they tried to Read me and failed. Chance and I stopped and made as if to go into the bushes on personal business, watching them from cover. When the distance had widened a little, we came after them, all innocence. If they really intended to use the Witch, she would make her Move soon.

And she did.

We watched them pull up, saw the broadly acted consternation as the Witch searched through her clothing, miming something lost. My, oh, my, what had she lost upon the road? Something important. Oh, yes; wide gestures of loss and concern; equally wide gestures to the others to go on, go on, she would ride back and then catch up to them. "Watch her," I said to Chance. "She'll head back toward us pretending to search the road for something lost."

"What did you say she looks like?" panted Chance.

"Black nails, black painted eyes, body like a bolster and hair like wires. 'Ware, Chance. She'll eat you."

"Up to you to prevent it, boy."

When she was a hundred paces from us, she turned to us, smiling, blazing. Lord, she was beautiful. My mouth almost dropped open, but then I felt around for the pattern that let me see clear even while my fingers fumbled for Wafnor in the pouch. Far ahead on the road the Armiger's horse was now riderless. I trusted not, tra-la. The Witch pouted, prettily.

"Oh, Sir Shifter, I beg your assistance. I know that Shifters can make their eyes keen like those of the flitchhawk to see a coin dropped in a canyon from a league away. Can you find for me the bracelet I dropped along the way here, perhaps at the edge of the trees?''

Then she turned to Chance, casting that smile on him like the light of a torch. Almost I saw him melt, but then I caught the tucks in his face where he had his cheeks between his teeth, biting down. "Pawn," she said, "would you help your master find my bracelet by walking along the trees. What he can see, you can retrieve, and have my thanks as he will. . . .''

Chance's eyes were out a finger's width, and he gave every appearance of being about to fall off his horse. Meantime, I smiled, bowed, and oozed desire in her direction while I called up Didir to sit in her head and tell me what she planned. I knew the Armiger was above us, somewhere, ready to fall upon us when we came within the trees. I gave a gulping prayer that I had enough power to do what I intended, then turned my eyes to the grassy verge of the road as the Witch came nearer. Under my fingers Wafnor came alive and reached up into the branches. I worked my way almost to the forest.

"Oh, lovely one," I called. "Here. Could it have caught on a branch? See the sparkling there where the sun catches it, not so bright as your beauty, but able to adorn it. . . .''

Witches are, for the most part, stupid. They tend to come into their Talent early, and this early accession to beguilement gives them too easy success in their formative years. At least so Gamesmaster Gervaise was wont to say. This particular Witch could have served as an object lesson. She came into the trees after me, still glittering and beguiling for everything she was worth. I was reminded of Dazzle, and, yes, of Mandor, and when I turned toward her she must have seen it in my face, for she flew at me with a scream of rage and those black nails aimed for my eyes. There was no time for thought. I grabbed her wrist, ducked, twisted, and felt her fly over my head to land with a whoosh of expelled breath on the leaf-littered ground behind me. Then Didir did something quick and clever inside her head and the Witch lay there unconscious. Physical combat is not something we ever learned in a School House, but Himaggery believed in it. He had pawnish instructors giving classes every afternoon in the Bright Demesne. I hadn't seen the sense of it until now.

Chance looked at her where she lay. "Ugly," he said.

"I told you," I muttered.

"What now?" Chance always asks me what now when I have no idea what now. I shook my head, put my finger to my lips, concentrating on what Wafnor was doing. Fingers of force fluttered the bright leaves above us. The noise would be the Armiger. I could feel Wafnor searching, then there was a harsh "oof" as though someone had been roughly squeezed. I felt a shaking in my head, then Wafnor speaking in a cheerful grumble. "Stuck. Got him between two branches, and he's stuck!" One of the tree tops began to whip to and fro as Wafnor continued growling cheerily. "Won't come loose. Stupid Armiger . . ."

"Whoa," I said, weary of the whole thing. "Chance, hold the horses while I climb the tree."

I found the Armiger hanging by one badly bruised foot in the cleft of a tallish tree. Wafnor assisting me, we thrust one limb aside to let the Gamesman fall, none too gently, into the forest litter. He lay there beside the Witch, the two of them scruffy minor Gamesmen, not young, not well fed. The idea of killing them did not appeal to me. They were not players of quality. I said as much to Chance.

"They haven't the look of Huld about them somehow. He has more sense than to send such minor Talents."

"Maybe, lad. And maybe they were hired as supernumeraries by those up ahead. Hired fingers to touch you with, see if you sizzle."

Chance's remark had merit. I explored with Didir a possibility which would allow us to let them live, something she might plant in their heads which would take them away. After a short time the Witch and Armiger picked themselves up, dusted themselves off, and limped away to the south leading the Witch's horse. "They will believe they are going to meet others of their company," whispered Didir. "The notion will leave them in a day or two, but by that time they will be far distant from this place."

"Now," I said, "we can ride in a wide circle south which will take us around those two ahead. We'll leave them behind us...."

"Oh, lad, lad," sighed Chance. "Go around 'em and they're behind you. Lose a Pursuivant and he'll find you. What are you playing at?"

I sighed, pulled up my boots, looked at the sky, sucked a tooth. He was right. One doesn't "lose" a Pursuivant easily, and the trick of sending the other two away south wouldn't fool anyone long. Besides, if Chance's notions were correct, the two ahead of us were the real threat and came from a real opponent. The more I thought of it, the more I wondered if Huld was behind it. It didn't feel like Huld, but undoubtedly Huld would have to be dealt with sooner or later. I struck Chance a sharp blow on one shoulder. "Right you are, Brother Chance. Well then, it's back to the road, ride on, and let them wonder."

Which we did. The Pursuivant and the Invigilator had moved on a little, leading the Armiger's horse. I went through a dumb show of waving as though taking leave of someone hidden in the trees. They wouldn't believe it, but it might confuse the issue still further.

We were a moving Demesne, the Game was not joined. Between the two men ahead of us on the road were five Talents and not inconsiderable ones. This reminded me of my own depleted state, and I fingered Shattnir, feeling the warmth of the sun beginning to build in me. I might need all I could get. The two ahead might be as shoddy as the two just defeated, but they might be the real foe, the true opponent, the True Game. If so, then what? What did I want to happen?

"Young sirs," Gamesmaster Gervaise had often said. "When you confront True Game in the outmost world, remember what you have been taught. Remember the rules. Forget them at your peril." Well, so, there was time during this slow jog along the road to remember the rules.

Game had been announced in two ways. By the Witch thinking of it and by the Armiger riding awkwardly. The Witch would have thought what she thought whether ordered to do so or not, but the Armiger would have ridden in that fashion only to attract attention. Therefore, the announcement was directed to one who would see the announcement with his eyes, not Read it. So presumably they had announced Game to a Shifter—which was, after all, what I seemed to be.

Now the Armiger was gone. Presumably, therefore, they knew that their opponent, the Shifter, had played. They knew I was in the Game. I knew they were in the Game because of what Didir had Read in the Witch's head, but *they* did not know that *I* knew what was in the Witch's head, therefore . . .

"I never had any head for covert Games," I complained to Chance. "Whenever I get to the third or fourth level of what I know and they know, I lose track."

"Look, lad. They know you're a Shifter. They're expecting that. They may have been *told* you're something else as well, but nobody knows exactly what, so they can't expect everything. Just be original and surprising. My granddad, the actor, used to say that. Original and surprising."

"Follow the rules." I sighed again. The rule was to take out the Pursuivant first, because he had the power to change place in an instant, and one might find him behind one with a knife before one could take a deep breath. Two of the Gamesmen of Barish and I had a little conference, waiting for a turn in the road. It might have been quicker to use Hafnor the Elator, but I had never 'ported from one place to another. The thought made me queasy, like being seasick. Besides, I didn't know the area ahead, and those with that Talent could only flick to places they could visualize. Which was another reason they were moving ahead of us. They had seen the road we traveled, but we hadn't seen the road they were on. No. I would use Tamor and Didir. I was used to them. And Shattnir, of course, to provide power, which she'd been doing for the last hour or so. It was moving toward evening before the road set as I wished it to.

We were moving between close set copses, dark trunks still half masked in drying leaves. One could not see far into them, a few paces perhaps. Just ahead of us the road swung around a huge rocky outcropping to make a loop to the left. Shortly before the riders ahead of us reached this place, Chance and I began a conversation which turned into a loud argument— Chance's voice much louder than mine. Old rogue. He was an actor as much as his granddad had ever been. As soon as the two ahead had ridden out of sight, I grasped the figure of Tamor and flew up from my saddle, darting away through the trees like an owl among the close trunks while Chance's voice rose behind me in impassioned debate. From time to time a softer voice would reply, Chance again, but those ahead would have no reason to think it was not me, Peter the Shifter, riding along behind them.

I had to intercept them before they had any opportunity to become suspicious. The trees were close, too close for easy flight, but I came to the edge of the road silently only a few paces behind them. I drew my knife and threw it, launching myself at the same moment, Shifting in midair. The Pursuivant went down, skewered, even as my pombi claws swept the Invigilator from his saddle. Then I sat on him. Beneath me he screamed, struggled, tried to fly. I let him struggle while I drooled menacingly into his face. He screamed a little more, then fainted. At least Didir said he really fainted, sure I was going to eat him. Shattnir drained him of any power he had left, and then we tied him up after going through his pockets. I found the thing almost at once. It was another of those constructions of glittering beads and wires like the one Nitch had sewn into my tunic in Schooltown, like the things Riddle had shown me outside Bannerwell. It was rather like the thing Huld had used against me in the cavern of the bodies, away north. It was shaped like a hood or cap, with a strap to go beneath the chin.

"What does it do?" asked Chance.

Didir sought in the Invigilator's unconscious mind even as I started to say I did not know. The man stirred in discomfort. She was not being gentle with him. I repeated to Chance what she told me.

"It guarantees docility," I said. "If they had put it on my head and fastened the strap, I would have obeyed anything they told me to do." I stood there for a time, thinking, then asked Didir to search further. Did the man know who sent him? Once I was "docile," where would they have taken me?

Whispering, she told me, "There are some ruins near the river which bounds the land of the Immutables. Old ruins. North of here. He would have taken you there."

Ah. I knew the place. I had found the Gamesmen of Barish

there. Dazzle and Borold and Silkhands had stayed there. Well, I would go there. It would be original and surprising.

"Put the cap on him," I told Chance. "I'm going to get into the Pursuivant's clothing." So much for my fine fur cloak and my pombi head, lost in the mad flight through the trees. I stripped the Pursuivant and put his clothes on, sorrowing for him as I did so. I had not intended to kill him. The knife had turned in flight. When I had done, I carried him into the woods and laid him in a shallow scrape and covered him over with leaves before we rode away.

In a little time three men rode on: an Invigilator, very silent, the strange cap hidden beneath his leather garb; a Pursuivant, whose clothes fit none too well; and a pawnish servant who rode along behind leading two extra horses.

"Do we go on to Xammer, then?" the servant asked, humming to himself.

The Pursuivant, I, merely nodded. We were indeed going on to Xammer, to meet Silkhands, and then we were going farther on to those ruins I had visited once before. Behind us in the forest the real Pursuivant's body was food for ants, and before us was food for thought. I hoped it would not give me indigestion.

2

Xammer

We rode into Xammer, each taking a part in our little play.
Chance was playing the grieving servant for all he was worth.
The Invigilator, wearing the mysterious contrivance, played
himself, though with only such verve as we ordered him to
display. I, Peter, played the part of the Pursuivant, trying to
convey with every attitude the heartfelt regret I felt at having
killed the young Gamesman, Peter, during some unspecified
and unfortunate occurrence upon the road. If we were being
observed, this bit of acting should have gone further to confuse the observers. We took a room at an inn on the edge of
town. I changed aspect and clothing in our rooms and sneaked
out the back way, having been able to think of no good excuse
for a Pursuivant to visit Silkhands the Healer. Chance was
happily immured with a supply of wine and a perfectly bid-
dable audience to listen to his reminiscences. He could have
been happier only if the sportive widow from Thisp had been
present, so I felt no need to hurry.

It was as well. The town of Xammer may be unique among
Schooltowns. There was much to observe.

There are no Festival Halls in Xammer. Vorbold's House is
one which specializes in teaching the daughters of the powerful, daughters of Queens and Sorcerers who have risen to first
rank, of eminent female Armigers and Tragamors. They are

taught how to play their own Games at Vorbold's House, the
game of survival and reproduction. No Festivals for them, to
be impregnated by nameless pawns or bear young at random.
No. These maidens are the prizes of alliance and are as protected within the walls of Vorbold's House as they might be
within a fortress guarded by dragons.

So much I knew, for it had been discussed at the time that
Silkhands was sent to the place. I had not considered the implications of it, however, and it was these which made the
town unique. It was full of shops, shops dealing in luxuries
which were purveyed to the School House and to those who
visited there. It was full of inns, not scruffy roadside inns but
hostelries built with magnificence as the objective. It was full
of travelers, powerful travelers entering the town under death
bond that no Talent would be used within the walls. It was
full, therefore, of courtesies and veiled malevolence as Gamesmen pursued their strateg·es through earthbound Heralds forbidden to Fly and a pawnish class of merchants who called
themselves negotiators and arbitrators. I had never heard so
much talk, not even in Himaggery's council hall.

I had known enough to bring proper dress, a little ostentatious and overdone, and was received with some courtesy for
that if for no other reason when I presented myself at Vorbold's House. It had a high graceful gate leading into a sunny
courtyard where a cat and kittens made endless play through
the flower pots. I expected to be invited into the School but
was instead shown to a small audience room off the courtyard
and told to wait. The time was made less onerous by the arrival of a pretty waiting girl who brought wine and cakes and
lingered to flirt with me. This was enjoyable for both of us, so
much so that I almost regretted the sound of Silkhands' step
on the tessellated pavement. That is, regretted until I saw her.

She was—yes, still Silkhands, but something more. At first I
thought she had somehow Shifted herself to become so lovely,
but then I saw it was only a matter of a little more flesh
smoothing her face and gracing her neck and arms, a little
more sleep in a softer bed than the campgrounds we had
shared, less worry and stress and sorrow, a little more silk
against the skin to replace the rough rub of traveling clothes.
She did not even notice the retreating servant girl—nor did

I—but came straight into my arms as though I had been some long lost love. "Peter," she said, "I am so happy to see someone from Home. How is Himaggery? Did they finish the new swimming pool in the orchard? Is your thalan still at the Bright Demesne? How is your mother? I heard about Windlow—ah—" and she was suddenly crying on my neck. I could feel the warm trickling wetness of her tears.

I felt as though two years had disappeared and we were traveling from the ruins where I had found her to the Bright Demesne once more. The best I could manage was a mumbled, "You haven't changed at all, Silkhands," while my body and my mind jigged with the notion that she had changed entirely, utterly. Of course, it was not she so much, but I figured that out later.

She asked if I were alone, and I told her that Chance and another fellow were at the inn, giving no details beyond that at first. She asked if I wanted to stay in the Guest House of Vorbold's, and we talked of that. I murmured something about the place being secure, and she looked at me slantwise, a look I remembered from the past.

"I see you have something to tell me, Peter. Well, the Guest House of Vorbold's is as secure a place as exists in all the purlieus and demesnes. We have guards against trifling as you would be astonished at. So. Will you go to the inn for your baggage, or shall I send for it?"

I thought it best to sneak in and out and to tell Chance myself. It was as well I did so, for the Invigilator had fallen into some kind of a trance, and Chance could not make him move or speak. We took the wicked little cap off of his head and put him to bed, bent up as he was in a sitting position. I told Chance to tie him and gag him loosely if Chance left the room, just in case the fellow came around, but otherwise to do as he pleased for the day or two I would spend at Vorbold's. "Tell anyone who asks that your Pursuivant companion suffers from a flux," I suggested, "and if this fellow hasn't moved in a day or two, I'll ask Silkhands to take a look at him." I could have called forth Dealpas, of course. She was preeminent among Healers, but she was so tragic and sorrowful that it was a pity to wake her. The fellow was breathing well enough, and his heart beat steadily. I thought a day or two would not change him greatly if he were kept warm and quiet.

And then I went back to Vorbold's House to find a guest's room made ready for me (not in the House itself) and a servant standing ready to unpack or clean or press or whatever I chose. I was glad to have brought clothes with me and thanked Mavin for so directing me. I had thought of traveling without any. The man advised that dinner would be served in the Hall at the evening bell, and he took himself off. I luxuriated in my bath, listened to the music from the courtyard, and tried to shake off the very uncomfortable feelings Silkhands had stirred up in me. After the bath I leaned in the window to watch the musicians. Vorbold's House collected artists, musicians, and poets from all the lands and demesnes. A representative group of them were gathered in the courtyard below me, all demonstrating their skills. The poets wore their traditional ribbon cloaks, looking something like boys let out of School for Festival, though more ornate and grand. There is some controversy about musicians and artists. Some hold that they are Talented, while others hold that it is merely a skill. In any case, they are not under bond in the town as the more ordinary Talents are. They may use whatever it is they have in a School-town or anywhere else, and it is not considered proper to Game against them.

Below me a musician played short phrases of melody over and over while a poet set words to them, and across the yard another poet declaimed a long verse, phrase by phrase, while another musician set notes to that. It seemed there was to be a song contest in the evening on a subject assigned by Games-mistress Vorbold herself the evening before. In Mertyn's House, where I was reared, we would have disdained such trifles, and I formed the intention of twitting Silkhands about it. That was before I saw the great Hall.

It lay in the area to which guests are admitted, one ceremonial entrance for the guests, one even finer opposite which led into the School. I found my assigned seat and sat back to watch the spectacle which had aspects of Festival and of a bazaar. The guests were almost all male. Many were there on their own behalf, but others were there as agents. The products which they bargained for sat at other tables, on low

daises of ivory hued stone, young women clad in silks and
flowing velvets, each table of them with a Gamesmistress at its
head. Silkhands sat at a table near my own. I could look
across the glossy heads between and wink at her. Somehow the
intensity of the atmosphere around me—though it was all
covert, glances and sighs and whispers—made a wink seem improper. I satisfied myself with an unsatisfactory smirk and
bow. I was, by the way, clad most sumptuously and wearing a
face not entirely my own. I had cautioned Silkhands against
knowing me too well or obviously in this public place. She
bowed in return, I thought more coldly than was necessary.

The evening's entertainment began with welcoming words
from the Lady Vorbold, Queen Vorbold. She wore the crown
of a Ruler, but her dress was much modified. As I looked
about the room I noted that all the women of the House were
clad in light delicate gowns under robes of heavier richer stuff;
that all the young women who were of an age to have man-
ifested Talents wore appropriate helms or crowns or symbols,
but all reduced in size and bulk to the status of mere orna-
ments. The heavy silver bat-winged half helm of a Demon
might be expressed as a mere bat-winged circlet, airy as a spray
of leaves. I saw a Sorcerer's spiked crown, tiny as a doll's
headdress, and a Seer's moth-wing mask reduced to a pair of
feathery spectacles drawing attention to the wearer's lovely
eyes. It was as though they sought to make the Talents less important than the women who wore them. Well. In this House
that was probably the case. Why did I suddenly think of the
consecrated monsters which Mavin and I had seen in the
caverns of the magicians? Was it some similar blankness of
eyes? I did not quite identify the thought.

The song duels began, one against one, the musicians playing and singing in turn while the poets sat at their feet. At the
conclusion of each song, the diners tapped their silver goblets
upon the table to signify praise, and the judges—a table of
elderly Gamesmistresses—conferred among themselves. I
heard one of the phrases I had listened to from my room,
woven now into a complete fabric of song. The singer was
young and handsome, and his voice was pure and sweet. I
thought of the singers among the magicians, lost now under
the fallen mountains, and grew sad. The song was one which

evoked sadness in any case. He finished in a fading fall of strings and was rewarded by a loud clamor of goblets upon wood. He took the prize. It was fitting. His was the most melancholy music of the evening. All the ladies loved it.

After this entertainment came an intermission during which the young women circulated among the tables to talk idly to the guests. One elegant girl wove her way to the table where I sat, body like a willow waving, garments swaying, face showing that smiling emptiness I had noted before. We greeted her, and she sat to take a glass of wine with us. She was obviously interested only in the tall chill Sorcerer who sat with us. He asked her politely what she was studying.

"Oh, ta-ta." She pouted. "It is all about Durables and the Ephemera, and I cannot get it in my head. It stays about one instant and then goes—who knows where."

The Sorcerer smiled but said nothing. Thinking to fill the silence, I said, "My own Gamesmaster gave us a rule which made it easier to remember. If a Talent is continuous, as for example it is with a Ruler or a Sorcerer, then the Gamesman is one of the Greater Durables or Adamants." She smiled. I went on, "Those in whom the Talent is discontinuous but still largely self-originated are among the Lesser Durables. Seers, for example, or Sentinels."

She cocked her head prettily and looked up into the face of the Sorcerer. Still he said nothing. She made a little kiss with her mouth. "The Ephemera, then? What is their rule?"

"Those Gamesmen who take their Game and power from others, sporadically, are of the Greater Ephemera," I said. "Demons, for example, who Read the minds of others but only from time to time, not continuously. And finally there are the lesser Ephemera, those who take their only value from being used by other Gamesmen. A Talisman, for example. Or a Totem."

"I see. You make it sound so interesting." She gazed up at the Sorcerer again after a quick ironic glance at me, and in that glance was all I had not understood until then. It was not that she failed to remember, not that she lacked interest in the subject. She *knew*, perhaps better than I, but had been taught not to show that she knew. I caught a sardonic smirk on the face of the Sorcerer and turned away angered. There was not that much difference between these, I thought, and the consecrated monsters of the magicians. I wondered how Silkhands could lend herself to this—this whatever it was. There might be time to ask her later, but now the intermission had ended and we were to be granted another song by the evening's champion.

He stood among us, smiling, relaxed, not touching his instrument until all present had fallen silent. When he touched the strings at last it was to evoke a keening wind, a weeping wind which focused my attention upon him and opened my eyes wide. He faced me as he sang, coming closer.

> "Who comes to travel Waeneye
> knows what makes the wild-wind cry.
> Whence the only-free goes forth,
> shadow-giant of the north,
> cannot live and maynot die,
> sorrowing the wild-wind cry."

The wind music came again, cold, a lament of air. He was very close to me, singing so softly that it seemed he sang for me alone.

> "Wastes lie drear and stone stands tall,
> signs are lost and trails are thinned,
> abyss opens, mountains fall,
> Gamesman, Gamesman, find the wind...."

Then he moved away, walking among the tables, humming, the music reminding me of night and bells and a far, soft crying in caves. He was standing next to Silkhands as he sang:

> "Who walks the Wastes of Bleer must know
> what causes this ill-wind to blow.
> Shadowmen play silver bells,
> krylobos move in the fells,
> gnarlibars come leat and low,
> listening to ill-wind blow."

He looked up to catch my eye again, sang:

> "Mountains mock and mystify,
> hiding Wizard's ten within.
> One more walks the world to cry,
> 'Healer, Healer, heal the wind.' "

The music ran away as a wind will, leaving only a dying rustle behind it. There was a confused moment, then a barely polite tapping of goblets upon the table. They had not liked it. At once he struck up a lilting dance song with a chorus everyone knew. Within moments virtually everyone in the room had forgotten the wind song, if they had ever heard it, except Silkhands and me and a young woman who sat at Silkhands' table and now regarded me with an expression of total comprehension. She had large dark eyes under level brows, a pale face with a slightly remote expression, and a tight controlled look around her mouth, like one cultivating silence.

I, too, had found the song disquieting, though I could not have said why. All the evening's entertainment had done nothing but leave me irritated and cross. When Silkhands came to my room in the Guest House later, this irritation remained and I made her a free gift of it, not realizing what I was doing. I was speaking about the girl who had come to our table, about what I presumed to call her "dishonesty." Silkhands disagreed with me.

"Ah, Peter, truly you expect too much. Who was it came to your table? Lunette of Pouws? I thought so. Her brother wishes to establish an alliance with the Black Basilisks at Breem. So he seeks to interest Burmor of Breem in Lunette. She is his full sister, and she is no fool. She seems like to manifest a Talent which will fit her well enough among the Basilisks; however, Burmor wants no competitor in Beguilement at the Basilisk Demesne. Thus she plays witless before those he sends to look her over. What would you have her do? Stand upon her dignity and Talent, as yet unproven, and so cause her full brother annoyance and grief? If she goes to Burmor, she will be of value there as symbol of the alliance. She will be protected, and there will be time for her Talent to emerge.''

This argument did not sit well with me, and I said so with much reference to the "consecrated monsters" I had seen in the place of the magicians. "They, too, were taught to be passive, or were so changed in the hideous laboratories that they could be nothing else. They, too, existed for nothing except to breed sons. . . .''

"You may recall," she said, "that Windlow once told us of the rules of the Game? How those rules had been made originally to protect; how those rules came to be more important than what they protected; how those rules came to be the Game itself! Well, those rules were made by men, Peter. Lunette chooses to make her own safety and her own justice within the Game. It is her choice.''

She was so annoyed with me that I thought it wise to change the subject. "Who was that minstrel who won the prize? Did I mistake him, or did he sing to you and me alone of all that crowd?''

"Ah, one of my students, Jinian, thought the same. He has sung this wind song before. It seems to follow me wherever I go, into the orchards, the gardens. His name is Rupert of Theel, and he is well known among the musicians. Yesterday in my bath I heard 'Wild-wind weeps and ill-wind moans. Has the wind an eye? A hand? Has the wind sinews or bones? Healer, Healer, understand.' It so infuriated me I leaned naked from the window and told him to cease singing 'Healer' or 'wind' in my hearing.''

"Well, last night he sang 'Healer,' but he also sang 'Gamesman,' '' I commented. "He sang to me as well as you if he sang to either.'' We wondered at it a bit. What was there in it, after all? A song. There was this much in it: it linked the two of us together as did Windlow's prophecy. Musing on this I reached out to take her into my arms. She sighed upon my shoulder and we sat there for a long time in the candle shine and starlight, lost in our own thoughts. When she drew away at last, I began to tell her what had brought me to Xammer.

Thus Silkhands learned about the blues, and about Windlow's blue, the only person besides myself who knew of it, the first person beside myself to know the sorrow of it.

"I take the blue into my hand," I whispered. "Windlow comes into my mind, a gentle visitor, gentle but insistent. Silkhands, he struggles there. I feel his struggle. He inhabits my mind as a man might inhabit a strange house—no, a strange workshop where nothing is in its accustomed place. I feel him search for words he cannot find, seek explanations for things which are not there—connections and implications which might have been obvious to Windlow in the flesh but which he cannot find in me. He struggles, and it is like watching him drown, unable to save him."

"Not your fault," she soothed me. "Not your doing."

"No," I agreed. And yet it was my doing. "If I do not take him up, then he lies imprisoned in the blue, a living intelligence imprisoned as intelligence is imprisoned in these students of yours who must hide it to protect themselves. Oh, Silkhands, worst of all is when he wants me to read to him."

"Read? As a Demon Reads?"

"No, no. Books. A book. He wants me to read the little book, the one he called the Onomasticon, over and over. As though there were something in it he needs to know and cannot find. Oh, he is gentle, kind, but I can feel the sorrow like a whip."

At that she came into my arms again to comfort me, and we lay there upon the wide windowseat staring at the stars until we fell asleep. When I woke, stiff and sore, it was morning and she had gone. I went out to the necessary house behind the Guest House. (A silly place to have it. We had toilets near our rooms at the Bright Demesne.) The singer was there, Rupert, and I thought to find out about the wind song, perhaps find why it disturbed me so.

"I am interested in the song you sang," I said politely. "The one about the wind?"

"Better you than I, Gamesman," he said, making a face. "Would I could forget the thing."

I evinced surprise, and he laughed a short bark without amusement. "I heard it first at the Minchery in Leamer. They make shift there to train artists up from childhood, and there is a summer songfest at which many of us assemble to lend encouragement and judge the contests. There are always new songs, some written by students, some brought in from the

Northern Lands. Many are of a caliginous nature, dark and mysterious, for the students love such. Well, this wind song was one of them. I heard it, and since have been unable to get it out of my head. I find me singing it when I eat, when I bathe, when I . . ." he gestured at the necessary house behind him.

"The places mentioned in the song? Waeneye? The Wastes of Bleer? Where are those?"

"Oh." He seemed puzzled. "I do not know that they exist, Gamesman. I took them for more mysteries. They may exist, certainly, but I know nothing of them." He smiled and bowed. I smiled and bowed. We took leave of one another. I believed he had told me all he knew. Considering how the song ran in my own head, I could believe it had haunted him.

When I saw Silkhands later in the morning, I asked, "Have you a cartographer at the School?"

"Gamesmistress Armiger Joumerie," she said. "A good Gamesmistress. A difficult person."

"Difficult or not, I would like to see her."

And I did see her that afternoon in my room at the Guest House, for no male may enter the School House. As the girls there were much valued for their ephemera they were much protected against its premature bestowal.

I asked the Gamesmistress whether she knew of a place called Bleer, or one called Waeneye. Also did she know of Leamer, or of any place where creatures called krylobos or gnarlibars might live. I had heard, I said, that gnarlibars lived in the north, but that might have been only talk.

"Bleer, Bleer," she mumbled to herself, stroking her upper lip with its considerable moustache as an aid to concentration. She was a big woman, larger than many men, and her face had a hard, no-nonsense look about it. "Yes. That jostles a memory."

"Possibly a mountainous place," I offered. The song had mentioned mountains and stone, an abyss, fells.

"No help, Gamesman," she said tartly. "If one excepts the purlieus around the Gathered Waters and Lake Yost, virtually all the lands and demesnes are mountainous. You are not untraveled! Surely this has struck you. How much flatland have you seen?"

I had to admit having seen little. The valley of the Banner was fairly flat, as were the valley bottoms leading into Long Valley in the southwest. Other than that I could think only of that vast, tilted upland which lay above the River Haws and south of the firehills and Schlaizy Noithn. I would not speak of that to the Gamesmistress, but the thought had reminded me of something. "Shadowpeople!" I said. "Where are shadowpeople said to dwell?"

"Find me a place they are said *not* to dwell," she replied. "They live in the far north and west, in the southern mountains below the High Demesne, in the lands around the Great Dragon purlieu far east of here. No, that is no help to you, Gamesman. Give me a bit of time and I will find it for you. The name Bleer echoes in my mind. I have seen it on a chart before." It echoed in my mind, too, but I could not remember where I had heard of it. Had I asked the right question, I would have had quicker answers.

As it was, Gamesmistress Joumerie returned to me that evening to say she had found the place.

"The Wastes of Bleer," she informed me, licking her lips at the taste of the place, "lie to the north. A highland, the canyons of the Graywater to the west, the vast valley of the River Reave to the east where lies Leamer or Leamers, called variously. If you intend to go there, I could recommend the road to Betand and the eastern route from there over Graywater. There is a high bridge there at Kiquo, the only one for many leagues. Or, River Reave is navigable as far as Reavebridge, or even Leamer in season. There are trails into the high country from there."

"What Games, Gamesmistress?" I asked her. "Is there any troubling there? What Demesnes are active?"

She snorted. "Wary are you? You are young to be so wary. My latest charts show little enough. The Dragon's Fire purlieu lies north on River Reave, but there is no Game there currently or presently expected. Who knows what hidden Games may be toward? Or games of intrigue or desperation?" She fixed me with an eye yellow as a flitchhawk's. "If you are that wary, lad, best enter my School House here and learn to dissemble as these girls do."

I flushed at that. She went stalking away to the door, making the floor shake. In the doorway she stopped to speak more kindly, seeing she had hit me fair. "There is a cartographer in Xammer, in Artists' Street, by name one Yggery. He is honest, so far as that goes, by which I mean he will not put anything in a map he knows to be false nor leave out anything he knows to be true. This means his maps are rather more blank than most. Still, if you have treasure enough, buy a map from him before you go north. And if you take Silkhands with you (for I can see the tip of my nose in a mirror in a good light), care for her. She has had more of Gaming than many of us, and has burned herself in caring for others."

I had not honestly thought of taking Silkhands with me until that moment. I had not thought she would want to leave Vorbold's House. Testing this notion, I asked her and was surprised to hear her say she would have made a trip north in any event.

"I go north to escort Jinian, my student," she said. "I need a time away from Vorbold's House. There are some here who turn their eyes from the students to the Gamesmistresses, and I am . . . weary of that."

"Have you been molested?" I was angry and therefore blunt. I should have known better, for she laughed at me.

"In Vorbold's House? Don't be silly. Of course not. I have been sent proposals at intervals, and I have had to listen to a few representatives for the sake of . . . diplomacy. The offers have not been . . . unflattering." She fell silent, thinking of something she did not share with me, then, "Save to those like us who do not value flattery. I know I do not, and I presume you have not changed."

The expression on her face as she uttered this last was one I knew she used in the classroom, alert, polite, both encouraging and cautionary. I could hear her speaking thus to her students, "Now, young ladies. We do not value flattery. . . ." I giggled at the thought.

She stared at me for a moment as though I had lost my wits, then giggled with me. We ended up rolling onto the carpet to end in front of the fire, heads pillowed on various parts of our anatomies as we talked it over.

"I did sound properly Schoolhousy, didn't I?" she asked. "Well, being Gamesmistress does that to you. Perhaps I am too young for it. I am only twenty-one after all. Many of the students are older than I.'' She did not consider this remark at all important, but to me it came as a revelation. Only twenty-one. I was seventeen, almost eighteen, and she was only four years older? I had thought of her as . . . as . . . well, older-sisterly at least. I was suddenly aware of her thigh beneath my head and of a quickening pulse in my ears. I sat up too hastily, dumping her.

"Come now,'' I said overheartily, trying to hide the fact that my hands were trembling. "We must make plans. I am going from here to the ruins where I first met you because the men who attacked me on the road would have taken me there.''

"Dindindaroo,'' she said, blinking in the firelight like an owl. "That's the name of the place, or once was. Dindindaroo, the cry of the fustigar. It is said the place was once a main habitation of Immutables.''

"Truly? Why was it abandoned?''

"A flood, I think. And a great wind which laid waste to the land about there. At any rate, it was abandoned some three generations ago, perhaps eighty or a hundred years. We used to find old carvings and books when we were there. Himaggery spoke of sending a party of Rancelmen to explore, but he never did.''

"So the Immutables once occupied this place, Dindindaroo. Well, some villainy is centered upon it now, and I must go there in the guise of the Pursuivant to see what I can find. After that, however, if no sign of Quench has been found, why should I not go with you to the northlands? Windlow's vision sees us there together, and the song directs us there. Let us go.''

She agreed hesitantly. "I must take Jinian to the court of the Dragon King at the Dragon's Fire purlieu. He and another Ruler, Queen someone—I've forgotten her name—set up a Rulership there, a kind of King-Demesne. Having no sisters, he chose to build his strategy around sons rather than upon thalani, but all his sons save one were eaten in Game over the years. He has only one left, at school in Schooltown, Havad's House, I believe. He is desirous of children to replace those lost.''

I remembered out of dim mists having heard that name. "Ah. So the Queen died. Or was lost in Game?"

"Died. Of too much childbearing to too little purpose, some say. Now he desires a strong young Gameswoman to bear him sons."

"Who will also die of too many babies?"

She smiled a secret smile at me. "No. Our students learn better than that. We may teach them covert game, Peter, but we teach them to survive at it and their children as well. Jinian will not over-bear."

I did not pursue the matter, though I thought with a pang of the girl who had given me that long, level, understanding look at the dinner. She had not looked like one who would go uncomplaining into such a life. Well. Who could say.

Silkhands went on: "It will be a few days before we are ready to leave. You have your own trip to make. How shall we combine our journeys later?" She looked at me, hopeful and luminous in the firelight. I would have promised to combine a journey with her to the stars, and she seemed to know that, making a pretty mouth at me in mockery. I gestured hopeless and resigned acquiescence, and we spent the remainder of the evening talking of other things. I think both of us thought then that we would become lovers. No. I think she thought it and I hoped it. We did nothing about it except stargazing. There seemed to be time, and no reason occurred to either of us to think time would run out. I can still remember the shape of her in firelight, half of her lit with a soft melon-colored light, the other half in darkness.

So the morning after that found me back in the inn with Chance. The Invigilator had come around to some extent. He would sit up when told, and walk, and eat, and relieve himself. He would do nothing at all unless told to do so, and the strange cap had been on him only one full day. When Didir looked into his head she found an emptiness. "As though untenanted," she said. I was sorry then that we had put the thing on him. "Perhaps if it had not been on him so long," whispered Didir, "the effect would have been less."

We thought this likely. My assailants could not have wanted to make me witless. What good would I have been to them in that condition? I could not even have served as bait. No, the

Invigilator had simply been caught in his own trap, but I mourned nonetheless that his body lived while his mind was gone.

Before leaving Xammer, we went to Artists' Street to buy the chart Gamesmistress Joumerie had suggested, and also to the Gamehall to hire a Tragamor. Silkhands had arranged for the few blues held at Vorbold's House to be packed and delivered to the inn. The Tragamor, escorted by an Armiger, took them off to the Bright Demesne along with a message from me.

"I am going north," I wrote, "to stop at the ruins of Dindindaroo. Thence to the land of the Immutables to leave the messages entrusted to me by Himaggery, and thence on the Great North Road in company with Silkhands, traveling to the Dragon's Fire purlieu. Word may be sent to me in the care of the Gamehalls on the way. Let me know if you find Huld, or Quench. I have found something odd I think Quench would know about." By which I meant the cap, of course, a thing made by magicians or techs, if I ever saw one. I sealed the letter, then unsealed it and added a postscript. "All affection to Mavin Manyshaped and to my thalan, Mertyn."

I thought privately that it was a good deal easier to feel affection for them both when I was a good distance from them.

3

Dindindaroo

We rode out of Xammer with me in the guise of the Pursuivant once more. He had been a man with lines in his face all crisscrossed from scowling, hard round cheeks and eyebrows which slanted upward over his nose to give him a falsely mournful expression. It was not a face which pleased me nor on which a smile fit easily, and after a time Chance told me to quit twitching it about and settle on something more comfortable for travel. "You can always gloom it a bit when we come to the ruins, lad," he said. "No sense making me the benefit of it while we're on the way." The Invigilator had no comment. We were still having to tell him when to drink and when to go into the bushes to pee, but Didir said there were glimmers of personality deep within which were beginning to emerge again. Evidently the evil little cap had done the same thing a devilish Demon might have done, wiped out all the normal trails in a brain to leave it without any tracks at all. My conscience still bothered me about that. There are worse things than being dead, and this might be one of them.

Once my face smoothed out into my own once more, it was a more comfortable trip. The ruins—Dindindaroo—were not far from Xammer, a short day's ride, no more. There was a lot of traffic on the road, too, for the comings and goings to and from Xammer were constant. Not only by emissaries of alliance hunters, either, but by merchants who found Xammer a profitable stop and a convenient place to buy luxuries for shipment farther north. One day I would go north on the road, I resolved, and see the jungle cities. Meantime, we amused ourselves, Chance and I, identifying Gamesmen in the trains. I saw a pair of Dragons, the fluttering cloaks painted with patterns of wings and flames and the feather crests snapping in the breeze. They nodded to us as they trotted past, hurrying away somewhere north, perhaps to the Dragon's Fire purlieu which was known for its population of air serpents. There were a good many exotic Gamesmen. I saw a Phantasm, gray and blue, faceplate faceted like a jewel, and a bright yellow Warbler who caroled a greeting at us as he passed, the subsonics and supersonics shivering our horses and making all the fustigars in the forests howl. There was a troop of brown-clad Woodsmen, a common Talent among the Hidaman Mountains where they are much valued to fell timber and fight fires because of their ability to foretell where fires will happen and move earth and start backfires of their own. Though I had heard of a Woodsman taking his troop halfway down the range in pursuit of a fire he had Seen which was accidently caused by his troop only after they arrived. Even old Windlow had said that Seeing was not dependable, and I considered it a good part flummery. Perhaps it was this opinion which made me reluctant to call up Sorah as I felt it would not make her think well of me.

We saw a Thaumaturge and a Firedancer and a Salamander and then about evening came to the fork in the road where the winding trail led away to Dindindaroo, overgrown with weeds and not appearing to have been traveled at all for many seasons. I did not want to come upon the place in the dusk, even with Didir in my pocket telling me she could not Read any minds at all in the place. So we camped, Chance, the idiot Invigilator, and I, with me doing the cooking. Chance amused himself by having the Invigilator make the fire and gather firewood. I think he was making a pet of the creature. Come morning we were up and on the trail at early light, me with my face carefully shifted into a good likeness of the Pursuivant. I felt my Shifting slip away even before we saw the ruins swarming with men. Chance said, "Immutables," and I knew at once he was right. Well, Riddle might be among them, and he knew Chance, and it probably didn't matter that I could not hide my own face. Let me go as myself and tell part of the truth.

The men working on the ruins had it marked out with pegs and string and were busy digging and hauling loads away in large barrows. We stopped a distance away from the turmoil, waiting to be decently noticed, and a man came down the pile toward us, wiping his forehead and looking oddly familiar to me. When I told him who I was, he started a little and gave me an extremely curious glance which I put down to his not having expected a Gamesman to visit. I took pains to be polite, coming down from the horse and making no extravagant noises.

"Would Riddle be here?" I asked. "I have a message for him from the Bright Demesne."

The man went back up the tumulus, peering at me over his shoulder in a way that reminded me unpleasantly of the way the Armiger had ridden ahead of us on the road. Still, that feeling left me when Riddle himself came from some hideaway and stopped to peer at me nearsightedly as though he couldn't believe what he saw.

"Peter? You? In Pursuivant's dress? But—what does this mean? . . ."

I saved him his puzzlement, not wanting him to start thinking about my Talents or lack of them. He had turned quite pale in his confusion. "We had a bit of trouble on the road," I said. "A Pursuivant was among our attackers. He is dead now, poor fellow, and I put on his clothes to confuse those who had hired him. Whoever it was, they should have been here. So said this Invigilator." I pointed the man out, explaining his lack of interest in what was going on. "He's not very useful at the moment. He had a kind of cap thing in his pocket, a thing like those you showed me at Bannerwell. Well, we put it on him, and it's had this awkward effect. . . ."

Riddle was nodding and nodding at each thing I said, looking very uncomfortable and grim, which I thought still might have been caused by my appearing thus suddenly in the guise of another Talent. At any rate, he collected himself and asked what brought me. I repeated what I had said before, that I had expected to find whoever plotted against me in this place. "Haven't there been any Gamesmen about, Riddle? Have you seen anyone lurking?" To which he mumbled and said something or other about having been too busy to have noticed.

It was obvious he was preoccupied, so I gave him the messages Himaggery had sent (something to do with the search for Quench, in which some Immutables were assisting Himaggery) and told him I would stay in the vicinity for a day or two in case Himaggery sent a message for me. And, finally, he managed to shake off his discomfort, from whatever cause, and become hospitable.

I asked him what they were doing, and he offered us tea while explaining. "We are growing more and more crowded in the purlieu, Peter. Our councilmen decided we should expand our territory, and this ruin marks the southern edge of the lands our people once occupied. They called it Dindindaroo, after the sound of the fustigars who den in the canyons and forests. At any rate, my own grandfather was the leader here in his time. It is our intention to build here once again."

"Wouldn't it be easier to build to one side of this ruin? Why all this digging and delving?"

He hemmed and hawed for a time before saying, "Oh, there may be artifacts here which are of interest to our archivists and historians. We thought it a good idea to take a little time to salvage what might be left from a former time." Then he changed the subject. His explanations sounded weak to me. They did not seem to be salvaging. They were searching for something particular. At any rate, Chance drew me away to speak privately.

"There seems to be no Gamesman here now, lad, no one to do you harm. So it seems. But there is nothing to keep someone from coming in the night, and even if no Talent may be used with all these Immutables about, still there are knives and arrows that can do a good bit of damage. I'd like it better to be inconspicuous."

I humored him. We took our leave of Riddle and rode away to the east. Once under the cover of the trees, however, Chance insisted we turn in a large circle which ended us west of the ruins. We found a cavelet well hidden behind tumbled stone, and when we had found the place, Chance asked that Didir look around us to see if anyone lurked. She reported only beast minds and bird thoughts, and I privately thought Chance must be among them to be so concerned. He disabused me of that notion.

"I had a suspicion," he said when we had settled down. "We came to that place expecting to find one there who Games against you, Peter. No one was there but that Riddle and his Immutables. So what if that Riddle had not been a so-called friend of yours? What would we think then? We'd think, well, here is the one who set that Game on us. So what I want to know is, how do we know he didn't?"

"Riddle? Ridiculous."

"Well, how so ridiculous? I dare say those Immutables have reasons and purposes of their own. Can't you imagine some reason he might want you all quiet and obedient to his will, for him to use some way?"

I could not. I tried. Riddle knew me as a Necromancer. What need or use could he have for me which I would not have fulfilled for him gladly at the asking? I thought of all possible combinations and alliances and strange linkages which could have come about—Huld, Prionde, the Council, Quench, the techs, Riddle, even the minor Gamesmen such as Laggy Nap and his like. Nothing. I said so. Chance was not satisfied.

"Well, just because we can't think of what it might be doesn't mean it isn't. Would you give me that, lad?" I said yes, I could give him that. He went on, "So 'ware what you say. Don't go telling everything you know about where we're going and what we're about. Say we're going along with Silkhands to that Dragon's Fire purlieu because you and she are—well, give him that idea."

In the lands of the Game it did make sense not to trust too much. The only thing that bothered me was thinking of Riddle as a Gamer. Somehow, because he had no Talent, I expected him to be simple. When I said this to Chance, however, he corrected me with a hoot of laughter.

"Out on the sea, lad, where I spent many a season, we'd know a man by what he proved to be, not by what his mouth claimed for him. A man could be a devil or a good friend, and sometimes one and another time the other. Some Gamesmen are honest enough, I don't doubt, though they have the power to be all else without any to say them no, and some Gamesmen are evil as devils. So I doubt not the Immutables have their good and their bad, their complex and their simple. Well for you to suspect so, anyhow.''

And with that, he left me to lie there, aroused by the puzzle but too weary to stay long awake. We went back to Dindindaroo the next morning to see if a message had come from Himaggery and to take leave of Riddle, for if he was what he pretended to be, a simple and honest man, then he would think more kindly of me for the courtesy. And if he was not what he pretended—well. We found him down in a hole, pale and frustrated of face, and he showed such discomfort at my arrival that I thought perhaps Chance was right. I dissembled. For all Riddle could have told, we were still his dearest friends.

''What are you doing down there, Riddle,'' I demanded. ''Burrowing like a grole? Have you lost something? Or found it?'' Even as I said it, I realized that the hole he was in was probably the same hole I had fallen into some several seasons ago when I had found the Gamesmen of Barish and the book Windlow called the Onomasticon. I gave him my hand to help him out, and he blinked at me as he brushed dust from his coat.

''I thought for a time we might have found some valuables left here by my grandfather,'' he babbled. ''All the inhabitants of the place fled, leaving everything. There was great loss of life, a flood, a great wind. . . .''

''What exactly are you looking for?'' I asked him, all polite interest and bland lack of concern. ''Would it help to raise up the dead here and ask them?'' Aha, I thought. If you do not want me to know what you are doing here, then you will not accept this offer.

And also aha, said a quiet voice in my head. If Riddle had wanted you to raise up the dead in this place without knowing what you were doing, might he not have arranged for you to be put into that strange cap the Invigilator carried? Hmmm? Chance gave me a look, and I turned away as Riddle shook his head and fussed and said no, no, the only one who had known was his grandfather and his grandfather was said to have died elsewhere, and besides, he doubted a Gamesman could raise

Immutable dead. I nodded my acceptance of this while privately thinking that I could do it if I chose. Whatever it was that made them immune to Talents, I wagered it went away when they died.

I shook my head for the benefit of those standing about. "It is probably just as well, Riddle. The longer they are dead, the less they remember of life. They hunger for life more the older they are, but they remember less. How long ago was the destruction?"

He thought some eighty years. His father had been a young man at the time.

"Well, you have waited a good time to seek what was lost," I said, all kindness and concern. "A good long time."

He mumbled something. I think the sense of it was that if he had known earlier what was lost, he would have come earlier to look for it. And this told me much. Riddle had lately learned something new. So. I was not of a mind to hang about making the man sweat. There would be better ways to find out. Besides, I was without Talent in this company and had only one man to stand beside me. It could be less dangerous to be elsewhere. I gave Riddle my hand and bade him farewell, putting the Invigilator in his care.

"He will dig for you, if you put the shovel in his hand," I said. "And if any Gamesmen come here who seem to know him, I would be grateful if you would send word to the Bright Demesne." I did not want Riddle to think I suspected him of anything. In truth, I still did not know that I *did* suspect him of anything. All I could believe was that Chance was wiser than I, and that I would be wiser—far wiser to be more careful. If only I had remembered that later.

We rode away without talking, both of us preoccupied with our own thoughts. After a time I turned to Chance and said, "I don't necessarily believe it."

"Well, don't then," he said. "But it'd be smart to act as though you do."

"You know what he was looking for back there." I made it a statement, not a question.

"For those things you found, I guess. I notice you didn't offer them to him."

"The thing I noticed was that he said his grandfather left them there. How came his grandfather by them? And why did

Riddle not know of them until recently? For I will bet my lost fur cloak that he did not.''

Chance shrugged, mumbled to himself. Finally, "Would anyone else among those Immutables know? Or is it only Riddle who knows? What about his family?''

"He had only a daughter," I said. Then there was a long pregnant silence of such a quality that I looked back to find Chance's eyes upon me, brooding and hot. "Oh, no," I said. "I will not.''

"She's buried nearby," he remarked. "Almost in sight of the ruins.''

"I couldn't do that," I said flatly. It was true. I could not even think of raising the ghost of Tossa. It would have made me feel like a Ghoul, and I said as much.

"I didn't say you should take her with us," Chance said in mild reproof. "I didn't say you should drag her around.''

I swallowed bile at the thought. Ghouls did raise certain kinds of recent dead and drag them into a kind of fearful servitude of horror, a thing which no self-respecting Necromancer would think to do. There were others who raised ghosts—Thaumaturges, for example, or Revenants, or Bonedancers. If what old Windlow and Himaggery had told me was true, full half of all Gamesmen would have some Talent at Deadraising. Full half of all Gamesmen would share *any* one Talent. If so, it was not a Talent generally used in the way Ghouls and Bonedancers used it, and I felt unclean at the thought.

"No," I said. "She died, Chance, without ever knowing she was dying. Often the dead do not know they are dead until we raise them up." In that instant I thought of Windlow with a kind of stomach-wrenching panic, then sternly put that thought down. "The ancient dead are only dust; they have forgotten life and possess only a kind of hunger which the act of raising gives them. I do not feel thus about the ancient dead. But the newly dead—ah, Chance, that is a different thing. With Tossa, she would know herself dead, and it would hurt her.''

The memory of Mandor's ghost was recently with me. I was prepared to be as stubborn as necessary, but Chance only said, "Well, then we'll have to think up some other way to find out. How about someone dead for eighty years or so?''

"I don't know," I said.

"Do you think you could raise an Immutable?"

"You're thinking of Riddle's grandfather? Riddle said he didn't die in the ruins."

"Riddle said a lot of things. Don't know whether I believe him or not is all."

So we rode along while I thought about that. Riddle was digging in Dindindaroo. He had recently found out that something lay in the ruins which he needed? Wanted? Someone else wanted? Well, which he cared enough about to go to some trouble over, put it that way. Where had he found out, and when? Perhaps on that northern journey he and I had started to make together, when he had turned off toward the east just above Betand? Or in his own land? Perhaps someone had told him? Who? Or he had found old papers?

After a time Chance interrupted this line of thought to say, "You know, these Immutables are just like the rest of us. They drink a little and they talk. Get a little jolly, they do, and they talk. Pawns travel through their land on business. You and me, we could travel there."

Which was an answer, of course. We would need to disguise ourselves. Riddle knew me as a Necromancer only, or so I believed. Chance and I had been seen together once before in the Land of the Immutables, but only briefly. So suppose we went into that land as two pawns, traveling on business. What business? I put this to Chance.

"Well, as you left me to my own devices in that town of Xammer, boy, and without a hello, goodbye, how was your dinner, I got into a little game or two."

"Chance!"

"Now, now. Mustn't react hasty-like. A quiet game with honest folk is always good fun. Anyhow, I took my winnings in various small bits and pieces. A little gold, some gems, fripperies and foolishness. Thought I might turn a profit, up north."

"So that's what's in your saddlebags. I thought you were heavy loaded for having no pack beast."

He nodded to himself happily. I never knew what pleased Chance most—winning a game of cards or dice, finding a woman who was a good cook, or locating a wine cellar put together by a master vintner. Whatever else the world offered, he would choose one or more of those three.

He instructed me: "Enough in the bags to make us legitimate, lad. If you can change your face some and get out of those dusty black clothes. Wouldn't hurt to change horses, too. As may be possible not far from here."

Which was possible with Chance in charge of the trade. He went away leading my lovely tall black horse and came back with a high-stepping mare of an unusual yellow color with nubby shoes such as they use along the River Dourt, or so Yarrel had once told me. It was not an inconspicuous animal. However, he had obtained a pack beast in the trade and had done something to his own face while away from me, stuffed his cheeks to make them fatter and darkened his hair. He looked a different man, and it was easy to disguise myself as a younger version of the same. When we were done with this switching about we turned west to cross the Boundary River into the Immutables' own Land. We had decided to be the Smitheries, father and son, and Chance told me to ride one stride behind and mind my manners toward my elder, which so amused him in the saying he almost choked.

So that night I sat in a tavern and learned a lesson in gossip. Chance talked of the sea, and of horses, and of trading in general, and of the goods he had picked up in Xammer, and of the young women in that city and elsewhere, and of how the world had changed not for the better, and of a strange wine he had tasted once in Morninghill beside the Southern Sea, and of an old friend of his in Vestertown, and of a man he had known once who used to live in Dindindaroo.

"Oh, that makes you a liar indeed," said an oldster, sucking at a glass of rich dark beer which Chance had put into his hand. "If you knew such a one, he was old as a rock. Dindindaroo has been wreck and ruin this hundred year."

"Not a hundred," interrupted another. "No, Dindindaroo was wreck and ruin in the time of my mother's father when my mother was a girl, and that was no hundred year."

"Oh, you're old as a rock yourself," asserted the first. "For all you're chasing the girlies like a gander after goslings, which you will never catch until the world freezes and Barish comes back. If it were not a hundred, it were near that."

"Ah, now," said Chance. "The man I knew was old indeed. Old and gray as a tree in winter. But he said he was there when ruin came down on the place, he said, like the ice, the wind, and the seven devils. Caught a bunch of the people, the ruin did. Or so he said."

"Oh, it did. Aye, it did. Caught a bunch of 'em."

"Caught old Riddle's grandfather, I heard," said Chance. "That's what the fellow told me."

"Oh, so I've heard. Free and safe he was, out of the place, then nothing would do but he go back for something he'd left there, and then the ruin came. That's the story. Buried in it, they said. Buried in it when the flood came down, and no sign of him and his contrack after that. Oh, a man'll do strange things, won't he, when ruin comes."

"He will, indeed he will," agreed Chance, nodding at me over his beer. At which I nodded, too, and agreed that a man will indeed do strange things.

"What was it he went back for, do you suppose?" asked Chance, as though it didn't matter at all.

"Who knows, who knows," murmured the second oldster, who was growing very tipsy with the unaccustomed quantities of free beer.

"His contrack," the loquacious oldster said. "That's what I heard. Was his contrack from the long ago time of Barish. That's what they kept at Dindindaroo. Charts and books and contracks to keep 'em safe until Barish comes back for 'em. That's what." And he hiccupped softly into his glass before looking hopefully to Chance once more who bought another round and changed the subject. They got into an argument then as to whether Salamanders are really fireproof. After that was a good deal of calling on the seven hells and the hundred devils, after which we went to bed to lie there in the swimming darkness talking.

"So he died there in the ruins, Chance. I have no bad feeling about calling him up. I didn't know him, and he's dead this eighty years, but Dorn himself couldn't call anyone up with all those Immutables about. All of them would have to leave."

"As they may do," suggested Chance, "if they heard that the thing they're looking for had come to light elsewhere."

"Elsewhere?"

"Somewhere far off. Leave it to me, Peter. We'll spend one more night here."

The which we did. And there was more buying of beer and

more talk, and this time Chance made the circle of acquaintances larger so that there were more listeners to what was said. Middle of the evening came, together with jollity and general good feeling, and into a pause in the noise, Chance dropped his spear.

"You know, it was odd your mentioning Dindindaroo last night," he said to the oldster at his side.

"Odd? Was it? Did I? Oh, yes. So I did. What was odd?"

"Oh, only that I met a man in Morninghill, not a season gone, and he told me he'd dug up treasures around Dindindaroo."

At this there was general exclamation and interest. Chance turned to me for verification, and I said, "Oh, he said so, Father, yes. Dug up treasures, he said, and was selling them moreover."

Chance nodded, said nothing more, waited. The questions came. What had the man found? The Smitheries, father or son, did not know. Something small and valuable, they thought. Something wonderful and rare, for the man was a famous dealer in such. Old things, certainly. Then, when interest was at its height, Chance led the conversation away from the subject onto something else. I saw two dark-cloaked men leave the place immediately thereafter, and when I went to the window for a bit of air I could hear the pound of hooves going away south.

We slept there that night, and on the morning went out of the Land of the Immutables, riding publicly east toward the Great North Road. Once out of sight, we turned into the forests and began the circle which would bring us into the cover of the trees nearest the ruins of Dindindaroo.

We spied upon the place, I with my Shifter's eyes, keen as any flitchhawk's, and Chance with a seaman's glass he carried with him. Sure enough, there were two dark-cloaked men talking with Riddle, the three of them standing upon a mound of crumbled stone and soil, Riddle gesturing as though he were in a considerable turmoil. Troubled he was. His face was white with frustration. After a time they settled down, and by noon they had reached some decision, for many of them went away north into their own land while others, Riddle among them, rode south. So. He was going to look around in Morninghill, and a long weary journey that would be.

We waited until early evening, until the westering sun threw long golden spears across the tumbled stone, and then we came to the ruins and walked about on them. The industrious diggers had changed them about somewhat. Still, the crumbling walls were there where Dazzle and Borold had sheltered to watch the fire dance, and so was the high slit window where I had hung my shirt to counterfeit a ghost. I stood, looking at it, feeling that deep brown emotion made of dusk and smoke and sorrow which is so piercing as to be sweet beyond enduring. Then I shook myself and took Dorn into my hand.

"Well, Peter," he said to me in my mind. "Here lie many dead. Would you have us raise them all?" He knew what I had thought of, but he was ever courteous, treating himself as a guest. Besides, in clarifying for him, I made clear to myself as well. "A name," he said. "Did you neglect to learn the man's name?"

I uttered an oath, disgusted with myself. If we were to draw out one from among so many, a name would be needed for we did not know precisely where he lay. "What was his name?" I growled to Chance. And he answered me, soft as pudding, well Riddle of course, same as his grandson. So we went with that.

I began to sense the dead about us, the feeling of them, the luxuriant quiet of them. They were at peace in the long slow heat of summer and the long slow cold of winter, the ageless waft of the wind and the high cry of the hawk upon the air. In them the leaves moved and the wavelets of the river danced. In them sorrow had no place; time for sorrow had gone with the turn of the seasons and the fall of the leaves. "Pity," said Dorn, "to disturb this peace."

Still, he called the name of Riddle into the quiet of the place, drawing out and up, and at last we saw a little whirlwind of dust turning itself slowly upon the tumulus before us, spinning and humming a quiet sound into the twilight. Through this whirling dust the sun fell, turning it golden, so that we confronted a shining pillar and spoke as with a Phoenix, for so those Gamesmen whirl into flame and are consumed before rising once again.

We asked, and asked again. This revenant was not so old as those we had raised in the caves beneath Bannerwell, so we had created no monster of dust which hungered for life.

Neither was it so short a time after death as the raising of
Mandor, so there should have been no remembered agonies.
Despite this, it seemed disinclined to speak with us, resisted
being raised. I was about to give up when I heard Didir within,
unsummoned, feeling—was it excited? Surely not. Impetuous.
"Let me." She reached into that whirling cloud and seemed to
fumble there as though Reading it, making some tenuous connections of sparkling dust.

Then the humming cloud took the shape of a man, a wavery
shape, still resistant, not unlike Riddle in appearance, looking
at something I could not see.

"I see Dorn," the phantom said. "Barish promised us immunity, Gamesman. He promised, but I am raised from the
dead by Dorn. Ah, but then, I broke my pledge, my oath to
Barish. All unwitting, all unwise. Forgive and let go. . . ."

Chance and I looked at one another, a hasty, confused
glance. This was not what we had expected. I stuttered,
reaching for a question to clarify. "Riddle, tell me of your
pledge to Barish."

"Barish . . . Barish. He gave us immunity from your power,
Gamesman, for us and our children forever, immutable
throughout time, so he said. And in return we must keep his
body safe, keep the bodies of his Gamesmen safe where they
lie, north, north in the wastes, north in the highlands where
the krylobos watch. We must keep the Wizard safe, and the
Wizard's eleven. But he went away and did not return. I
brought the Gamesmen here, Barish's book here, thinking to
find him somewhere, find him and return them, but the waters
came, the waters came and I died. . . ." The figure writhed,
became the humming cloud once more. From it the voice came
in prayer and supplication, "The contract broken, all unwitting . . . and Barish's promise broken as well for I am raised by
Dorn to suffer my guilt. Ah. Forgive. Let me lie in peace. . . ."

It was not my voice that said it, and not Dorn's. I thought it
was Didir, though I could not be sure. "You are forgiven,
Riddle, faithful one. Go to your rest."

The cloud collapsed all at once and was gone. The sun
lowered itself below the undulant line of hills. Dark came
upon the tumulus and in the forest a fustigar howled, to be
joined by another across the river. A star winked at me, and I
realized that I saw it through brimming tears. Something had

happened. I was not sure what it was, or why, and the Gamesmen in my pocket did not know either. It was as though they and I had listened in upon some conversation from another time, a thing familiar and strange at once—familiar because inevitable and strange because I could not connect it to anything I knew. Chance was watching me with a good deal of concern, and I shook my head at him, unable to speak.

"Well," he said when I could hear him. "What went on there?"

I tried to tell him. All I could get out was that the answers to all our puzzles seemed to lie in the Wastes of Bleer.

"Riddle's grandfather brought some things here from the Wastes of Bleer," I said.

"I think it would help us if we stopped talking around and around," he said thoughtfully. "Let's not say 'things'. What was brought here was those little Gamesmen you found and the little book you gave Windlow."

"I have it with me," I said. "There may have been other things as well."

"No matter. What was lost was the Gamesmen and the book. Now did this Riddle fellow steal them?"

"No!" I was shocked. "No. He was supposed to have them. Supposed to keep them safe—them and the . . . bodies."

The light that engulfed me then seemed to be around me in the world, but it was only inside my head. The bodies. Didir's body. Lying in the northlands, waiting for her. *Her*. Her I had in my pocket, not merely a blue, not merely a Gamespiece, but a person awaiting . . . what? Resurrection? Awakening? Tamor, there in the northlands, Tamor who had saved my life more than once. And tragic Dealpas. And Trandilar. Oh, Gamelords, Trandilar! Voluptuous as boiling cloud and as full of pent energies, erotic, beguiling Trandilar. And Dorn. Dorn who was almost my elder brother in my head, lying there in the northlands, awaiting his renewal.

And all the while that part of me thought yes, oh, yes they must be found and raised up, awakened, another part of my mind said—no. No. They are mine, mine. My power comes from them. *My* Talents. I will not give them up. And the first part of me recoiled as though a serpent had struck at me inside myself so that I gasped, and gagged on the bile that rose in my throat. I struggled while Chance shook me and demanded to know what was wrong, what was wrong. Oh, Gamelords, what was wrong was me!

And then, somehow, I managed to thrust the conflict away, to stop thinking of it. I knew, knew it was there, but I would not think of it. Not then.

"Riddle's grandfather had a covenant with Barish," I choked. "But Barish disappeared, didn't come back. So Riddle's grandfather brought some things here—maybe hoping to find Barish. Maybe for safekeeping. Only wreck and ruin came on Dindindaroo."

Chance objected. "The covenant couldn't have been with Riddle's grandpa only." I shook my head. Obviously not. The contract must have been with the Immutables, father and son and grandson, generation after generation. Chance went on, "Those bodies have been there how long?"

I was careful not to think when I answered. "A thousand years. More or less. And do not ask me how Barish survived or came and went during that time for I don't know, Chance. It does not bear thinking of."

"So now what's our Riddle searching for? What's he up to?"

"Duty," I replied. "The covenant. The contract. The pledge his forefathers made to Barish. Oh, Chance, I don't know. I can't think of Riddle as anything but honorable. It's too confusing."

"Well, lad, don't get into an uproar over it," he said, giving me a long measuring look. "Whatever we don't know, we do know more than we did."

"Not enough more," I mourned, thinking of the hundred questions I should have asked the ghost. I could not call him up again. Would not. He had been given absolution by someone, and I would not undo it. I felt tears slide down my face.

"Maybe not enough more," Chance agreed, "but some more." He built a fire then and gave us hot soup, then some wine, and then an interminable story about hunting some sea monster during which I fell asleep. When I woke in the morning, I was able not to think about the disturbing thing, and the day was sharp-edged enough to live in.

4

The Great North Road

I told Chance about the singer in Xammer who had sung about wind to me and Silkhands. A mere song seemed a foolish reason to go exploring the northlands, and I hoped Chance, who was never loath to declaim upon foolishness in general, would say so. This would give me reason not to go, but I did not ask myself, then, why I wanted such a reason. Instead I made excuses. Himaggery and Mavin would need me, I said to myself, waiting for Chance to say something to give substance to my rationalization.

But he said, "What was it made you think the singer sang to you?"

"Only that he sang of the far north," I said without thinking, "and in the Bright Desmesne a Seer told me my future lay there . . . with Silkhands." I did not say the Seer was Windlow.

"Well then, that's twice," said Chance. "And Riddle's grandpa is three times. Remember what I always said about that. Once is the thing itself, twice is a curiosity, but three times is Game."

I did remember. It had always been one of Chance's favorite sayings, particularly when I had committed some childish

50

prank more than twice. "Whose Game? Who would be pulling me north?"

"Well, lad, there's pulling and there's pushing. The ghost was lamenting the loss of those things you carry. And maybe those things you carry are lamenting the loss of their bodies. I would if it was me. Maybe it's them want to get back where they came from."

So Chance was no help, no help at all. The knife of conscience twisted, and the serpent of guilt writhed under the knife. Was it possible? Could they be pushing me without my knowing? I tried to say no. "They have to use my brain to think with, Chance. They are only—what did old Manacle call it—patterns of personality. They are whatever they were when they were made. Didir comes into my head always the same Didir. She uses my mind, my memories to think with, but she does not carry those memories back into the blue. They stay in my mind, not hers. What I forget, she cannot remember. They couldn't pull or push without my knowing!" I said this very confidently, but I was not sure. "And I'm not sure that Silkhands and I ought to go north for such a reason. It's probably very dangerous."

He looked at me in astonishment. "And what do I hear? Peter talking about dangerous? Well, and the daylight may turn pale purple and all the lakes be full of fish stew. I thought never to hear such stuff after Bannerwell. If we are not here to seek out mysteries and answer deep questions, why are we?"

"Why, Chance." I laughed uncomfortably. "You're a philosopher."

"No." he rubbed his nose and looked embarrassed. "Actually I was quoting Mertyn."

I might have known. Oh, Gamelords, I could not turn my back on this thing without feeling cut in half. I could at least pretend to go wholeheartedly, even if I were torn. Why not follow the scent laid down for me as a fustigar follows a bunwit, "Head high and howling," as Gamesmaster Gervaise was wont to say. These agonized thoughts were interrupted.

"Where did you and Silkhands arrange to meet?"

"She will be leaving Xammer soon, tomorrow or the next day. I thought it better not to travel together so close to the Bright Demesne. If someone is watching and plotting, let them work at it a little. I told her we would meet her below the Devil's Fork of the River Reave, at the town there. Here, let us see.''

I burrowed out the chart we had been at such pains to buy, spreading it upon the ground with stones at the corner to keep it flat. It was well made, on fine leather, the lettering as tiny and distinct as care and skill could make it. I found where we were, between the ruins and the Great North Road, then traced that road north with my finger to the place it split below the fork in River Reave. The town was there. Reavebridge.

"Well," I said, "we can go in disguise, on the road or off it; or in our own guise, on the road or off it. You are the wary one. I leave it to you."

"Then let us continue as Smitheries, father and son," he said. I agreed to that, and we packed up our things to ride away northeast where stretched the Great North Road.

The river which the Immutables call the Boundary came out of the northeast, and we followed it through the pleasant forests and farmlands north of Xammer. Ahead of us we could see the frowning brows of Two Headed Mountain, two days' ride away, which cupped the Phoenix Demesne at its foot. Farther north were the bald stone tops of Three Knob, hazed with smoke from the foundries there. These were both landmarks I remembered from my years at Schooltown, though I had never yet seen either of them much closer than we saw them on our way. Behind Three Knob, between it and the rising range of eastern mountains, was said to be what Himaggery called a Thandbarian Demesne made up of Empaths, Mirrormen, Revenants . . . I couldn't remember the other four Thandbarian Talents by Himaggery's scheme of Indexing. His scheme depended upon listing all the Talents which shared porting as a Talent, first, then all those left which shared Moving, then Reading, and so on. I wasn't sure it was any easier to remember than the old Indexes which listed each Talent as a separate thing, unique of its kind. One didn't seem to make any more sense than the other. There were still thousands of different Gamesmen. If the Talents were evenly distributed, said Himaggery, then half of all Gamesmen would have any one of the Talents. Still, Himaggery was attached to his scheme, and according to him there were seven Thandbarian Talents and over a thousand Elatorian ones. And no Necromantic ones at all except for Necromancers themselves. Which was idiotic, because there *were* Necromantic ones, Ghouls and Bonedancers and even Rancelmen.

Oh well, and foof. Still, since I'd been thinking about them, I asked Chance if he'd ever seen a Mirrorman (I never had), and he gave me a look as though he'd bitten into something rotten. "Yes, lad, but don't ask about it. I was a time being able to sleep at night again, after, and I don't relish the memory." Well. That was interesting.

It was less than a day's ride to the Great North Road where it crossed the Boundary River over a long sturdy bridge which had a look of Xammer about it, the railings being turned and knobbed like the balcony railings I had seen in the town. Its building had undoubtedly been commissioned by the town leaders in order to make travel—and trade—easier. Past the bridge was a campground, a place with a well and toilets and a place providing food and drink and firewood. The night was warm, so we bought food ready cooked and sat in a quiet corner of the place to eat it. Since we had chosen to sit fireless, our eyes were not flame dazzled and we could see who came in. Who came in was a Bonedancer, black and white, helmed with the skull of some ancient animal long extinct. He had either left his train of skeletons outside the place or currently had none, for which I was grateful. Bonedancers have enough Talents, including Necromancy, to raise dry bones and make them dance—or to do other things if moved to malice. Mostly they prey upon pawns in remote villages, telling fortunes and threatening horrors. I wondered how they could do it, wondered if they were ever reluctant to do it, wondered if perhaps there were many Bonedancers who simply did not exercise their Talents at all just as some Ghouls refused. Still, having the Bonedancer there did not upset me much. At first.

Then, however, came three more together: an Exorcist, a Medium, and a Timereacher. Chance drew in breath in a long, aching sigh as the three joined the Bonedancer, all at one fire, all talking together. "Game toward," he murmured. I was inclined to agree with him. Why else so many dealers with the dead in this one place?

"What is it Timereachers do?" I asked. "See the past?"

"It's said so," he whispered to me. "Mediums as well. A combination of Seeing and Deadraising? So I've heard."

"Exorcists too," I said. "Seeing, Healing, Deadraising. Able to settle ghosts, I recall, and perhaps to See where a ghost may trouble before it actually begins haunting. Still, to have all three, plus a Bonedancer? Someone means to raise something great, and he wishes to be sure he can put it to rest again. Who do you think?" The four were taking no notice of anyone around them, but there was something almost familiar about one of the figures. What was it made my skin crawl?

"Do you wish we were away from here?" I whispered.

"Enough to get away from here," he murmured in reply. It needed no discussion. He stood and walked away to the toilets, merely another one in a constant stream of toing and froing. After a moment, I went the same way. We met at the picket line, loosed our horses, and led them quietly into the night. Inasmuch as we had prepared no food for ourselves, nothing had been unpacked. When we had led them far enough for quiet's sake, we mounted and rode northward again, seeing the yellow glows of the little fires dwindle behind us in the dark. I was thinking, suspecting, wondering about the Gamesmen we had seen, the way they had moved and walked, the order of their arrival. Four. A Bonedancer, an Exorcist, a Medium, and a Timereacher. Three with Seeing; two with Healing; one to hold Power; one to raise Fire; and all four to Raise the Dead. I groped for Dorn in my pocket and read him this list.

"If such a four can find a battlefield," he whispered in my mind, "or the site of a great catastrophe in which many died, not so long that bones have fallen to dust yet long enough that flesh has left the bones, why then, were I Gaming, I would guess those four will raise a multitude and will seek, thereby, to do some evil work. . . ." I waited for him to go on. After a long time, he said, "A Healer may Heal. Know also a Healer may Unheal. Do not let the Medium or Exorcist lay hands upon you. . . ."

I had already learned that in School House, the unwisdom of letting those with the power of the flesh (another name for Healing) lay hands upon one. An Exorcist could lay hands on one and leave a bloody handprint where he had broken every little blood line in one's flesh. It was said, among boys, that Mediums could raise the dead and set them on your trail, and that they would follow forever. I asked Chance if he believed that.

"Well, there are haunts set, lad. You told me you put down one such in Betand. And there are Ghostpieces."

"I have yet to hear one straight word about Ghostpieces," I said with considerable asperity. "Windlow mentioned them once, and others have talked of them. I have never learned what it is they can and cannot do. Perhaps in your wide travels, Chance, you've learned the answers to all this." I was being sarcastic.

He became very dignified at once. "Lad, don't get all exercised at me. So there's Deadraisers on the Great North Road, and so you think they have something to do with you. Well, I'm not ringing any great bell to tell them where you're hid. I don't know a midgin more about Ghostpieces than the next one; what we've heard is all. We've heard of things raised up which could not be put down again. We've heard of things that turned on those that raise 'em. Himaggery would say to put your reason to work on it, and I can't say better than that."

When Chance got offended like that, there was no use trying to get anything out of him, so I rode along feeling ashamed of myself. Reason said that anything raised had to take power from somewhere. Reason said that, and so did experience, for when Dorn had raised up the dead under Bannerwell, I could feel the power flowing from him—me. But then once they were raised up, they went on their own—at least those in Bannerwell had. It had been like pushing a wagon from the top of a hill, a hard push to get it started, then it rolled of itself. So at least under *some conditions* things raised up would move on their own. Well, reason had not led me far. I would have to think more on it.

Meantime, we had come so far on the road that the Phoenix Demesne stood due east of us. It was time to rest, for us and for the animals. Here and there in the flat farmland, crisscrossed by a thousand little canals which flowed down from the east fork of the River Reave, were small hillocks covered with trees, woodlots left to provide fuel for the farms. In one of these copses we took cover for what remained of the night, tethering the animals so they could not wander out to be seen from the road. I went to sleep in discomfort and foreboding. Gamelords know what I dreamed, but I was so wound up in my blankets that Chance had to help me out of them in the morning, and the sweat had soaked them through.

We breakfasted over a small fire, built smokeless and quickly extinguished when the first travelers appeared on the road. We lay behind a shield of dried fern, peering through. There was an hour or so of usual travel, farm wagons, a herd of water oxen, a girl leading three farm zeller by the rings in their noses, their udders swinging full before milking. Then came a burst of travelers from the south, all riding speedily without looking around them, then another three or four, then a space, then a bunch riding with eyes ahead as though intent upon covering the leagues. There was another little space, then two men riding hard and whipping their animals. After them, the bones.

They came in a horde, a hundred, perhaps more, complete skeletons, so loosely joined that the arms and legs might go off dancing on their own, jerking and rattling, only to come back to the other bones and accumulate once more into more or less complete sets, the grinning skulls bouncing and lunging at the tops of the backbones as though on springs. Behind this clattering aggregation rode the Bonedancer on a shabby black horse, and behind the Bonedancer the Exorcist, the Timereacher, and the Medium— No! It wasn't a Medium. In the firelight the night before I had seen only the dark gray cloak pulled forward, hiding the face. Today the cloak glittered with gold spiderweb embroidery and the hood was thrown back to reveal the magpie helm beneath. A Rancelman—same Talents as a Timereacher, but with Reading added. I sharpened my Shifter's eyes to see more clearly, then muttered an oath as I saw more clearly than I liked.

"It's Karl Pig-face," I said. "A Rancelman!"

"No!" Chance fiddled with his glass, easing it through the dried fern so as not to betray us where we lay. "So it is! But what's wrong with his face? That isn't the Karl you knew!"

I looked again, more carefully. It was Karl Pig-face, right enough, but the face was . . . empty. Pale. Dry, rather than sheened with sweat as I had always seen it. At that instant, his head began to turn toward me, and as his head turned every skull in that endless train of bones began to turn also. Without thinking, I reached for Didir, felt her flow into me, and made my own mind dive down like some depth-dwelling fish to let her shield me. Through my eyes, I felt her watch the skeleton heads swing restlessly to and fro, like pendant fruit, the wormholes of the empty eyes seeking me. Then Karl's head faced forward once more, and they went on, on to the north. I did not move or speak until they were vanished in dust, beyond even a Shifter's ability to see them.

"That one sought you, Peter," whispered Didir. "Sought you out of hate, malice, and because he is forced to do it. He wears a cap, like the other one you are remembering. He felt you, Peter."

"But he did not tell them. . . ." I replied wonderingly.

"They are fools," she said. "Whoever wears the cap will do only what he is told. They told him to find you, not to tell them he had found you. So he found you, lost you, and went on seeking. Their stupidity has saved you, this time."

"Who?" I breathed.

She did not answer. I had not thought she would. Karl had not known who sent him, and for her to attempt to Read any of the others would have been to signal our presence.

"So we are behind them now," said Chance.

"Behind *them*," I said. "But who knows how many have been set on my trail. It began the minute we left the Bright Demesne. I am not such a fool as to think these boneraisers are the end of it. Someone has gone to considerable trouble."

"Ah," said Chance.

"Huld!" I said. I was certain of it. It had all the marks of Huld, all his energy, his relentless malice, his fascination with the mechanisms of the techs. Who else could have learned from Mandor that Karl Pig-face was my enemy? Who else would have known of my association with Silkhands . . . *Silkhands!* "Silkhands is in great danger," I said. "Huld would not let the chance pass to use her against me. He will take her when she leaves Xammer, depend upon it, and she is all unwary of this."

"Well, lad, I wouldn't let him do that if I were you."

Curse the man. No sympathy. No hooraw and horror, no running about squawking. Merely "don't let him do that." Tush. Xammer was more than a hard day's ride south, and she might be leaving at any time. Or have left already.

"There's that Hafnor," said Chance, fixing me with his beady little eyes. "In case you've forgot."

Damn him. Of course I hadn't forgotten. The idea made me sick to my stomach was all. Stopping existing in one place. Flicking away to another place. Starting to exist there. All in an instant. It was worse than the bones. I felt my inner parts lurch and sway, a kind of vertiginous gulping of the guts.

"No other way I can see," said Chance, still staring at me.

With no sense of volition about it at all, I reached into the pouch to find Hafnor, knowing him in the instant by the unfamiliarity of him. I clenched my hand around him and took a deep, aching breath, only to have my mind filled with a gust of mocking laughter. "Well, and where are we here?" I felt someone using my eyes, my nose, my tongue to taste the air, my other hand to feel the ground beneath me. I saw the shape of every tree, the volume of the leaves against the sun, felt the texture of the dried grasses. "That's here," said the laughing voice. "Where do we want to go?" I tried to explain about Silkhands, about Xammer, but felt only a mad, laughing incomprehension and impatience. "Where, where, where? What walls? What smell of the air? What floors? What doors leading in and out? What windows? Draperies? Furniture? What landmarks seen through those windows? Where, where?"

All I could think of was the room in the Guest House, and I tried to remember it in a way that would suit Hafnor. Sudden memories surged up, ones I had not known of, the color and sound of the fire, the feel of the woolen carpet on my hands, the smell of the polish used on the furniture. The memories assailed from every side, and I dropped the tiny figure of Hafnor in panic, to stand heaving like an overridden horse. When I had panted my way back to a kind of sanity, I said to Chance, "If I go, and if I am gone when night comes, then go to . . . to Three Knob. Get rid of that yellow horse and his strange shoes. Tell anyone who seems interested that the young man who was with you has gone away . . . to Vestertown, or Morninghill. But you go to Three Knob and wait there, however long it takes me. We'll meet you there, Silk-hands and I."

He did not argue or make any great fuss about it, merely watched me, nodding the while, as I took Hafnor into my hand again. I summoned up the memories of that guest room and saw them take visible shape before me, as though framed in a round window. From the corner of my eye, I saw another window which looked out onto a flame-lit cavern, and another which showed the attics of Mertyn's House in Schooltown, and another which showed the long, half-lit corridors of the magicians' lair beneath the mountains. I spun, seeing these windows open about me, as though I stood at the center of a sponge or a great cheese, all around me holes reaching away to every place I had ever been or known of. "Where?" whispered Hafnor, and I turned to the hole which showed the guest room in Xammer, stepped through it, and stumbled upon the rug before the cold fireplace to fall sprawling.

When I had stopped shaking and had time to get up and brush myself off, for I was still covered with half dried grasses from that hill beside the road, far to the north, I sneaked down to the courtyard and appeared there to the first person I could find from Vorbold's House. It was Gamesmistress Joumerie, who looked me over curiously and answered me words I did not like.

"Silkhands? Why, no, Gamesman. She rode out this morning with young Jinian and several servants and two Armigers for safety's sake, riding to King Kelver's purlieu, away north. They will not move over fast, not so far you may not catch them up, ride you swiftly."

I left her with scant courtesies to find a hidden corner and take Hafnor into my hand once more. "What do I do now?" I begged. "I must find her, but I don't know the road well enough to . . ."

"Hoptoad, lad," came the laughing voice with more than a hint of malice at my discomfiture. "Hoptoad. Do you look far ahead, keen as your eyes will go, and I will do the rest." That is what we did. I looked as far down the road as I could see, sharpening my vision to the utmost, spying the place ahead, the trees, the canals, whatever might be about, bit on bit, and then we *flicked*, and I was in that spot. Then I did it again, and

flick, and again, and flick, each time scanning the road between to be sure we did not miss her. Until we saw the confusion and heard the screaming and *flicked* to find ourselves
among a crowd, all shouting and running about near the unconscious body of one Armiger and the bleeding, perhaps
dead, body of another.

I shook one of the bystanders and demanded that he tell me
quickly what had happened. He pointed a trembling finger at
the forest edge. "Ghoul," he whispered. "Came with a horde
of dead out of the trees. The Armigers tried to fight them, but
you can't fight that. The Ghoul took the women. Dragged
them away into the trees."

Though obviously frightened, he had kept his wits about
him. I ran for the forest, knowing that Hafnor could not help
me there. It would take Grandfather Tamor, swift flyer, to lift
me up where I could see. So it was. He caught me up like a
feather, moved me like a swooping hawk to peer this way and
that, seeking the movement of leaves or the rustle of under-
growth below, quartering again and yet again, hearing only
silence, working slowly westward, a little faster than a man
might run.

It was the cold first, then Silkhands' voice which led me to
them. The Ghoul could not stop her chatter any more than I
had ever been able to do, and her voice went on resolutely,
almost as though she knew someone would be searching for
her. I came into a tree top to watch them. The Ghoul dragged
them along, one on either side of him, his host of dead following in a shamble of rotting flesh. Ghouls do not move clean
bones; they have the Talent of Moving, of Power, of Raising
the Dead. How much power did this one have? Plenty, it
seemed, and was drawing more, for the place was icy as
winter. I hung above them judging the distance.

Then as he passed below I stooped upon him, screaming as I
flew, "Ghoul's Ghast Nine, I call Game and Move!" as I
snatched the two girls from him and launched myself upward
toward another tree. . . .

Only to know in one hideous moment that I had played the
fool, the utter, absolute and unGamed fool. I had called a risk
play, an Imperative, unwise and unready as I was, and the

Ghoul would not ignore it. I hung there in the tree, the girls reaching out to cling to the branches as the strength left my arms. There was no power in the place to draw and I was weak . . . weak. I was in the Ghoul's Demesne, and he had drawn it all. Such power as I had I had expended prodigiously in the flick, flick, flick of Elator's hunt in finding them, in the reckless flight and swoop and call. Now there was no more strength in me than enough to move myself away a few yards, myself only, and no way to get more. I gasped, unable even to think what might be done.

I saw him reach for his power. He had more than I would have guessed, for two of the rotting liches staggered to the tree where we clung and began to climb, clotted eyes fixed upon us. They climbed awkwardly, leaving parts of themselves stuck to various small twigs and branches, but they came higher by the moment. Beneath them, others assembled, waiting, lipless mouths gaped in silent grins of amusement at the fruit about to fall into their hands and jaws. I heard Silkhands whimper, saw the girl, Jinian, glaring down at the Ghoul while rumbling curses in her throat. I wanted to close my own eyes, half dead as I was with cold and terror. I could fly myself away to another place, me, alone, with no burden. Or move Silkhands away without me. No more than that, and the place cold, cold.

Below me the Ghoul laughed and screamed into the quiet forest, "Armiger's Flight Ten, fool flyer. Armiger's Flight Ten." He was calling my death and the death of those two with me, and I knew it as did they.

I wondered if I would have the strength to move Silkhands away. My hand clenched in my pocket, clenched, and then gripped again as I felt that other unfamiliar shape in my fingers. Buinel. Sentinel. Firemaker. He came into my mind like a bird onto an unfamiliar nest, fussing and turning. I felt the thousand questions he was about to ask, anticipated the lengthy speech he was about to make. Oh, something within me recognized him, knew him for that Buinel whom Windlow had called Buinel the flutterer.

The branch under my foot swayed. I looked down into the face of one of the liches as it fastened a partly fleshed hand upon my boot. I kicked wildly, and the thing fell away as Jinian shouted shrilly at my side.

"Buinel," I cried silently. "Fire. Or we die, you die, we all die. Forever."

"Who?" he fussed. "Who speaks? What authority? What place is this? Who is that Ghoul? What Game?"

"Buinel," I shouted at the top of my voice, startling a flight of birds out of the trees around us, "if you do not set fire to the Ghoul and to all the liches in this tree, we are dead and you with us."

Something happened. I think it was Tamor, the pattern of Tamor, though it may have been Hafnor. Some pattern in my head issued a command, said something harsh and peremptory to the pattern which was Buinel, and the tree behind the Ghoul burst into flame, all at once, like a torch. The Ghoul turned, startled, but not too startled to begin storing the power of flame. Shattnir was in my hand in the instant drawing from the same source. "More," I demanded. "By the ice and the wind and the seven devils, Buinel, more fire. Burn these liches at my feet." For another of the corpses had reached to lay hands upon me. The cerements on the creature began to smoke, the very bones began to glow and it dropped away silently as other trees went up in explosive conflagration. Meantime, Shattnir and the Ghoul fought it out for the available heat. There was more than was comfortable.

The Ghoul sent up a clamor, "Allies, allies!" into the roar of the flames. I thought I heard a Herald's trumpet away somewhere and turned to catch a sudden dazzle of light reflected off something, but I could not see it and could not wait. I had enough power by then to lift the women and flutter away through the columned forest like a crippled bat, bumping and sliding across branches in a search for water. Behind me I could hear the Ghoul screaming, and I muttered "Ghoul's Ghast Ten," to myself. "Move and Game." I had never planned to die as Armiger's Flight Ten in a strange wood, eaten by liches. But it had been close.

We found a little islet in a pond, and there Silkhands Healed our burns. I drew more power and Searched as the fire burned in all directions, wider and hotter. It would stop at the river on the south, and there were only flat fields to the east, but it would burn long to the north and west unless some sensible

Tragamors brought in clouds and wrung them out. I could do nothing about it alone, chose not to in any case, for I wanted to see who ran before those flames. Twice I caught that dazzle of light, but I could find no one. Whoever it might have been had flown away. At last I gave up and returned to the women.

They had made a couch of grasses behind some fallen trees. All three of us lay there in the late afternoon sun to let it quiet us. Later I was to think it strange that I did not inquire what Talent the girl, Jinian, had. Silkhands had not mentioned the matter in my hearing. If she had had any headdress, it had been lost in the attack. In any case, I did not ask and she did not offer. She did ask to borrow my knife in order to set a snare, but I told her I would furnish a meal before I left them to go away and arrange our farther travel. I did it by Shifting into pombi shape and murdering some foolish farm poultry who had wandered into the woods to brood. While the fowl popped over the flames, we spoke of alternatives. I could have gone back to Xammer to procure horses, supplies, a replacement carriage, even guards and servants. We chose not to do so. Instead, when we had eaten, I Shifted myself into a middling ordinary human shape and went off to find some settlement where goods and beasts would be available.

After that was only a weary time of looking and bargaining and going elsewhere for this thing and that thing which no one, ever, would have thought of having when and where it might be wanted or convenient to any other thing which might have been wanted. The evening spent itself into night and the night into morning. It was noon the following day before I led Silkhands and Jinian out of the trees to see what I had accomplished.

"By the pain of Dealpas," said Silkhands reverently, "I have never seen such a tumbletrundle in my life."

I nodded, pleased. The wagon did look as though it might fall apart at any moment, but it would not. I had fixed certain parts of it myself. The animals hitched to it were probably mostly water oxen, though the parentage of either could have been questioned. They were large, ugly, and looked too tough to tempt hunters, too rough to tempt thieves. The clothing in the wagon was of a kind with the rest, ugly and boring.

"No one would want it," said Jinian. I cast her a quick

look, thinking it a pity she was so plain-looking for she had a perceptive mind. "Exactly," I said. "Now we must make sure that no one would want any of us, either."

I believed that we succeeded. Time would prove, the occasion would tell, but we had certainly changed the conditions of our travel more than a little. No one would be interested in the old man or either of the two mabs at his side. All three had dirty faces and gap-toothed smiles. The girls' teeth were blackened out with tar; from an armslength away they appeared to be missing. When evening came of this day after I had left Chance, we were on the Great North Road once more, only a little north of the Boundary bridge. Looking back at it, I sighed. We had spent much time and effort coming a very small way, and there were still twenty leagues between us and Three Knob.

I had only one real satisfaction. The episode with the Ghoul had decided me firmly and finally that Huld was responsible. The earlier episode with the Witch might have been Riddle's doing, but it was Huld who set Bonedancer and Ghoul upon my trail. He had made a fool's call once, in the ice caverns. He had called Necromancer Nine on me, but he could not Play to fulfill it. Now, he was determined to fulfill it, to fulfill it in a way I could not mistake, using Ghoul and Bonedancer, Rancelman and Exorcist—all of them with Necromantic Talents. I had used the dead against Mandor and Huld; now he would use them against me to the death. He had underestimated me before and again this latest time, though not by much. He still did not know what I was or could do.

It was rare to find Gamesmen who did many things well. Sometimes there are children born who, when they reach puberty, seem to have bits and pieces of many Talents. Often they turn into ineffectual idiots who sit in the sun playing with themselves, endlessly moving one stone atop another or floating a handswidth above the earth or porting tiny distances around a circle to the accompaniment of loud laughter. Having more than four or five different abilities seemed to carry destruction with it. Minery Mindcaster was sometimes called a twinned Talent. The way we had all learned to think about Talents made it easier to accept her as being a combination Pursuivant and Afrit than simply as having seven separate

Talents. I, who had all eleven chose I to use them, would not be thought of as a possibility by Huld. Not yet. He had known me first as Necromancer, and he was stuck with that notion for some time. Perhaps he knew me as Shifter, but I thought not. He had seen me fly in the ice caverns, but did he think it was my own ability or that some Tragamor lurked out of sight and Moved me? When I blasted out the barrier Huld had set across the exit to that place, did he know I had done it, or did he think some Sorcerer was involved? If he thought I had done it, then he was judging me as an Afrit, for these were the Afrit Talents.

However, he was not a fool. He might be misled for a time. His Bonedancer and his Rancelman had not found me on the road. His Ghoul was dead. Nonetheless, Huld was an implacable enemy who grew stronger and more clever with time. Could I lay all my powers down in the northlands and confront him with nothing . . . ? Nothing but myself? Inside me I whimpered and cowered until at last I was sickened at myself. I had been more courageous at Bannerwell than I was being now, and I reflected that a little taste of power could take a reasonably sensible person and make some kind of groveling, cringing thing of him.

A SAMPLE OF THE INDEXING SYSTEM USED BY WINDLOW

	Elatorians: (sample list)				Tragamonians:								Demonics:		
	Pursuivants	Churchman	Phantasm	Archangel	Divulger	Midwives	Herald	Woodsmen	Warbler	Ghoul	Bonedancer	Afrit	Rancelmen	Invigilator	Basilisk
NECROMANTIC — Power of the Dead										×	×	×	×		
HEALING — Power of the Flesh															
CLAIRVOYANCE — Power of Seeing	×				×		×			×			×		
SHIFTING — Power of Shape															×
FIRESTARTING — Power of Flame		×	×				×								
SORCERIAN — Power of Storing										×	×	×		×	
BEGUILEMENT — Power of Ruling	×								×						×
FLYING — Power of the Air		×					×					×	×		
TELEPATHY — Power of Reading	×			×	×	×							×	×	×
TELEKINESIS — Power of Moving		×			×	×	×	×	×	×	×	×			
TELEPORTATION — Power of Travel	×	×	×	×											

	1	2	3	4	5	6	7	8
Armigerians:								
Dragon				X				X
Cold Drake				X	X			X
Prophet			X			X		X
Trandilarians:								
Talisman					X	X		
Thaumaturge	X	X					X	
Firedancer		X		X			X	
Halberdier							X	
Priest/Witch					X		X	
Trader			X			X	X	
Shattnirians:								
Phoenix				X	X	X		
Oneiromancer			X			X		
Dervish		X		X		X		
Buinelians:								
Salamander	X			X	X			
Gazer		X			X			
Exorcist			X		X			
Thandbarians:								
Empath		X		X				
Mirrorman	X			X				
Revenant			X	X				
Sorahians:								
Timereacher	X		X					
Medium	X	X	X					
Dealpasian:								
Mourners	X	X						

5

Three Knob

I have said that the land to the east of the Gathered Waters is
flat. It was no less flat and unenlivening the second time I
traveled it in the space of a few days. The pace of the water
oxen may have been as much as a league an hour, when they
hurried, which they were inclined to do only toward evening
when it grew cool and they sensed water ahead. I had coached
both Jinian and Silkhands in the use of jiggly rhymes or songs
should any Demon or other Talent with Reading skills come
by, and I had set myself a persona, Old Globber, in expecta-
tion of some such event. As a matter of fact, one Demon did
ride by toward dusk of the second day. So far as I could tell,
he cast not even a passing look toward us. We were, indeed,
very unattractive.

Boredom began to oppress us early. In midafternoon of the
second day, Silkhands and Jinian began to share confidences
concerning their emotions and feelings toward those of my
sex, and I found myself alternately titillated and embarrassed
by their frankness, finally being made so uncomfortable that I
sought some way to change the subject. Some idea had been
fluttering at the back of my head for several days, and I
thought the little book in which Windlow had set such store
might net it for me.

"Jinian," I said, thrusting my request into a brief niche in their conversation, "I have something I've been studying, a little book. Would you read it to me?" She said she would, though I could tell that she was surprised at the request. I dug out the Onomasticon and gave it to her. My hope was that hearing it in another voice might let the words fall into some pit of comprehension. Thus Jinian, and when she tired, perhaps Silkhands.

"Shall I start at the beginning?" She was doubtful, having dipped into it and found little sense there.

"Pick a page," I said. "At the beginning, or anywhere. There is supposed to be some deep meaning or content in these pages, so an old friend of Silkhands and mine thought. However, I've been unable to find the key to it. Perhaps you'll find it for me."

She began. " 'When the Wizard returns for the ninth or tenth time, there will be much work to do.' " She stared at the page, then turned to me. "Which Wizard is that?"

"Barish, I suppose," I said. "You've heard it. So have I. People saying, 'When Barish returns.' I heard one codger in a market say he would drop his prices at the twelfth coming of Barish."

She nodded thoughtfully and went on. " 'The greater power these Gamesmen have, the more they are corrupted . . . yet there are still some born in every generation with a sense of justice and the right . . . so few when compared to the others. I would that they become many!' And I say so-be-it to that," said Jinian. "I would there were more like you, Peter, and Silkhands, and fewer like that Ghoul."

I think I may have flushed, conscious as I was of my own struggles to perceive and do the right. Gamelords! It is not hard to risk your life when you have nothing to live for, but it is a hard thing when life is sweet. I tried to catch Silkhands' eyes, hoping for a lover's glance from her, but her eyes were closed and she breathed as though asleep. Jinian went on reading, unaware.

" 'In the meantime, Festivals will provide opportunity for reproduction by young people . . . School Houses will protect them . . . I fear that those at the Base have lost all touch with reality. They are breeding monsters in those caverns and they do not come into the light. . . .

" 'I have met some of the native inhabitants of this place. How foolish to think there were none. They leave us untroubled in this small space but will not do so forever. . . .

" 'I have set this great plan . . . a thousand years in the carrying out . . . centuries of the great contract between us and the people we have set to guard us. . . .' "

"Read that last part again," I said to her.

" ' . . . a thousand years in the carrying out. It will depend upon a hundred favorable chances, the grace and assistance of fate and those who dwelt in the place before we came, and the perpetuation through the centuries of the great contract between us and the people we have set to guard us.' "

"Nothing ponderous about that," I said in an attempt to be witty. "Lords, but the man took himself seriously."

"What man? Who wrote this? I thought at first it was printed, like some books, but someone wrote it by hand in tiny printing in old style letters. In places it's all smudged, as though the person was tired or confused." She thrust it at me, pointing with one strong finger, and I saw what she meant. Over the years the ink had faded and the paper discolored to make the whole monochromatic and dim. Her question triggered that evasive thought which flickered at the edge of my mind. It was too late; we were too weary. I could hardly see the road verge, much less the pages in the failing light.

"I believe Barish wrote it," I said. "A kind of diary of his thoughts? Though why such a diary should now be considered so important is beyond me. Windlow the Seer searched for this book for decades and read it constantly once he had found it, searching in it for—what? Right now I believe the Immutables are searching for this book. Perhaps others search for it as well. Oh, it's an important book, I'm sure. If I could only find out why. I thought hearing it in your voice might help, but the solution won't come. . . ."

And then, while Silkhands dozed, I told Jinian all that I knew or guessed about this book and about the Gamesmen of Barish while she asked sensible, penetrating questions in a manner which reminded me much of Himaggery on his better days. In the dusk her face had a pale, translucent quality, a kind of romantic haziness, and I remembered I had thought her plain before. Though what was it Chance always said? Any hull looks sound in the dark? Well, her hull was sound enough, dark or light.

"Windlow said something about words changing their meaning over time," I told her. "He said that if we knew the words, then we would know what things once meant—or words to that effect. He mentioned, for example, that in this book the word 'Festival' meant 'opportunity for reproduction,' and he said that was important. I don't know why."

She was a sober little person, very serious and intent. When she considered things, two narrow lines appeared between her eyes and her mouth turned down as though she chewed on the idea. It made me want to laugh to see her so earnest with the dirt on her face and her teeth blacked out. It was as though she had forgotten how she looked. Silkhands had not. Every time she wakened, she made some petulant remark about it.

"It is true that powerful Gamesmen are careless of the lives of others," Jinian offered. "We all know that, of course. It's part of the Game. So if we did not have School Houses, then young people without Talent yet, or those who don't know how to use their Talents, would be eaten in the Game in great numbers. And if they were shut up always in School Houses, then they would not have babies. We were taught at Vorbold's House that it is easiest for women to bear children when they are young—the women, I mean, not the babies. So, when women are young, they are in School Houses, and if they must have babies then, we must have Festivals. Otherwise there would be few babies and everything would stop." She sighed. "If Barish wrote this, he is saying that School Houses and Festivals are necessary, and further he is saying that he, personally, has invented both. But—that was so long ago. It is a very old book."

"Very," I murmured. "Very old. What was that bit about the native inhabitants?"

She did not answer for some time. I thought she had gone to sleep. I thought of going to sleep myself. The water oxen were now plodding along in starlight, and we had to give serious consideration to stopping for the night so they could browse and we could eat and sleep, preparatory to our mad gallop into tomorrow behind the faithful team. When Jinian spoke at last it was conversation extended into dream.

"Did you ever hear the story of faithful-dog?" she asked. I nodded that I had. It was a nursery tale. "Did you ever see a dog?"

"It's just another word for fustigar," I said sleepily.

"No it isn't," she said. "In the story of faithful-dog, the dog wags his tail, his tail, you know? Remember? Fustigars can't wag their tails. They don't have tails."

"Well, maybe at one time they did," I objected. I had never thought of that, though indeed the old story did have a wagging tail in it. That was the point of the story for children, for it was the wag of our bottoms as we acted it out which made it fun.

"Pombis don't have tails," she continued. "Cats do. Mice do. Owls and hawks do, but flitchhawks don't. Horses do. But zellers don't."

"We don't," I said.

"I know. That's what's confusing, because I think we belong with cats and horses and faithful-dog. But we don't have tails and they all do. Anyhow, it's as though there are two kinds of animals and birds and creatures, one kind from here and one kind from somewhere else. Only I don't know if we're the kind from here or the kind from somewhere else. Do you?"

In the place of the magicians, I had learned an answer to this. "We're from somewhere else." She accepted this, as she did almost everything I said, very soberly. "The shadow-people are from here, however. And they have no tails."

"Have you seen them?" She was as excited as a child seeing the Festival Queen for the first time. I told her I had seen them, and what they were like, and she laughed when I told her of their songs, their flutes, their dances, their huge eyes and wide, winged ears, their appetite for rabbits (which have tails) and bunwits (which don't). I told her of their language, the sound of them crying "Peter, eater, ter ter ter," in the caverns of the firehills. The water oxen had found a convenient wallow at the side of the road where a canal spilled into a little slough, and they refused to plod another step. I shook Silkhands awake, and we burned charcoal in the clay stove I had bought to heat our food. Somewhere to the north of us a shuddering growl came out of the earth, and we felt the vibrations under us. "Groles," said Silkhands. "Have you ever seen them, Peter?"

I told her I had not, though I had heard the roar often as a child when I had lived in Mertyn's House.

"Sausage groles?" asked Jinian eagerly, and both Silkhands and I laughed.

"No. Rockeaters. From Three Knob. For sausage groles, one must go on up to Leamer, where the Nutters live. Only rockeaters make that noise, and there will be no fustigars or pombis within sound of it, for it drives them away."

"Do they have tails?" This from Jinian, so sleepily that I knew she would not hear the answer. And she did not, making a little sighing noise which told me she was asleep. I covered her with a blanket and let her lie where she was. The ground was at least as soft as the wagon bed, and probably cleaner. I didn't know whether groles had tails or not. I thought not. I went to sleep making an inventory of all those birds and beasts with tails, thinking how odd it was that I had learned this from Jinian when none of my Gamesmasters seemed to have known or thought anything about it.

On the morning, we composed ourselves to ugliness once more and got back into the wagon. If the water oxen could be kept to a steady pace, we would arrive at the Three Knob turn off by midday. I hoped Chance had arrived there safely, and I wondered what guise we might travel in as we went farther north which would not betray us to the Boneraisers. I had no doubt they still searched for me, and I had not yet thought of any convenient way to go through the minions which had been sent against me to reach Huld, who had sent them. It would do no lasting good to Game against mercenaries. Huld could wear me to a nubbin sending bought men against me. So, thinking this and thinking that, we rolled along. Almost I missed seeing the skeleton train ahead, but Jinian thrust a sharp elbow into my ribs and began to sing. Silkhands picked up the song, and they two began nodding their heads in time to their hushed la, la, la as I dived deep and grasped Didir to cover me.

"Larby Lanooly went to sea," they sang. "Hoo di Hi and wamble di dee. Did not matter he would or no, did not matter

the winds did blow, put him into the boat to row, Oho for Larby Lanooly." There were at least thirty verses to the song, and
Silkhands knew them all. While I drove, letting Didir manage
Peter while Globber held the reins, the skeleton train came
toward us, back down the road from the north. Old Globber
was terrified, as he should have been. He clucked and cried
and drove the wagon off the road, almost into a canal. He sat
there and shivered in his socks while the bones danced past
him, the two women next to him clinging together and singing
under their breath, "Larby Lanooly went to farm, Hoo di Hi
and wamble di darm. Did not matter he knew not how, put
him behind an ox and plow, he'll do well or not enow, Oho for
Larby Lanooly."

If Karl Pig-face had been wearing the strange cap before, he
was not wearing it now. His face was red again, shiny with
sweat, and he tugged angrily at a cord which bound him to the
Bonedancer on one side of him. As they passed, Didir heard
one of them say, "If you will not do as you are told, we can
put the cap back on you, Rancelman."

"I've told you," blustered Karl. "When you had that stupid
cap on me, I thought I felt him down the road here. But I
couldn't tell you. You need no cap, nor no cord to bind me.
Pay me, as you'd pay anyone, and I'll seek Peter Priss to the
end of the lands and purlieus for you. No love between him
and me, and I'm glad to do it."

"Earn our trust, Rancelman. Earn it if you can, and no
more sneaking away in the night. Now, stop tugging at the
binding and lead us to the place it was you say you felt him
last." And they went on by us, not looking at us at all. It was
many a long moment before Globber got himself together to
drive the oxen back onto the road. Meantime we had taken
Larby Lanooly from farm to shop to mine to devil-take-it.

"If they have anyone in that group who can track," I said at
last when the Boneraisers were gone and we were plodding
northward once more, "we may see them again. I doubt not
that Chance left readable tracks when he came north from the
copse."

"Three days' traffic on the road?" asked Jinian. "Would
that not cover?"

I clenched my teeth, trying to remember. So far as I could

recall, only the yellow horse had had distinctive shoes, nubby ones such as they use along the River Dourt, but the yellow horse should have been sold or traded or simply set loose long since. "Perhaps," I said. "Though I would feel better about it if there had been rain and a bit of wind."

"Well, that may happen soon enough," said Silkhands. "Watch the sky west of us where the black clouds gather and pour. I doubt not we'll have more rain than is comfortable before nightfall."

"Before nightfall, we'll be at Three Knob," I promised them. We kept that schedule with time to spare, for the sun stood short of noon when we came to the turn off to the right which led away toward three bald stone hills grouped above the foundry smokes. Stone pillars marked the turn, and we drove between lines of long, low brooder houses where they hatched the groles. There were few of the creatures about during the day, most of them being down below ground, gnawing their way through the stone with their adamant teeth, chewing the rock into gravel and packing it into their endless gut. At night they would digest it, roaring the while, and on the morn the dung gatherers would wash the night's gravel for powder of iron and nuggets of occamy and silver, less only the light metals which the groles had nourished themselves upon. As we drove, we began to see large groles feeding on piles of broken stone and bone and charcoal. These were the toothlings, just growing their teeth of adamant, soon to be promoted to work in the mines. Handlers stood beside each, stroking the creatures with long iron-tipped staffs, crooning grole songs to them. I shuddered. Imagine a great gut, as wide as a man is tall, as long as five men laid end to end, with a dozen rows of teeth and no eyes, and that is a grole. Still, how would we have metal for our axles and weapons did we not have groles?

"Stop," said Jinian. "I want to pet one."

I pulled up the wagon, amazed, and she hobbled over to one of the beasts, staying in character the whole way, to feel its huge side. Nothing would do but that I come as well, and Silkhands, to feel the stony hide of the beast and wonder at its size. The handlers seemed well accustomed to such marveling from travelers, almost uninterested in us.

Then we got back into the wagon and Jinian surprised me

further. "You are Shifter, are you not?" Well, of course I had told her I was. "I thought it wise for you to lay hands on the creature. That is how it works, does it not? You must lay hands on it? So I have heard?"

So she thought it wise, did she? She must have seen something of my irritation, for she flushed, then shrugged. "If I have misunderstood, forgive me." She had not misunderstood. That was how it worked, or at least one way it worked. But Shifting into something like that! The bulk, alone, would take hours to build. One could do it by starting small, eating rock and converting it to bulk, then more and more. I thought the process out, step by step, lost in it, and then blushed, embarrassed, to catch her eyes on me. She knew very well what I had been thinking.

"No need for forgiveness," I said. "It is an interesting thought." As it was. I did not ever intend to do anything about it, but it was interesting.

The mines and many small foundries were scattered along the gulches and upon the ridges around the three mountains, but Three Knob itself lay cupped among them like a child's toys spilled upon a dish. I chose not to ride into the town as we were. Instead we would engage in further deception. We found a twist in the road behind a long, crumbling wall, unharnessed the water oxen and drove them away down the slope of the meadow toward a distant line of trees which marked a stream. Then I took the hammer I had brought for the purpose and beat the wagon into several pieces, separating these from the wheels. When stacked along the wall, it looked like what it was. Wood fit for the fire. Perhaps a wheel or two worth salvage by some desperate wagoner. Our rags were buried beneath the wagon, and we cleaned the dirt from our faces and the tar from our teeth before walking into Three Knob as a middle-aged buyer of something or other and his two daughters. I hoped I would not have to look far for Chance.

As it was, I did not have to look far enough. The yellow horse I had told him to get rid of was cavorting in a paddock near an Inn, nubby shoes and all. Chance was toping wine, red of nose and bibulous, full of good cheer and unresponsive to my annoyance.

"Why, my boy, the Bonedancers are all long gone on ahead. He's a good horse. No need to trade him off just yet."

"They're behind us again, Chance. Behind us. They passed us on the road. Karl Pig-face, with his nasty little mind hunting me, and he did feel me back there when you and I lay up in the copse and watched him. Further, he *knows* you!"

I wasn't getting through to him at all until Silkhands reached out to take his hand with an intent expression. She was doing something intricate and intimate to his insides. I saw the flush leave his face and gradual awareness seep in to him. "Ah. Ah, well, lad. I'm sorry about that. Truly, I had not thought they would return. And they may not have one among them who can track."

"Rancelmen do," said Jinian. "They have a skill for it. We must think quickly what to do, for they could be on the start of our trail and back here by evening."

Silkhands nodded agreement to this sadly. Her face was quite drawn, and I felt a quick pity. The way had been hard on her. I could not help her, however, and Chance interrupted the thought.

"It was my doing, so fair it be my undoing. I'll take the animal with much hoorah and ride off on the back roads. Once far enough along, I'll get rid of the animal and continue so far as Reavebridge. You all lay by here until you're rested—Silkhands needs a night's sleep in a bed—then come on north to meet me. Have you barter enough for new mounts, lad?"

I told him truthfully that I did not. The last coin I had had been spent on the wagon and water oxen. So he dug down and gave me a pouch which seemed well filled. Part of his gain from Xammer, no doubt, and he did not deny it. He was generously quick to offer it, and I knew he felt guilty. At the moment, I was in no mood to forgive him, though no great harm had been done if he would ride swiftly away. We had all been talking quietly, so we separated ourselves from him as would any travelers who had made casual talk upon the road and busied ourselves finding lodging. Meantime Chance gathered his string of animals together and got himself gone with much loud joshing and suchlike, to draw attention.

As for the rest of us, we found two rooms adjoining, upstairs above the stable yard, and set about having a bath in deep tin tubs before the fire. Afterwards, wrapped in great, rough towels, we sat in the window to sip warmed wine and watch for the Bonedancer, hoping he would not come. It was after dark that he came, him and his colleagues, but come he did. They did not leave. The bones lay in a drift against the stable wall. The residents of Three Knob cowered in their homes. The Boneraisers, including Karl Pig-face, sat in the common room below, eating and drinking with much cheer. We, Jinian, Silkhands and I, stayed in the rooms above, quiet and inconspicuous.

As for me, I was hung between two pillars. On the one side, I was as angry as I have ever been, angry at Karl Pig-face for sitting below in the common room, undoubtedly eating and drinking his fill without any need to hide or sly about. On the other hand, I remembered clinging to that tree while the Ghoul pranced beneath me, as close to death as I have ever come. I felt no desire for audacity, but I hungered for vengeance against Huld and all his minions. Across the room from me Jinian sat, staring at me, the fire dancing in her eyes. Silkhands slept. I do not know where I got the idea that Jinian knew what I was thinking. There was no Demon tickle in my head, and it wasn't that kind of mind reading anyhow. I simply thought that she knew. I was certain of it when she said, "They don't know me at all. If they ride out tonight, I could lend them a lantern to light them through the dark . . . tunnels."

I was not at all sure I liked her knowing what I thought, but it would work better if she did help. "Tonight would certainly be best," I agreed.

"They must be encouraged to leave soon, then," she said. "Perhaps they would be so encouraged if they heard that the horse they are following is soon to be sold or traded? If they heard this from someone?"

"Someone being you?"

She smiled. "Oh, I don't fear the Bonedancer. I am not pretty enough to attract that kind of attention, either. I can try."

"They may Read you."

"I think not. I will do it simply. But not until you are ready."

I thought about that. "Midnight, then. Or earlier, if it looks like they are going off to sleep." Privately I thought it fairly risky, but better than doing nothing. I slipped out the back way, walked at the side of the road Chance had taken, able to see the prints of the nubby shoes even in the light of the lantern I had brought with me. The road wound and climbed back into the gullies above the town, dodging behind this bank and that hillock. I had not gone far before I found what I was looking for, a narrow defile where the roadway cut through a bank. I put out the lantern and got to work.

As I did so, I visualized what was undoubtedly going on back at the Inn. Silkhands would stay quietly asleep. As a former Gamesmistress of Vorbold's House—to say nothing of her being a Healer—she might be known to someone in the place. Jinian, on the other hand, would be only an anonymous girl, of Gamesman class by her dress. She would go into the common room to the place the Innkeeper sat in the corner adding up his accounts and keeping an eye on the man who poured the beer and wine. She would wait for a lull in the conversation, then say, "Innkeeper? The man who left this afternoon, the one who owned the pretty yellow horse with the nubby shoes? Do you know if he is coming back? He said he intended to sell or trade the horse at once, and I thought I might offer for it."

The Innkeeper would say something about the horse, or about Chance. They would talk of his having ridden north on the back road. Jinian would evince disappointment. "Well, the man will have traded the horse by the time I could catch up to him tomorrow. Ah, well. I will not worry on it further." And then she would take herself off upstairs.

Behind her in the common room, the Bonedancer would snarl at Karl Pig-face. Then, if all went as I thought it might, they would decide to ride out after the man and the horse with the nubby shoes to catch him before the trail was lost. If they hurried, they would say, they might catch him as he slept somewhere, and find they had captured Peter without further effort. I went over this scenario in my head several times, finding it both likely and satisfying. Some time went by. I began to doubt and fidget, never ceasing to chew away at the work I was doing. The moon rode at my back, curved as a blade. In the dim light I saw the shadows at the turn of the road, then heard the clatter, clatter of the bones as they rounded the corner. They had a lantern, for the Bonedancer led them in a puddle of yellow light, Karl trudging sullenly beside him with the others. Then Karl's head came up.

"I Read him," he whispered excitedly. "Petey Priss. I Read him. Not far off. Near us. Oh, what a fool to go sleeping by the road! He's close ahead of us."

"Well then, walk quiet, little Rancelman," a whispered reply from the Bonedancer. "At the end of this tunnel here we'll spread out and seek him. Then you'll be paid as promised and a good job done." I saw the gleam of moonlight in their eyes, then lost the light as they entered the tunnel, Gamesmen first, bones after.

Only then did I shut my mighty grole mouth and let the grole innards grind. In the two hours which had passed, I had managed to add enough bulk to grow a man and a half high and nine men long. I had made a believable tunnel. One without an end, unfortunately for those who entered.

I lay there in the darkness, a great, black bowel in the night, trying to decide whether I felt sadness over Karl Pig-face. I decided that he was more digestible to me dead than alive and hunting me. When I had finished the light metal in the bones (delicious to a grole—they taste with their stomachs, I learned) I pulled the net and gave up bulk, having first heaved myself out of the defile and onto a broader patch of ground. What was left was only a long, vaguely cylindrical pile of rock and some powdered ores. So much for one more of Huld's reaches in my direction. I was not fool enough to think it was the last or the strongest. Next time would not be this easy.

Next time, I thought, he may send a Game I cannot win.

6

The Grole Hills

Since Jinian had already spoken to the Innkeeper about buying horses, it was she who went to the beastmarket the following morning to get mounts for us once again. Silkhands
assured me it was wisest in any event, for Jinian had been
reared at the southern end of River Jourt, where horses are a
religion and a way of life. The whole town was talking of the
Bonedancer, visits from such Gamesmen being unusual in
Three Knob, and it took her some time to accomplish her
business. Meantime, Silkhands and I finished our breakfast,
and I taxed her with being a mope and poor companion.
Truly, she had been growing quieter and sadder with each step
of our journey.

"Oh, Peter," she sighed. "This traveling about is worse
than I remembered. I have grown used to luxury at Vorbold's
House. The beds are soft, the rooms warm. There are good
cooks in the kitchens there, and excellent wines in the cellars.
It is a quiet, interesting life, and one need not fear being taken
by Ghouls or pursued by monsters. I have grown soft and un-
willing to bruise myself upon stones."

"Well," I said heartily, "you'll get used to being rough

upon the road again. It will not take long."

There was no enthusiasm in her answering smile. She did not dispute me, but it was plain to see she had no heart for it. The look of her gave me a quick, half despairing sense of loss, and I kissed her. She returned the kiss, but it was more sisterly than our kisses had been in Xammer. I could hardly tax her with not being loverlike when she had never signified she intended to be, so I satisfied myself by swatting her behind. Not, I suppose, the best way to convey the depth of my feelings. Later I thought of that.

When Jinian returned with the horses, she went over them point by point with me, full of enthusiasm, with sparkling eyes and a quickened voice. She pointed out their rough coats, good, she said, for the season, and their common shoes. "They are sturdy, not fast," she said, "as we may travel back roads. What do you think of our going to Reavebridge by way of the Boneview River? I looked at the map last night while you were . . . busy, and if we go overhill from Three Knob to the northeast, we will come into the river valley. Once there we can go west to parallel the Great Road some little way before we must cross it to come to Reavebridge."

Her face was smudged. I had a witless desire to wipe the smudge away. She seemed so eager that I thought, well, why not. It would be easier going on the North Road, but we might be bothered less if we went by back ways.

The women had lost everything they carried in their encounter with the Ghoul, so we had next to replace some garments and cloaks, though Silkhands said there was no selection at all in a place like Three Knob. Well, by judicious use of Chance's winnings, we refitted ourselves for travel. When Silkhands saw the horses, she gave a rueful rub to her backside, and I knew she was regretting the light carriage they had lost on the road. I put my arm around her. "Don't be despondent," I said. "There will be luxury enough when we come to Reavebridge. Chance will have won another fortune, and we will all live on his luck for a few days."

She laughed. "When Chance wins, it isn't luck. No, I am not that concerned at having to lie on the ground for a few nights, Peter. It is this wild, dreamy feeling I have. I woke last night and went to the window for air, only to dream that I saw a misty giant moving across the stars as though he strode at the edge of the world. And the wind song haunts me. And I cannot settle at anything.''

Over her head I could see Jinian, watching us and listening intently. I smiled at them both, trying to be light and unconcerned. ''Well, that is the way with prophecies. I was told in the Bright Demesne we would go north, and the wind song sings of the north, and in Dindindaroo a ghost spoke to me of the north. Wild and dreamy, indeed, and reason enough for sleepwalking.''

''Three times,'' said Jinian, surprising me with this echo of Chance. ''Three times is Gaming. Who Games against you?''

I shook my head. ''The minstrel learned the song in Leamer. Perhaps there we'll find the root of it.'' Jinian frowned at this, as though she might weep, and I could not think why she should be so unhappy at the thought of Leamer. Later I asked Silkhands, and she replied.

''King Kelver is to meet us in Reavebridge. He will take Jinian north from there, so she will not be able to go to Leamer with us. She is undoubtedly disappointed at being left out of the mystery and its solution—if there is one.'' She sounded very offhand about it, as though it did not matter what Jinian thought. I thought it did matter. If Jinian were disappointed, so was I.

We traveled back through the Grole Hills, leagues of twisty road over which little black tunnel mouths pursed rocky lips, with gravel everywhere. It was the waste product left by the groles after men washed out the heavy metals which the groles don't use. Hooves on the gravel made an endless, sliding crunch, a monotonous grinding sound. There were a few dirty trees in the valley bottoms, so many gray dusters along the scanty water courses. Occasionally a bird would dip from one tree to another with a tremulous, piping call. The air was still, with no smell to it. Men called to one another across the valleys, long echoing sounds fading into silence, and we rode along half asleep with the endless crunch and jog.

Then, all at once, a shadow moved across us from the south, a chilly shade which removed most of the sound and color from the world. The crunch of gravel was still there, but far away as though heard through multiple layers of gauze. The call of the birds became dreamlike. We rode in a world of distance, of—disattachment. Something moved past us, around us, toward the north, and we heard a shred of music and a voice speaking inside us saying, "Kinsman, help." As soon as we heard the words a whip of air struck, and the quiet was gone. Dust swirled up around us, and we coughed, for the air was suddenly cold and smelled of storm.

Jinian gasped, "That was a wild, ill wind," leaning over the neck of her horse and trying to get the dust from her throat.

All three of us had tears running down our faces, all of us were crying as though utterly bereft. The voice we had heard had had no emotion in it at all, and yet we had *heard* it expressing a horrible loneliness and despair. It took us an hour or more to stop the tears, and I cried longer than the women did, almost as though the voice had spoken to me in a way it had not spoken to them. I was not sure I liked that idea or Jinian's compassionate glances toward me. That young woman seemed to understand too much about me already.

It was not long after that the dusk came down, soft and purple. Bird piping gave way to the *oh-ab, oh-ab* of little froggy things in the ditches. I heard a flitchhawk cry from the top of the sky, a sound dizzy with the splendor of high gold where the sun still burned. He made slow, shining circles until the darkness rose about him, and then it was night and we could go no farther. We talked then of the music, the voice, the wind.

"We must be sensible," murmured Jinian. "Things do not occur without purpose, without order, without Gamesense."

"If it is a thing which has occurred," said Silkhands, "and not some mindless ghost."

"A mindless ghost who calls us kinsman?" Jinian doubted.

"Kinsman to us all," I said, "or to only one? And which one?"

"And asking our help," brooded Jinian. "How can we help?"

"We can do nothing except wait," I said. I did not even bother to seek the advice of Didir or the others—not even Windlow. I simply knew that whatever *it* was, *it* would return, and no amount of cogitating or struggling would make anything clearer. I knew.

So we ate the food which had been packed for us in Three Knob, and let our talk wander, and grew more and more depressed.

"All day I have thought of Dazzle," Silkhands said. "When the Ghoul came with his train, the death's heads reminded me of her. Reminded me she may still be alive, there beneath Bannerwell in the ancient corridors. But she is likely dead, young as she was. There are so few old ones of us, Peter. Windlow was old, but he is gone. Himaggery and Mertyn are not old. There are so few old. I was thinking I would like to be able to grow old. . . ."

I tried to make her laugh. "We'll grow old together, sweetling. When you are so old you totter upon your cane, I shall chase you across the hearth until you trip and roll upon the rug." It was evidently not the right thing to say, for she began to weep, the same strong, endless flow of tears we had experienced earlier.

"Will any of us come to that time? Life in Vorbold's House is sweet! Need I lose it in some Ghoul's clutches, be arrow shot by some Armiger at Game? I think of all I knew when I was a child, and so few are left, so very few. . . ."

After that, I could only hold her until she went to sleep, then roll myself in my blankets and do the same, conscious all the while of Jinian's silence in her own blankets across the fire. I knew she had heard each word. And in the morning she told us that she had.

"I did not mean to intrude," she said, flushing a little. "But I have keen hearing, and a keen understanding of what is going on. We are all feeling terribly sad, lonely, and lost. We began to feel so when the whatever-it-was happened yesterday. We must not make the mistake of thinking those emotions are our own."

She sounded very like Himaggery in that instant. I was amazed.

Silkhands shook herself like a river beast coming out of the water, a single hard shudder to shed a weight of wet. "You're right, Jinian. Always good for the instructress to be taught by her student. Well. It is wise and perceptive of you, no doubt, and good of you to tell us so firmly. I am beginning to melt from my own misery."

"You and Peter and I," said Jinian, pouring herself more cider and taking another crisp, oaty cake from the basket, "feel the same, but I know my only reason for sadness is that the two of you have planned to share something in which I was to have no part, that you would go on to an adventure without me. Well, so I have decided I will not let you go on without me. I have heard your story, read your book, felt your wind, heard your music. I know as much of all this as you do. So I will not be left behind."

"But King Kelver will be in Reavebridge," objected Silkhands.

"So," said Jinian. "Let him be in Reavebridge." And we could get nothing further from her, even though Silkhands tried to argue with her several times that morning.

All day we waited for something to happen, another silence, another voice. Nothing. We rode in warm sunlight, bought our noon meal from a farmwife—fresh greens, eggs, and sunwarm fruit just off the trees—and came down to the banks of the Boneview River at sunfall. We were grubby and dusty, and the amber water sliding in endless skeins across the pebbles could not be resisted. We were in it in a moment, nothing on but our smalls, pouring the water over us and scrubbing away at the accumulated dust, when it happened again.

First the silence. River sounds fading. Bird song softening to nothing. Then the fragment of melody, tenuous, fading, at the very edge of hearing. *Kinsman, help.*

Just there the river ran east and west in a long arc before joining the northerly flow. We were near the bank, looking down the glittering aisle of sunset beneath the graying honey glow of the sky. Against that sky moved the shape of a man, moving as a cloud moves when blown by a steady wind, changing as a cloud changes. Time did not pass for us. We watched him against the amber, the rose, the purple gray, the vast swimming form filling the sky until stars shone through its lofty head, arms and legs moving in one tortuous stride after another, slow, slow, inexorably walking the obdurate earth toward the north. Fragments of mist shredded the creature's outline only to be regathered and reformed, again and yet again, held as by some unimaginable will, some remote, dreaming consciousness expressed as form and motion. The idea of this came to all of us at once so that we turned in the direction it moved, toward the north, to stare beyond the lands of the River Reave to the mighty scarps of the Waenbane.

"A god," whispered Silkhands.

I thought not. Or not exactly. Something, surely, beyond my comprehension, and yet at the same time something so familiar I felt I should recognize it, should know what it was —who it was. There was something tragic about it, pathetic for all its monstrous size. We were silent, in awe for the long time that darkness took to cover it. Then—

"Are we going there?" demanded Jinian. "Where it is going? North?"

"Peter and I," began Silkhands wearily.

"All of us," said Jinian. "I won't be left out, Silkhands. I won't."

"King Kelver . . ."

"Devils take King Kelver. I'll spend my whole life weaving an alliance for King Kelver, warming his bed, bearing his children, but not until I've done something for myself. I won't be left behind."

She brushed aside Silkhands' expostulations as though they had been cobweb concerns of no matter. I stifled laughter to see her, so sturdy and independent, so determined not to be left out. Oh, I understood well enough that feeling of being shut up in others' lives. "Let be, Silkhands," I said. "King Kelver will no doubt wait."

"He is to meet us in Reavebridge," Silkhands retorted, obviously annoyed. "He will not be pleased. Nor will your brother be pleased, Jinian. I have heard of the black rages of Armiger Mendost."

"Leave Mendost to me," Jinian said. "He knows how far he may push me and how far he may not. He has no other sisters, but I have other brothers who are fond of me and not overfond of Mendost. They know his black rages, too, and have reason to undo him if he proves unreasonable."

I thought, Aha, she is not so manipulable as I had assumed. And this led me to other thoughts and wonders about Jinian so that for a moment I forgot the giant, forgot the mysteries of our journey, only remembering it all when we had dressed ourselves and gathered at our fire. Then it was only to search the starry sky and wonder whether the misty form still walked north beneath its cover or whether it had come to rest in some far, high place—and in what form. Across the fire, Jinian sat crosslegged with the little book tipped to catch the light of the flames. She was so deep in it that I had to speak to her twice before she heard me.

"What are you finding there, student? You look like a newly named Thaumaturge, trying to figure your life pattern from perusing the Index."

She thought seriously upon this before answering me. "It is not unlike that, Peter. I am taking what you have told me, and what is in this book, and what I have seen and heard, and making an imagining from them."

"A hypothesis," I said. "That is what Windlow called it. A hypothesis; an imagining which might be true."

"Yes." She chuckled, a little bubble of amusement. "Though I had thought of it rather more like a stew. A bit of this and a bit of that, all simmering away in my head, boiling gently so that first one thing comes to the top then another, with the steam roiling and drifting and the smells catching at my nose." She wrinkled that nose at me, making me think of a pet bunwit. "A tasty stew, Peter. Oh, I am eager to go north and see what is there!"

"The song spoke of danger, Jinian. You have been at risk of life once on my account already."

"Well, but it was exciting in a sort of nasty way," she said. "And very surprising. I think I'm more ready for it now, knowing that wonderful things are toward. And, if danger comes, well, it is no little danger to bear children, either. And no one much concerns themselves about that."

Silkhands had retreated into an aggrieved silence which I did not interrupt. When we had lain down to sleep, I did ask, "Will those of Vorbold's House hold you accountable that Jinian chooses to make King Kelver wait upon her pleasure?"

She sighed, turned, and I saw the firelight gleaming in her wide eyes. "Not they, no, Peter. King Kelver himself may spend annoyance on me, but who am I to tell Jinian she must do this or that. The negotiations were complete; she agreed; now she says yes-but-wait-a-while. Who knows who will hold any of us accountable. Do not let it worry you." And she closed her eyes.

When we dropped off to sleep, we were three blanket bundles around the fire. When I woke in the morning, I sat there stupidly, unable to count fewer than four, startled into full wakefulness by a harsh cry from the riverside. There were two monstrous birds drinking from the ripples, spraddle-legged, long necks dipping. Birds. Yes. Two man heights tall from their horny huge feet to the towering topknot of plumes which crowned them, screaming greeting to the morning like some grotesque barnyard fowl, and the fourth blanket bundle across the fire had to be whoever—or whatever—brought them. I began a surreptitious untangling of arms and legs only to be greeted by a cheerful, "Ah, awake are you?" and a small round man tumbled out of the fourth roll of blankets to stand above me, yawning and stretching, as though he had been my dearest friend for years. I saw Jinian's eyes snap open to complete awareness, though Silkhands made only a drowsy *umming* sound and slept on.

He was good humored, that one, bearded a little, almost bald, dressed in a bizarre combination of clothing which led me in one moment to believe he had been valet to an Armiger, or that he was a merchant, or perhaps a madman escaped from keepers and let loose upon the countryside. His boots were one purple, one blue, his cloak striped red and yellow (part of an Afrit's dress) and he wore a complicated hat with a fantastic horn coming out the top, all in black and rust, Armiger colors. Aside from these anomalous accoutrements, he wore a bright green shirt and a pair of soft zellerskin trousers, an aberrant combination, but perhaps not insane.

"Allow me to make myself known to you," he said, stooping over me where I lay in the tangle, taking my hand in his to pump it energetically. "Vitior Queynt. Vitior Vulpas Queynt. I came upon the fading gleam of your fire late in the night and thought to myself, Aha, I thought, Queynt, but here is company for tomorrow's road and the day after that, perhaps. Besides, who can deny that journeys move with a speed which is directly proportional to the number traveling? Hmmm? Four move at least one third faster than three, isn't that so? And a hundred would move like the wind? Ah, hmmm. Ha-

ha. Or so it seems, for with every additional traveler is more to distract one from the tedium of jog, jog, jogging along. Isn't that so? Ah, to be alone upon the road is a sadsome, lonesome thing, is it not? Well, I'll get breakfast started."

Still talking about something else, he turned away to pick up a pot and take it to the river for water, to return, to build up the fire and put the pot to boil, never stopping in all that time his talk to himself or the birds or the river running. I struggled out of my blankets at last and set myself to rights, deciding I did not need to shave myself after a quick stroke at my jaw. I joined our odd visitor at the fire.

"Those . . . birds?" I asked. "Are they . . . I mean, what kind are they?"

"Ah, the krylobos? Surely, surely, great incredible creatures, aren't they? One would not think they could be broken to harness, and, indeed, they have their tricks and ways about them, pretending they have broken a leg, or a wing—not that they use their wings for much save fruit picking and weaving nests—and lying there thrashing about or limping as though about to die, and then comes the predator with his hungry eyes full of dinner, and then old krylobos pops upright with plumes flying and swack, swack, two kicks and a dead pombi or whatever. I've seen them do gnarlibars that way, be the beast not too mature or fearsome bulky. Ah, well, the one on the left is Yittleby and the one on the right is Yattleby. I'll introduce you later so they know they cannot pull any tricks on any friend of old Queynt's. How do you like your egg?"

He had an egg, only one, between his square little hands, but that egg looked enough to feed us four and several fustigars beside.

"They—they laid that?" I asked, awed.

"Oh, not *they*, young sir, no indeed, not *they*. Why, Yattleby would be ashamed at the allegation, for he is a great lord of his roost and his nest and would not bear for an instant such an imputation. No, it is Yittleby who lays the eggs, and Queynt who eats them, from time to time, except when Yittleby goes all broodish and demands time to hatch a family, which is every other year or so and during that time old Queynt must simply do without his wagon, hmmm? Nothing else for it but do without. How do you like your egg?"

I suggested to him that I would be happy to eat egg in any form he cared to offer it, and then I went off into the bushes to think a bit. I sensed no danger in the man, no hostility, but Gamelords, what a surprise! I thought of calling on Didir, but rejected the idea. Was he Gamesman or not? Might he detect —and resent—such inquiry into his state of mind? Better leave it for now, I decided, and wandered back to the fire, stopping on the way to look at the wagon he had mentioned, peaceably parked beneath the trees and as odd a collection of derangement as the man himself. It had a peaked roof and wheels as tall as my shoulder, windows with boxes of herbs growing beneath them, and a cage hung at the back with something in it I had never seen before which addressed me gravely with "has it got some thrilp? some thrilp?" before turning head over tailless behind to hang by one foot. No tail, I thought. The krylobos had none, either. Nor, of course, did Queynt, which told me nothing at all.

Jinian was waking Silkhands, murmuring explanations in her ear as I rejoined them. The krylobos were picking nuts from the trees with their wing fingers, cracking them in the huge, metallic-looking beaks which seemed to have some kind of compound leverage at their hinge. Pop, a nut would go into the beak, then crunch, as the bird bit down, then *crrrunch* as it bit down again and the nutmeat fell into the beak or the waiting fingers. "Kerawh," said one of them conversationally to the other. "Kerawh, whit, herch, kerch."

"How do you tell them apart?" I asked Queynt, unable to see any difference between Yittleby and Yattleby at all.

"Ah, my boy, one of the great mysteries of life. How does one tell a male krylobos from a female krylobos? No one knows. Oh, but they manage to do it, the krylobos do. Never make a mistake. A female will tell another female across a wide valley and challenge just like that, but she'll let a male come into her very courtyard, as it were, without a threatening sound. And what's to see in difference between them? Nothing. That's the honest truth. Not a thing. Isn't it so?"

"But you know them apart. You said Yittleby was on the left?"

"Ah, my boy, when they drink or eat or talk with one another, Yittleby is always 'pon the left, indeed yes. When they

are hitched to the wagon, Yittleby is always pon the left. Yes,
indeed. And when I find an egg, it is always pon the left, my
boy, certainly, which is how I know it is Yittleby. But if they
were not properly arranged, why then, my boy, I could not tell
Yittleby from Yattleby or either from the other. And if there
were more than two, why, my boy, I would be totally lost
among them. Indeed I would.''

Thereafter, I watched them, and it did seem that the same
one of them was always to the left, the other to the right,
though I could not be sure. Nor could I be sure that the two incredible creatures did not know exactly what I was thinking
and were not laughing at me the entire time without opening
their beaks.

We had the egg scrambled. Somehow we managed to eat it
all, and it was very good, with a mild, nutty flavor. I began to
gather our gear, wondering what would happen next, but
Queynt soon clarified that. He summoned Silkhands to ride
beside him on the wagon seat, holding up the harness so that
Yittleby and Yattleby could thrust their long necks through
it and pull the traces taut. They were hitched separately, one
to each side of the wagon, the harness running across their
prodigious chests. I thought it would be a strange, whipsawing
way to travel, but when they strode off it was a matched
stride, varying not a finger width between them as they went
down the road chatting with one another in an endless whit,
kerawh, whit, while Queynt lounged on the wagon seat talking
to Silkhands who, for the first time since I had known her,
could not get a word in edgeways. Smooth as ice they moved
along, Jinian and I following, coming up beside when the road
widened, falling well back when it was narrow and dusty. So
we went, west along the Boneview River toward the Great
North Road. When we saw it ahead of us, I suggested to Silkhands that we turn north, avoiding the Great Road and its
possible dangers, but she and Queynt forestalled me.

''Why, my boy, this young lady is too weary to go ahorse-
back another step, not a step will I allow, no, not at all. She
may go inside the wagon and the other young lady as well, if
you think it necessary which I do not, for as I understand it,
no one knows her at all, and as for you, you can Shift a bit not
to seem so familiar to any who may be hunting you, and with

Yittleby and Yattleby to carry us along, we will go leagues and leagues on the Great North Road in less time than you can imagine.''

If Silkhands were minded to trust this strange one enough to confide in him, which angered me a good deal, then what could I say against it? I would not leave her and turn aside with Jinian, though the thought did go through my head all in an instant. No, if I Shifted a little, we could ride on the Great Road in some safety, I concluded. The wagon and the birds were so outrageously unfamiliar that no one looked at the riders along of it. None who passed failed to turn and stare at the great birds, and to each Queynt called out with a greeting or a jest, all full of words and empty of much sense. The hours went by. Queynt gave us fruit and bread from the wagon, come noon, and we rode on, the birds striding tirelessly, the tall wheels turning, and it was not yet evening when we began to see scattered nut plants and the spires of Reavebridge shining across the silver of River Reave which had been drawing ever closer to the road with the leagues we had traveled.

"We'll make for the Tragamor's Tooth," Queynt told us when we came up beside him. "A fine hostelry with excellent food and a stable which I am happy to say both Yittleby and Yattleby have found to their liking. We have never before been so far south as during this season. We must seem very strange to all these people, who, I must say, seem not far traveled by the looks of them. Why, I'll wager not one in a hundred has been north to the Windgate nor upon the heights of the Waeneye or upon the Waenbane Mountains. 'Windbone,' you know. That's the 'Windbone' Mountains, so called because the wind has carved great skeletons of stone up there, ribs and fingers reaching into the sky as though the very mountain had lain down and lost its flesh upon those heights. Ah, one must go there by way of the Wind's Eye, Waeneye as they say in these parts, if one is to see krylobos which put these two to shame for smallness. There are krylobos there, mark me, which would make you shiver in your boots to see, half again as tall as these, and able to kick gnarlibars to death I have no doubt.''

"Wind's Eye," said Jinian. "That's the prophesy you heard in the Bright Demesne. Wind's Eye.''

She had remembered it before I had, but her words brought back the sound of Windlow's voice in my head. *"You and Silkhands. A place, far to the north, called Wind's Eye."* I dug out the memory of the other things he had said. *"A giant? Perhaps. And a bridge. You must take me along . . . and the Gamesmen of Barish."* A giant. Perhaps a giant of mist, of cloud, of sadness, a giant seen at dusk who begged for help of his kinsmen. I raised my eyes to the towering scarps which loomed to the west of Reavebridge. Sharpening my Shifter's eyes, I could see the curved spires and organic shapes which Queynt had spoken of, as though some great, unfamiliar beast had laid himself upon those heights to leave his bones.

And behind those bones the outline of a giant, misty and vast, striding, striding to the north. I heard Jinian catch her breath, heard the man, Queynt, fall silent only for an instant before his voice went on in its ceaseless flow. When I turned, it was to find his eyes upon me, insistent and eager, measuring me as though for a suit of clothes—or a coffin—while he told us about the town of Reavebridge and all that lived therein in greater detail and to a greater length than anyone of us could possibly have cared to know.

7

Reavebridge

Before we arrived at the Tragamor's Tooth, Silkhands busied herself in Queynt's wagon, making herself beautiful. I noted that she did not suggest Jinian do likewise. I put it down to vanity. Silkhands was a little vain, only a little, and not in any sense which was improper or false. She simply liked to appear at her best, and who could argue with that. Jinian, on the other hand, seemed determined to make the King as little sorry for the delay as possible. Knowing that he awaited her at the Tragamor's Tooth, she had drawn her hair, which was plentiful and brown as ripe nuts, back into a single thick braid and had neglected to wipe the road dust from her face. Also, she was dressed for travel and looked as though she had slept in her clothes, which she had. She looked very good to me, very staunch and dependable, but she would have won no prize for style, that one.

So we arrived at the Inn with Silkhands looking a vision, Queynt appearing no less fanciful than he had done at dawn, and Jinian and me, the followers, dirty and sweaty and caring not who cared. Someone must have been watching for Jinian's arrival, for the King appeared as we were having our things taken to the rooms we had hired, a lean, elegant man, with a curly red beard and eyes that gleamed with intelligence and

humor. He came to the place Silkhands stood and called her
by Jinian's name, offering his hand and smiling. When she
disabused him of the mistaken identity and introduced him to
Jinian, his face changed no one whit though his eyes did. I saw
a flicker of disappointment there, and Jinian saw it as well.
She made her courtesies in a well schooled manner, however,
and her voice was all anyone could have wished, soft and
pleasant, without the whine of weariness or rancor at the mistaken recognition.

"I greet you, King Kelver," she said. "Many kind things
have been said on your behalf, and though I do not merit your
courtesies, I thank you for them."

He bowed, perhaps a little surprised at her calm and poise.
She was not at all girlish, as I have remarked heretofore. I
myself sometimes found it surprising.

"I greet you, Jinian. If you have received any courtesies on
my behalf, then be assured they were given freely and in pur-
suance of continued friendship between your people and my
own." It was delicately put, and I found myself liking the
man. He was telling her that he had not presumed to buy her,
that he had only tendered an offer of friendship and the final
decision was still hers. Jinian smiled at him, and I saw his eyes
lighten. She has a wonderful smile.

Queynt bustled in. "Ah, well then, ladies, young sir, so all
friends are met, are they? Good, good. One does not like to
stand upon ceremony at the end of a long ride when dust and
the day conspire to rob one of whatever youth and spirits one
may have hoarded long ago in the dawn—when the skin cries
for the waters of the bath and the throat yearns for the
marvelous unguents of the vintner's art. Ah, sir, forgive these
weary travelers for the moment, and I who have come with
them this lengthy way, until we are refreshed and cleansed suf-
ficient to be a credit to the honorable company which you so
kindly bestow upon us. . . ." And Queynt bowed us away
from the King, who stood with mouth open to watch this aberration lead us to the stairs and whip us upward with the lash of
his tongue. "Go now, Peter, to the room at the head of the
stairs where a bath will soon be brought, and you, ladies, to
the second room where a bath even now awaits, and these
lack-a-daisy pawns swift as flitchhawks rise, rise with your

burdens that my young friends be not inconvenienced at the lack of any essential garment or lotion or soothing medication which might be contained therein. Ah, when all is sweet again, and pure as the waters of the Waenbain which plunge in eternal silver from the heights, then let us return to this good King Kelver to partake with him of those viands his generosity and foresight cannot but have prepared.''

This last faded into silence, and I risked a glance over the bannister at that same King to find him with mouth still open but with a laughing look around the eyes. Well then, he was not offended.

I had scarce got into the room before hearing a quiet tap-tap at the door behind me which, when I opened it a crack, disclosed Chance in the get-up of a cook looking for all the world like a major servitor of some proud Demesne. He slipped into the room before I could greet him, stopped my mouth with his fingers, and hissed, "Who is this fellow with you? This clown? Where did you get him?"

I explained that I had not got him, that rather Queynt had got me; that, thus far, the man had done us no harm.

"Harm's known when harm's done," he said portentously, throwing himself into a chair and fanning himself with a towel. Indeed, he looked very hot and harried, and I guessed that the cook's garb was not a disguise. He affirmed this. "Seeing I caused such a hooraw there in Three Knob, I decided to be a little less obvious in future. So, come the outskirts of Reavebridge, I put the mounts in a stable and came into town like any pawn looking for work and well recommended.''

"Well recommended?" I didn't mean to twit him, but it did come out that way.

"Well recommended," he announced in a firm voice. "I had foresight enough to have Himaggery and Mertyn write me letters of reference and leave the as-what blank so I could fill it in myself. You'll be pleased to know they recommend me highly as a chef, and chief chef I am in this place since their last one got himself riotous during a recent family observance and hasn't got himself on his feet yet. May not, from what I hear. Terrible stuff, this Reavebridge wine, when drunk with grole sausage, which is mostly how they drink it.'' He went on fanning himself, pausing only to open the window behind him and lean out to take a deep breath. "I was beginning to give up on you."

"We came the back way," I said.

"Thought you must've come by way of the moon."

"Along the Boneview River, Chance. It was there that Queynt joined us. He's strange, all right, but it seemed less harmful to come along with him rather than make a fuss."

"Silkhands looks tired," said Chance. "Who's the girl?"

"Jinian? A student of Silkhands'. Promised to King Kelver by her brother, Armiger Mendost. However, she's not eager to be given to the King. Wants to come along with Silkhands and me to find the answers to the mystery."

"Oh, ah," said Chance, patting himself all over before finding the crumpled paper he was looking for. "Speaking of mystery, here's a message came by Elator from Himaggery. Says the blues are coming in from all over and they've found Quench. . . ."

"It's directed to me," I said mildly, seeing it was opened.

"Well," he said and shrugged, "you took a time getting here. Himaggery might have wanted an answer."

I unfolded the message, already ragged where Chance had ripped it, to read Himaggery's message. They thought they had found Quench—with the Immutables. "Gamelords," I snarled to myself. "That's why the fellow looked so familiar. It was Quench, Quench all the time."

"Who's that?"

"The fellow who came to meet us at the ruin, the one who went to get Riddle, the long-faced fellow. I'd never seen Quench without that square black hat the magicians wore and the long black robe and mittens. That's who that was: Quench."

"Well, that tells you what that hooraw was on the road. Must have been Quench trying to get you there without your knowing."

I didn't answer him. I was too angry with myself. I went back to the message. Riddle and Quench were being brought to the Bright Demesne together with some others of those who had escaped from the holocaust of the magicians. Riddle had decided he needed help of some kind, and so on and so on.

Peter was to feel free to go on to the north if he liked. They sent their affectionate regards.

"Why," I grated at Chance, "why did Riddle do that to me? I would have helped him if he'd asked me. Why! I can't believe he's an evil man."

"Well, if you won't believe him evil, then think up a reason why he's not."

That was Chance. Think of a reason. Before I had a chance to think of anything, we heard someone outside the door and Chance eased himself out with vague words about breakfast as Queynt oozed himself in.

"Well, young sir, so quick to place orders among kitchen staff? Hardly an instant, and breakfast ordered already? Ah, but what it is to be young! Isn't that so? Enormous energy, enormous strength, eat like a fustigar and sleep like a bunwit when one is young. One might ask why not wait to order breakfast until supper has been consumed. One might ask that, but Vitior Vulpas Queynt will not. No! Queynt has learned that each man has his oddities, oh, my yes. Ha-ha. Oddities, which if not questioned can be safely overlooked, but if mentioned must be dealt with, considered, judged! Isn't that so? Now, your tub, young sir, and me off to mine in the instant. Below us, supper soon awaits our pleasure."

He beamed at me and was gone, giving way to three struggling servitors, one bearing a tub on his back like some kind of half metallic turtle, the other two laden with tall ewers of water, one hot, one cold. All was set down and poured into and arranged to my satisfaction (to my annoyance, rather) before they trooped out to be succeeded by others bearing towels. I had never been so overserved in my life. Whether King Kelver was responsible or Vitior Queynt, I desired most heartily that all of them would leave me alone for a time.

But when I was scarce out of the tub—which the same servitors had come to haul away with much gesticulation and pour with loud shouting down some drain or other—the door was again tap-tapped and Jinian opened it a crack to whisper whether I were dressed or not. I told her I was not, but she came in anyhow. I was decent enough in the towel—more decent than we had been together several times on the road.

"My, you are in a temper," she said, seating herself on the

bed and arranging her flounces. "Silkhands made me dress up. She said otherwise would be an affront to the King."

"I am not in a temper," I growled. "I am perfectly all right."

She widened her eyes, played with her hair with one finger, fluttered and pouted. "Oh, ta-ta, Gamesman, but if you go on in this way, I will think I have offended you." She laughed, a high, affected little titter, then spoiled the effect by sneezing with laughter. I could not help it, but laughed with her.

"No," she went on. "You are in a temper. Do you know why?"

"Not really," I growled, "except that Queynt is too sudden an addition to our journey, and Silkhands seems too ready to trust him. She has told him too much, I think. He knew I was a Shifter, though I am not dressed so. He knew we were being hunted. How else did he know but Silkhands told him? She knows better!"

"Put not yourself in another's hands," agreed Jinian. "But she may not have done. You know, Peter, I don't think Silkhands wants to go on with you to Waeneye."

I felt my face turn red. "Nonsense. Of course she does. She's a little tired just now, but Silkhands would not let me go on alone to solve this thing."

"I think you're wrong," she said, her voice breaking a little at sight of my face. "She would rather not go."

"I have known Silkhands for years," I said, stiffly, and even more angrily. "I don't think it's appropriate for you to attempt to tell me what my friends would or would rather not do as it concerns me. If Silkhands did not want to go to Waeneye, she would tell me. She has not told me. Has she told you?"

"No. Not in so many words."

"Not in any words," I asserted, slamming my hand down on the sill and hurting the thumb. This made me angrier still. "You are *very* young, Jinian. I'm afraid you do not understand the situation at all." The last person I had heard use these honeyed tones was Laggy Nap, trying to poison me.

She did not answer. When I turned at last, it was to see a tear hanging on the fringe of her eyelashes, but she still regarded me steadily, even though her voice shook a little. "No.

Perhaps I don't.'' And she turned to leave the room. In the door, she turned. "However, Peter, it was not that I came to talk to you about. I came to say it is easy to stop listening to Queynt. He talks so very much, to so little purpose. One stops hearing him. However, it would be wise for us to listen to him carefully at all times.'' And she shut the door behind her, leaving me with my mouth open.

Oh, the ice and the wind and the seven devils, I said to myself. Now why did you do that?

You did that, I answered me, because Jinian is right. Silkhands does not want to go to Waeneye. Moreover, she does not want to journey like this at all. Moreover, her eyes when she looks at King Kelver are calm and considering, like the eyes of a cook choosing fresh vegetables for a banquet on which his reputation will rest. And the time when you and Silkhands might have been lovers is gone, Peter, and that is why you are angry.

That, at least, had the virtue of being true, whether I liked it or not, and I did not. Still, Windlow had seen me in the northlands with Silkhands. So what would she do now?

I could not make my face happy when I went down to the supper which King Kelvor had arranged. I bowed to Jinian and apologized for my bad temper. Her lips smiled in response, but there was something distant and dignified in her eyes. So. We went in to dinner.

We had sausage grole, of course. Anyone within fifty leagues of Leamer will eat sausage grole. I do not remember what else we ate. I do remember Chance being much in evidence, in and out of the room, directing this or that servitor; platters in, soup bowls out, flagons in, dessert bowls out. There were candles on the table. I saw Silkhands' face, dazzled in the light, rosy, laughing eyes turned toward the King. I saw Jinian's as well, hearty, simple, regarding me from time to time under level brows. Then we were drinking wineghost from tiny, purple vessels which were only glass though they could have been carved from jewels the way they broke the light, and the King was speaking.

"We are all well met, new friends all, and I have a wish that this friendship be not cut short without good reason. Therefore, as you go toward Leamer on this journey you have set yourself," (and I wondered what Silkhands had told him), "we of the Dragon's Fire Purlieu beg your consent to accompany you." He smiled directly at me. "You will not forbid me, young sir?"

I nodded my courteous permission, gnashing my teeth privately. If there had been any mystery better kept secret, the whole world seemed to know of it now, and it would be difficult to do anything secretly with such a mob gathered about us. Not to be outdone in courtesies, Queynt was talking.

"Ah, how generous an offer, King Kelver. How generous an offer and how kind an intent! Why, I have not seen such courtesy since the time of Barish, when courtesy was an art and sign of true refinement. Things change throughout the centuries, isn't that so? But courtesy remains the same, today as in any century past."

I would not have heard him except for Jinian's warning. As it was, only Jinian and I did hear him. He had not seen such courtesy since the time of Barish, eh? And where had he been in all that time? Was he a dreamer? Madman? Mocker? Or a Gamesman with a deeper Game than we knew? His eager little eyes were upon me, and I let my face seem as slack and wine-flushed as the rest.

The next morn I hired Chance away from the Tragamor's Tooth with much noise and many objections on the part of the innkeeper. We left the town, having seen none of it, to move in slow procession onto the road to Leamer, along the deep, silent flow of River Reave. It took the King out of his way, but not greatly. He could go on north of Leamer and then cut across country to the Dragon's Fire Purlieu, did he choose. Queynt set the pace for us, slower than I would have liked, with Silkhands riding beside him once more and King Kelver on a prancing mount alongside. Two of his Dragons followed behind, mounted, saving their Gaming and displaying for some better time. Far to the rear to avoid the dust came Jinian and I, with Chance and the baggage beast bringing up the tail.

"The King seems willing to follow you to Waeneye," I said to Jinian.

"The King isn't following me," she replied in a steady voice. "Though he is an admirable Gamesman. I had been ready for anger or threats, but he made neither. He is too wise for that. If our agreement is kept—or rather, if his agreement with my brother, to which I assented, is kept—he wants no memory of anger to stain the bed between us.''

Hearing her talk in this way put me in a temper again, though I was uncertain why. If it was Silkhands he was courting, why did Jinian's speaking of him thus upset me? It should rather have pleased me as though to say Kelver would not long be seeking Silkhands' company. Looking back on it, it seems that it should have pleased me, but the truth is it did not. I was flustered with myself, eager to fight with someone and ashamed for feeling so. So, we jogged and jogged until the silence grew tight and I sought to break it somehow.

''Have you made your stew yet?'' She looked at me with incomprehension, forgetting what she had said on the road from Three Knob. ''The stew you said you were making up, your hypothesis?''

''Oh,'' she said. ''That. Why, yes, Peter.''

We went on a way farther.

''Are you going to tell us what it is?'' I asked, keeping my voice as pleasant as possible. She was very trying, I thought.

''If you like, though it is only to tell you what you already know.''

''I? I know too little,'' I said, sure of it.

''Perhaps. But you know what you are going to find on the top of the Waenbane Mountains. You are going to find Barish's place, his Keep, his hideaway. You will go to find the bodies matching the blues you carry.''

''Yes, I suppose so,'' I gloomed. That much seemed unavoidably clear.

''So much we learned from a whirly ghost,'' said Chance. ''Of that much we may be certain.''

''Is there more?'' I asked.

''Some more,'' she said. ''I believe I know what plan it was that Barish had, what he intended should be the result of all this mystery and expense of time. We shall see if I am right.''

''You think we'll find Barish then?''

She shook her head. ''Everything indicates he was awakened last in the time of Riddle's grandfather. He left the northlands then, and he did not return. In which case, we will not find Barish himself. Only the eleven. Your Gamesmen.''

"The eleven," I murmured. "Barish's eleven. And a machine to resurrect them." I clutched at the pouch in my pocket. Perhaps, I said to myself, the machine is broken. Perhaps it cannot be used. The other ones, those the magicians had, were broken. If it is there at all, it will be centuries old. Rust and corruption and rot might have spoiled it. The serpent coiled cold upon my heart, and I thought of Windlow.

"Logic says it should be there," she said. "If it was used to wake Barish at intervals, it will be there, where he was."

"And what then?" asked Chance, eager for more mystery.

"And then," she said, serene as the moon in the sky, "we will do whatever it was Barish would have done if he had returned."

That one struck me silent in wonder at her audacity in saying it, even more at her colossal arrogance in thinking it.

"Barish was a Wizard." I laughed at her, the laughter fading as she turned cold eyes upon me.

"Well, certainly, Peter," she said. "But then, so am I."

8

Hell's Maw

One of the earliest things they had taught me at Mertyn's House in Schooltown was that one does not meddle with Wizards. Himaggery was the only one of the breed I had known, and I couldn't say that I knew or understood him well. Strange are the Talents of Wizards, so we are told, and I could not have told you what they were. Had anyone other than Jinian made claim to Wizardry, I would have laughed to myself, saying "Wizard indeed!" I did not laugh. Jinian did not joke about things. If she said she was a Wizard, then I believed her. Surprisingly, all I could feel was a deep, burning anger at Silkhands that she had not told me and had let me play the fool.

Oh, yes, I had done that right enough. I had said to Jinian that she was very young, that she did not understand. One does not say to a Wizard that the Wizard does not understand. I must have muttered Silkhands' name, for Jinian interrupted my anger with a peremptory, "Silkhands did not know, Peter. Does not know. I would prefer she not. You keep my secret, I will keep yours."

"I have none left," I muttered. "Silkhands has given them all away."

"I think not," she said. "Queynt knows what Queynt

knows, but not because Silkhands has told him." Then she smiled me an enigmatic smile and we jogged our way on to Leamer.

So, in the time it took me to consider all this, to feel alternately angry and guilty and intrigued, let me stop this following of myself about in favor of telling you what was happening elsewhere. I did not know it at the time, of course, but I learned of it later. What I did not hear of directly, I have imagined. So, leave Silkhands on the wagon seat beside strange Queynt; leave King Kelver and his men trotting along beside, full of courtesies and graceful talk; leave Jinian there upon the road, calm as ice; leave Chance—Oh, how often I have left Chance; leave Yittleby and Yattleby in their unvarying stride, their murmured *krerk*ing. Leave me, and lift up, up into the air as though you were an Armiger to lie upon the wind and fly toward those powers which assembled against us and which we knew nothing of.

Go up, up the sheer wall of the Waenbane Mountains, high against that looming and precipitous cliff to the place where they say the wind has carved monstrous, organic forms which they call the Winds' Bones. Do not look north to Bleer. We will travel there soon enough and stay longer than we would wish. Instead, cross the mountain scarp and the high desert to come to that gorge the Graywater has cut between two highlands. There is Kiquo and the high bridge, narrow as a knife edge, and the steely glint of the river, then high cliffs once more and another highland north of Betand.

Find the wide roadway there which leads into the northlands, see the strange monuments built along it, the greeny arches which hang above it. In spring, it is said, they glow with an undomainish light and have been known to drive travelers mad. Follow this road as it approaches the gorges of the River Haws and along the edge of that gorge to the town of Pfarb Durim. Hanging there high above Pfarb Durim, turn your head back toward the east and notice how all the lands between this city and the Wastes of Bleer lie flat and without barrier. A man might walk from one place to the other in two or three days, an Armiger fly it in much less time. Yet it is true that Peter did not think, nor Jinian, nor any in that company of the place called Pfarb Durim along the River Haws.

Look down now at that city. Come down to Pfarb Durim. The walls are high and thick and heavily manned. What do they defend against? What are these mighty gates closed against? Why do the balefires burn upon the parapets of Pfarb Durim? The city seems of an unlikely antiquity. Where else are these strange, keyhole-shaped doors found? Where else these triangular windows which stare at the world like so many jack-o-faces cut into ripe thrilps? Well. Leave it. Go aside from the walls and walk down the road which cuts the edge of the gorge, down to an outthrust stone where one may see what lies below—the place called "Poffle" because the people of Pfarb Durim are afraid to say its name. The place which is Hell's Maw, held now by a certain Gamelord, Huld the Demon.

Let us be invisible, silent, insubstantial as a ghost, to slide down that road to find the truth of what is there.

We will go down a twisting track, graven into the cliffside, sliced into that stony face by the feet of a myriad travelers over a thousand years—more, perhaps. Perhaps the city, the trail, Hell's Maw were there before the Gamesmen came. The trail winds down, deepening as it goes, until it is enclosed by stony walls on either side, shutting off any but a narrow slice of sky. Walk down this darkening gash until the rock edges above close to a sliver's width of light; find that dark pocket of stone which nudges the path with a swath of shadow; step in to find yourself at the upper end of a cloaca which bores its echoing way into the bowels of Hell's Maw.

It is dark, and the dark clamors, but as silent feet edge forward, sensible sound intrudes upon the cacophony of echo, and voices converse there in the terrible dark, voices of skeletons fastened to the walls with iron bands and the voice of their warder in hideous conversation.

"Take this torch, old bones. Pass it along there, pass it along. Some one of the high-and-mighties will be along that path soon, and they'll want light whether we need it or not." The warder may have been a Divulger. He is dressed as one, but flabby jowls droop beneath the black mask, flesh wobbles loose on the naked arms protruding from the leather vest. His eyes are blanked almost white with blindness, and he feels the end of the torch to know if it is alight. Behind him in the dark another Gamesman lies stretched upon a filthy cot, dressed black and dirty gray, a Bonedancer, empty face staring at the stone ceiling as acrid numbing smoke pours from his nostrils. "Hey, Dancer," the warder calls. "Kick up the bones there. They're slow as winter!"

The voice, when it comes, is full of sighs and pauses, long unconscious and unwitting moments. "Slow. Always slow. Well, why not? Bones should lie down, Tolp. Lie down. Slow and slow in the summer sun. Summer sun. I remember summer sun."

"I remember summer sun," cries a skeleton from the wall, waving the torch wildly before its empty eyes. "Summer sun. Winter cold. I remember pastures. I remember trees."

"Shush," says the warder, mildly. "Shush, now. Remembering is no good. It only makes you careless with the torches, Bones. Don't remember. Just pass the fire along there, pass it along to the end so the high-and-mighties can see their way."

"Who?" asks an incurious voice from the dark. "Who is it using the way to Hell's Maw, Tolp? They came yesterday, I thought. The legless one and the skull-faced one and the cold one. . . ."

"Came and went and will come again," replies Tolp, lighting yet another torch. "Legless one is a poor Trader, Laggy Nap. They put boots on him, he said, and sent him into the world. When the mountains blew up, so did the boots, and now he has no legs. . . ."

"No legs, no pegs; no arms, no harms. . . ." the bones sing from the dark wall. "No ribs, no jibs . . . "

"Shush. Cold King came yesterday, too. Old Prionde. Not liking what he sees here much. Well, he's not far from bonedom hisself."

"And the Demon, Demon Master, Huld the Horrible?" The Bonedancer laughs, a sound full of choking as the miasma pulses in and out of his cankered lungs.

"Went out, will come in again. Always. Since he was a child. For a while he was in Bannerwell with his pet prince, pretty Mandor, but Mandor's dead so Huld is here now, almost always. Hell's Maw has been Huld's place for a long, long time. . . ."

The Bonedancer sighs, coughs, sits up to spit blood onto the slimed floor. "Huld's been here forty years. Old Ghoul Blourbast brought him here first when Huld was a child, before he was even named Demon. You remember him then, Tolp. Used to help you in the dungeons.'' The Bonedancer laughs again, a hacking laugh with no joy in it. ''Liked the hot irons, he did, specially on women.''

''Oh, aye. I remember now. Forgot that was Demon Huld as a child. Mixed him up with Mandor. Well, Huld's only been here really since Blourbast died in the year of the plague in Pfarb Durim. He sent all the way to Morninghill for Healers, I remember. Caught some, too. I got them before he was dead.''

''Healer, healer, heal these bones,'' sing the skulls from the wall. ''Call the Healer, broken bones, token lones, spoken moans. . . .'' A clattering echo speeds down the line of them into the mysterious, endless dark.

''Hush,'' says Tolp. ''Hush now.''

''Wish I had one now,'' says the Bonedancer. ''Any Healer at all.''

''There's some up there with flesh power,'' says Tolp. ''One came through here not more'n two days ago.''

''Flesh power! That's how I've come to this pass, letting those with flesh power lay hands on me. They may be able to Heal when they're young, Tolp, but when they've laid bloody hands on a few, they forget how to Heal. All they can do is make it worse. No. I mean a real Healer.''

''Been long,'' answers Tolp, ''since a real Healer set foot in Hell's Maw. Those I Divulged for Blourbast were the last.''

''Those you killed, Tolp. Say what's true. You tortured them and you killed them because Blourbast wanted vengeance on them. They wouldn't Heal him. You killed them, and no Healer will lay hands on you ever because of it. Nor on me. Nor on any who's come here of their own will.''

''We could go away,'' says Tolp. ''Travel down to Morninghill ourselfs. They wouldn't know us there.''

''They'd know.'' The Bonedancer lies down with a gasp, takes up the mouthpiece once more to suck numbing smoke and release it into the dank air. ''Don't know how they'd know, but they'd know. Soon as they touched you, they'd know. Left a print in your bones, somewhere. Any time you hurt a Healer, they leave a sign on you. Even if they can't get at you right then, they lay sign on you. I always heard that.''

''Lay sign,'' sing the bones. ''Pray shrine, weigh mine. . . .''

''Hush,'' says Tolp. ''They're coming. I hear them at the end of the tunnel.''

And the light comes nearer as skeleton fingers pass the torch from fleshless hand to fleshless hand keeping pace with those approaching. First legless Laggy Nap on the shoulders of a bearer, a loose mouthed pawn wearing one of the jeweled caps of obedience; then cadaverous Prionde, tall crown scratching the rock above him, deep set eyes scowling over bony cheeks as he draws his robes fastidiously about him; then Huld in trailing velvets which his followers must leap and jitter to avoid. Followers—a Prince or two from the northern realms; a monstrous Ghoul from the lands around Mip; three or four Mirrormen in the guise of other persons; lastly a scarred Medium who drags a limp body behind. Tolp and the Bonedancer crouch in the redolent dark, drawing no attention. Huld does not look at them when he passes, merely calls into the swampy air, ''Let this body be hung with the others.'' To which the hideous Medium grunts a response as he lets his burden fall. Then they go on down the tunnel, the torches following them from bone to bone until they pass from sight and hearing.

''Now it'll stink again,'' says the Bonedancer. ''Stink for days. If he wants bones on the wall, why can't I take them from one of the bone pits? Why put bodies on the wall while they stink?''

''This one isn't even a body, yet,'' says Tolp. ''Still alive.'' He turns the lax form over with one foot to peer blindly down into a child's unconscious face. ''Isn't even grown. What'd he bring us this for?''

''So you can hang him on the wall and listen to him scream and then cry, then whimper, then sigh, then beg, then die,'' says the Bonedancer in a husky chant. ''Then rot, then smell, for he's come to Hell. . . .''

''Why? I just asked why?''

''Because he's Huld,'' replied the Dancer. ''Because this is Hell's Maw.'' Silent under the pulsing smoke, he reflects for a time and then speaks again. ''I think it would be good for you to take the one who isn't dead yet out of here. Up to Pfarb

Durim, maybe. Leave it on their doorstep."

"You out of your head, Dancer? Huld'd roast me."

"Huld's got lots on his mind. Might not even think of it again."

"Might not! Might not! And might, just as well. You stick to keeping your bones moving, Dancer. Leave the hanging up to me. Might not! Devils take it."

The Bonedancer shakes with another long spell, half cough, half laugh. "Oh, old Tolp, you'll be hung on that wall yourself, don't you know? You and me. Besides, I'm not keeping the bones moving. Haven't had the strength for that for a long time now. . . ." His words are choked off by Tolp's horny hands upon his throat.

"If you aren't, then who is, Dancer? Who is? Tell me that? Whose power?"

The Bonedancer's head moves restlessly from side to side between the choking hands. When Tolp draws away, growling, the Bonedancer only mumbles. "Ghostpieces, maybe. Who knows whose power?"

"Abuse power," cry the bones. "Blues devour. Choose hour."

Down the black gut of stone the bones cry, gradually subsiding into restless, voiceless motion, finger bones endlessly scratching at the wall, heels clattering on the stones, a ceaseless picking at the iron bands and chains which hold them. One day a skeleton finger will find the keyhole of the lock which binds them, will fiddle with it until the simple pins click and the lock falls open. Until that time, they remain chained to this stone. Pass it by. Go on beyond the last, small skeletons to the oozing stairs. So much I, Peter, have imagined from what I later saw and what Tolp was still able to say. What follows we have been told is true.

At the top of the stairs an anteroom opened to an audience hall, shadow-walled, its ancient stones dimming upward into groined darkness. Many powerful Gamesmen feasted at the lower tables. Huld and Prionde were seated upon a dais, Huld listening to Prionde with a semblance of courtesy, though his impatience could be judged from the hard tap-tap of a finger upon the arm of the massive chair.

"What meat is this?" asked the King.

"The animals are called shadowpeople."

"You eat them?"

Huld gestured at the raised hearth, the fire, the spits, around which were littered the wooly feet and wide ears discarded by the feasters. "Why should I not? There is no flesh forbidden to me, Prionde. Nothing is forbidden to me. Is it forbidden to you?"

"It seems near to human," said the King doubtfully. "Very near to human, in appearance at least."

"Why should that matter? When I hunger, I eat. Meat is meat, human or otherwise. It is all fuel to my fire, Prionde. I think it can be fuel to yours as well."

The King stirred the delicate finger bones on his plate with a finger of his own. Indeed the ones on the plate did look very kin to the finger which stirred them. "Why do you roost here?" he asked at last. "Why in this place, Huld?"

"Because it chills you," the Demon sneered. "You, and any who come here, and any who hear of it. It is the age old place of terror. It was terrible when I was a child and Blourbast brought me here. Mandor found it terrible, and fascinating, as I had in my time. It is the place of ultimate pain and horror, ultimate evil. From what better place may we strike terror into the minds of all? Our task will be easier when the world knows we move upon them from Hell's Maw. This is the place of atrocity, and power!"

"And yet your Ghoul did not return."

Huld shrugged, rubbed his greasy hands upon his velvets in complete indifference. "He was not expected to return. The Phantasm who flew in the trees and observed what happened, though, he did return," and Huld made a gesture of command to one of the Gamesmen sprawled in half drunken abandon in the hall below, a summons which the Phantasm was quick to obey. He knelt at Huld's feet, head bowed, the lantern light flashing from the faceted mask he wore.

"Tell the King what you have reported to me."

The Phantasm began: "I waited as I had been ordered to do, in the forest near where the Ghoul made his foray against the women on the road. When the Ghoul brought them into the forest cover, I followed, staying ahead of him and hidden in the boughs. He had not come far before someone came through the trees behind him. I heard the person cry Game and Move upon him, a risk call. I could not stay hidden and see clearly, but I heard the Ghoul cry out in triumph, as though the pursuer had played Gamefool.

"Then there was a cry from the pursuer, as though to some other Gamesman, words I could not hear clearly. Then a fire came up, all at once, as though a Sentinel had been present. I came closer to see, but the smoke and fire drove me away. I heard someone blunder away through the trees, and it was not the Ghoul. I did not let myself be seen, but came away as instructed to do." The Phantasm remained bowed down, awaiting the King's pleasure. Huld gestured him away.

"The point is," said Huld, "that the pursuer, Peter, arrived too quickly to have Flown. We must assume he Ported. Also, the fire came about because of him."

"What is he? I thought he was Necromancer named?"

"He was named Necromancer inaccurately. It misled me for a time. I believe him to be a twinned Talent. We have seen their like in the past. Minery Mindcaster, for example, was a strong twinned Talent, Pursuivant and Afrit. In my youth I knew of another, Thaumaturge Mirtisap who was, I know, both Thaumaturge and Prophet, though he denied it. Some say they start as twins in the womb, but the stronger swallows the weaker and is born with both Talents. Perhaps Peter is twinned Afrit and Archangel. When I encountered him in the caverns, I thought he was merely Afrit, but Afrits do not have a skill with Fire."

The King sneered beneath his beard, narrow lips curling in a mockery of humor. "You have forgotten that he seemed to have Beguiled Mandor's people at Bannerwell. I never learned that an Archangel has a skill with Beguilement."

Huld waved an impatient hand. "Churchman, then. Churchmen have both Fire and Beguilement. I do not intend to search the Index to find what combination of Gamesmen he is, or what obscure name is given to such a combination. He may be called Shadowmaster for all I care. Enough to know that now we know it, he will not escape me again. No, he will lead us as the arrow flies to that place we want to go, to obtain that which we want to obtain. . . ."

"Which you believe is . . ."

"Barish, King Prionde. Barish of the ancient times. Barish with his knowledge of the old machines, the old weapons, before which the knowledge of the magicians is as nothing. Barish who lies there in the northlands somewhere. Where we have not been able to find him, but where Peter can lead us."

"And how do you know all this, Demon? Whose head have you rummaged it out of?"

Huld chortled, a nastiness of tongue and mouth as though eating something foully delicious. "No person's head, King. I have put it together out of books, old books, books which lay unread in the tunnels of the magicians. Out of books, legends, and common talk. Out of things Nitch told me before he died, his intellect o'erleaping his pain to find things to tell me. I had an advantage Nitch had not. *I saw the machine.* I saw how the tiny Gamesmen are made! I saw the bodies stored away in caverns like so many blocks of ice. Well, they will not come to life again. The machine which could have brought them to life once more is dead and broken and blown to atoms."

"Assuming you are correct, then how will Barish be brought to life again? If the machine is gone, buried under the mountains?"

"I think the machine beneath the mountains was not the only one. There will be another, alike or similar, where Barish lies."

"And what is it makes you think Peter will guide you there? What is he that he should do this thing? What interest has he? His aim, what Game?"

"Only that he was mind-led by the old Seer of yours, King. Windlow the Seer was searching for the same thing I have been searching for, I'm convinced of it. He'd found something. He knew something, or had a Vision of something. Why else does Peter go north now, into the lands of mysteries?" He laughed, a victorious crow. "Why else does he go north, now, in company with my man? Mine!"

"Nothing more than that? It is all so indefinite and misty, Demon. I would hesitate to commit my men on such a Game had I nothing more than what you have told me. Perhaps it is not Barish who lies hidden in the north. Perhaps it is the Council."

Huld mocked. "There is no Council save ours, King

Prionde. When I had worked my way into the confidence of old Manacle, the fool, and his lick-heels, I asked how long it had been since they had heard directly from this Council. Not for seasons, he told me. The machine which brought the words of the Council no longer spoke. And so I told them *I* brought messages from the Council, and they believed me. So judge for yourself."

"You think if the Council still existed, it would not have let its communication be interrupted. Nor would your representations have gone so unquestioned."

"Exactly. Whoever, or whatever, the Council was, its last member has gone, or died, or found something else to play with. No, we are the Council, Prionde. I regret only that we have no more magicians to do our work for us. I found only those few tens of techs, scattered among the valleys." Huld gestured at a far wall where a few forms huddled in sleep. "I would like to find the one who led them, Quench. He knew things others did not. I would not have been surprised to learn that he knew of Barish, that his many times great forefather had passed some such knowledge along to him. Well, we may find him in time. . . .

"And meantime we build terror, Prionde, and utter despair. And when Peter has led us where we want to go, we will descend upon him in horrible power. I do not think he will withstand us. Even a twinned Talent is not immortal."

And so they went on feasting and drinking, while the people of Pfarm Durim kept watch upon their walls lest more innocents be swept up and chained in the endless tunnels of Hell's Maw where Tolp, even then, fastened the iron bands around the kidnapped child. In the blackness, the Bonedancer coughed his life away and lay quiet. When he had not moved for several days, Tolp fastened his body beside that of the child.

9

Nuts, Groles, and Mirrormen

There had been some discussion during the ride between Reavebridge and Leamer as to the route we might take to reach the top of the Waenbane plateau which hung above us in the west. Certainly, it would not be up the eastern face, a wall as sheer as that of a jug, almost glassy in places. My map showed the long notch coming into that tableland from the north, the way they called Winds' Gate, leading up into Winds' Eye, Waeneye. Queynt said he had been there, but I was not that trustful of Queynt.

When darkness came up and we had set camp only a league or so outside Leamer, I decided I would ride on into the town and make some general inquiries. It had the advantage of getting me away from Jinian as well. Something in our relationship now made me rather uncomfortable. As I left, I saw King Kelver riding away with a stranger, the King looking very angry and disturbed. I thought to call out, offering assistance, then told myself he had able assistance from his own Dragons if he wished help. I often have these good ideas which are as often ignored. So it was in this case, and I let him go. The results were unpleasant, but then, that's yestersight, which is perfect.

My way led down quiet lanes through the nut orchards. We were well into Nutland by then, so called because of the orchards which pimpled the flats along the river. The ground nuts bulge out of the ground like little hillocks, at first gray-green and shiny, a ring of flat, hairy leaves frilling their bottoms. As they grow wider and higher, the shells turn brown and dull and the leaves squeeze out into multiple ruffles. Some nuts are round, some elongated. When they have ripened, the orchard master drills a hole near the ground into the shell and feeds up to a dozen sausage groles into the hole. This is done at dusk. When they emerge at dawn, as they always do for some obscure reason of their own, their heads are lopped off and a lacing run through the skin of the neck. This is grole sausage, to be smoked or dried or otherwise treated to preserve it. Sausage groles are rather small as groles go, thick through as my thigh and a manheight long or more. Their teeth are formidable, however, for all the small size, and grole growers have terrible tales to tell about being caught inside a nut with unmuzzled groles. At the side of the road were piles of sawn nutshells, stacked like so many great bowls. I asked a nut sawyer what use would be made of his odd shaped pile.

"Why, Gamesman, these go down river to Devil's Fork, then up river again to the very top of the East Fork of Reave, then over the hill to the upper reaches of the Longwater and from there down to the Glistening Sea. We grow the best boatnuts here grown anywhere. It's a special strain my own grandad worked on to get it so long and narrow."

"I knew they made houses of them," I said. "I had not seen boats before."

"Oh, for housenuts you go over the West Fork to the orchards in the north of Nutland. People around there won't live in anything else. Warm and dry and smooth to look at, that's a good housenut. I saw one over there big enough to put three stories high in, five manheights it was, ground to top. There's vatnut groves along the river there, and one fellow had a tiny strain he calls hatnuts. Novelty item is what it is. Merchants buy them. But then, they'll buy anything to sell up north. Well, good evening to you, Gamesman."

And with that he shouldered his nutsaw and walked away

into the dark. I smiled at the notion of a hatnut and then stopped smiling as I thought how light it would be in comparison with a metal helm. Nutshells were said to be tough as iron.

I went first to the Minchery, the school for musicians and poets, run by a sensible group of merchants on the same lines as a School House is run, except that the students are pawns, not Gamesmen. Except for that, it was much the same in appearance. The young are very much the young, no matter where they are. Which was not quite true. Mertyn's House had never been so melodious as this place sounded.

I had thought out my story well in advance. A certain song, I said, had won a prize at a Festival in the south. The prize was to be given to the songwriter. I hummed a bit of it, sang a few words, and was taken into a garden to be introduced to a frail, wispy girl whose eyes were misty with dreams and songs. I put the gold into her hand and told her the same tale, glad I had thought of it for it brought her great happiness.

"Did it come to you all at once?" I asked, careful not to seem too interested. "Or did you compose it over a long time?"

"Oh, truth to tell, Gamesman," she piped, "I dreamed it. The tune was in my head when I woke one morning, and the words, too, though they took some working at to fit into the music. It is almost as though I dreamed them in another language."

Well, there was nothing more to be got there, so I thanked her, complimented her skill, and went away to find some place where merchants and traders gathered. It was not difficult. Leamer lies upon the main road between all the fabled lands of the north and south. I came soon enough to a pleasant smelling place, went inside and sat me down beside a leather skinned man with smile marks around his eyes. He was not averse to conversation, and by luck he had been up the Wind's Gate.

"Curiosity is what I did it for, Gamesman. Nothing up there to buy or sell, far as I knew, nothing to trade for, no people, no orchards, no mines. Curiosity, though, that's a powerful mover."

I told him I thought that was probably so.

"Well, so, I'd traveled along this road between Morninghill and the jungle cities for thirty years, boy and man. Saw these cliffs every time I came this way. Saw those old bone shapes up there. So, one time there wasn't any hurry about the trip south, and when we came to the notch there, the one they call the Wind's Gate, I said, well, fellows, we'll just turn in here and go up this notch to see what's there."

He seemed to expect some congratulations for having made this decision, and I obliged him with another glass and a hearty spate of admiration for his presumption.

"Well, Gamesman, there's a kind of road in there. No real trouble for the wagons save a few stones needing moving where they'd rolled down off that mountain. Little ones, mostly. We moved and we rolled and moved and rolled, and the ground began to go up. Now I'll tell you, Gamesman, there at the end of that notch the ground goes up like a ramp. Like it had been a built road. You'd think it would all be scree and fallen stuff, loose and slidy, but it isn't. It's hard and sure underfoot, just as though somebody put it there and melted it down solid.

"We didn't want to wear out the teams. We left them at the bottom and went on to the top, me and some of the boys. Right up where those bone shapes are, and aren't they something? I'll tell you: Unbelievable until you see them close and then more unbelievable yet. Wind carved, so they say, and that's hard to countenance. Well, we looked around. There's nothing there. Waste. Thorn bush and devil's spear. Flat rock and the Wind's Bones. That's it. Then, not far off, we heard that *krerk*ing noise the krylobos make, and a roar like rock falling, and one of my old boys says, 'Gnarlibar,' just like that, 'Gnarlibar.' Well, we hadn't seen one, but we'd heard about 'em, and we weren't about to stay up there and wait for a foursome to show up, so we turned ourselves around and came back down quick as you please."

"What have you heard about gnarlibars?" I asked. Perhaps I might find out, at last, what the beasts looked like.

"Big," he said. "And bad. Low, wide beasts they are. They come upon you four at a time, from four directions. Always hunt in fours, no such thing as a single gnarlibar. Contradiction in terms, so I've heard. Well, who knows. Somebody told me they're born in fours, twin ones to each female of a four, so every four is always related. It may be storytelling for all I know. We didn't stay to see." And he laughed over the limits to his vaunted curiosity.

I thanked him sincerely and left. There was no traffic at all on the road when I returned, guiding myself by our campfires which gleamed lonely against the dark bulk of the mountain. I found the place quiet, Silkhands busily talking to Queynt. I asked her where Jinian was, and she told me Jinian had ridden out a little time past in company with someone who had brought her a message from her brother Mendost. I went on to the separate fire where Chance squatted over his cookery, readying a bowl for me.

"Well, lad, did you find our way to satisfaction? Did some keen eyed merchant tell you the truth about our journey?"

This led to chaffing him at some length about gnarlibars and his former desire to have me Shift into such a beast. "They come in fours," I said. "You would have been riding an anomaly had I Shifted into a mere single beast, Chance. Your widow would have despised you for lack of knowledge."

"Ah, well, Peter, since you say it's a wide, low beast, it's as well you didn't. There's plenty of tall, dignified beasts what don't require all that company."

I chewed and gulped and gazed across the fire to the one where Silkhands sat. There, riding into that light was King Kelver, returning from his errand, face bleary and ill-looking as though he had been stricken with some disease or had been drinking since he left us. Chance saw it, too.

"Ah, now he doesn't look like he's feeling crisp, does he?"

"He doesn't," I agreed. "I wonder what the problem is?" And then, noting her absence, "I wonder why Jinian hasn't returned?"

Chance struck his forehead a resounding blow and fished around in his clothing to bring out a sealed message. "Fuss me purple if I didn't forget it in all this talk of gnarlibars. She left you this message and said give it to you soon as you returned."

"Chance! I've been sitting here over an hour!"

"Well, you got so stiffy about my opening the last message for yourself that I didn't open this one. What I don't know the contents of, I can't be overconcerned with, can I?" He was getting very righteous, and I knew he was angry at himself.

As well he might. The message read, *Peter, if I have not returned, it is because I cannot. This is a fool's errand, but I must find out. Say nothing to Kelver. Find me quickly, or likely I am dead.*

For a moment it did not enter my mind as making sense, then I screamed at Chance, "Which way did she go? Tell me at once! Which?"

"Which way? Why, lad, I wasn't watching! Somebody came and said they were from Armiger Mendost, and she should come along to the person carrying the message. Though that doesn't make sense."

It did not make sense. If her brother Mendost had sent a message, it would have been delivered to her in the camp. No need to ride elsewhere. "That was all a trap, a snare," I hissed at him. "Somewhere this minute she may be dying. Did anyone else see her?"

"They paid no more attention than I did, Peter. They were talking among themselves, Silkhands, Queynt, the Dragons."

"Not the King?"

"No. He'd gone away with some messenger before."

I was frenzied, not questioning the frenzy, not questioning why my heart had speeded or my mouth gone dry. I was lost in a panic of fear for Jinian, not thinking that a Wizard should be able to take care of herself.

It was very dark. No one could follow a trail in this dark, and yet she had said, "Find me quickly." To find her at all was beyond me. "How?" I demanded of him. "I must find her."

"A fustigar," suggested Chance. "Trail her?"

I had never tried to follow scent, was not sure I could. In any case, the fustigar hunts mostly by sight. I shook my head, frantically thinking. Could I use one of the Gamesmen of Barish?

"Not Didir," I mumbled aloud. "No one here knows where

she is. She misled them herself, purposely. Not Tamor. Who . . . " Even as I spoke, I fumbled among them. Oh, there was Talent enough to move the world, if one knew what one wanted to do, but I didn't know where, or how, or when. . . .

"If I had only seen which way she went," mourned Chance. "If I'd only seen . . . "

If he had seen. If I could See. I did not much believe in Seeing. It seemed unreliable at best, so much flummery at worst. I had never called upon Sorah, but what choice had I else? I could not find her with my fingers, so dumped the pouch onto the firelit ground, hastily scrabbling the contents back into it before Chance saw the blue piece among the black and white. Sorah was there, at the very bottom, the tiny hooded figure with the moth wings delicately graven upon her mask. For the first time, I wondered how it was that the machine had made blues dressed as Gamesmen when, to my certain knowledge, the bodies they were made from often wore no clothing at all? The question was fleeting. I gave it no time. Instead, I took Sorah into my hand and shut my eyes to demand her presence.

At first I felt nothing. Then there was a sort of rising coolness as though calm flowed up my arm and into my head and then out of it—outward. I seemed to hear a voice, like a mother soothing a fractious child or a huntsman a wounded fustigar. I could feel her stance, arms straight at her sides, shoulders and head thrown back, blind eyes staring into some other place or time, searching.

"What is she like?" the voice asked. "Think for me. What is she? Who is she?"

Likenesses skipped. Jinian in the river pouring water over her head, face rosy with sunset and laughter. Jinian speaking to me seriously on the wagon seat, telling me things I had not thought of before. Jinian angry and chill, turning in my doorway to instruct me. Jinian bent over a book; Jinian beside me laying hands on the great grole; Jinian . . .

Within me, Sorah turned and bent and reached outward once more. Evocation ran in my veins. A net of question flung outward toward the stars. Jeweled droplets ran upon this net, collected at the knots to fall as rain. An imperative upon the place. "World. Show me this!" Jinian a composite, a puzzle, breaking light like a gem.

And I saw. Jinian, held tight between two men. Dusk. Hard to see. They were beside a ground nut, taking out the plug, thrusting her within. I could hear groles inside, grinding.

Where? High to the west one bright star hung in an arch of Wind's Bones, fainter stars to left and right, above a close, high line of cliff. Around me only scattered hillocks of nuts, stones, wasteland . . .

The vision was gone. Sorah was gone. I dragged Chance off with me to the horses, and we two mounted to ride away. No one called after us to know where we went. It was as well. I do not think I could have answered. I could barely get the words out to instruct Chance what to look for as I sharpened my own Shifter's eyes to scan the rimrock silhouetted against the stars. "North," I hissed. "Closer to the cliffs than here." We galloped into the dark like madmen, our horses stumbling and shying at things they could not see.

I almost missed the arch of bone shapes upon the height. They were smaller than they had seemed in Vision, a slightly different shape seen from the side. Also, the stars had fallen lower against the rimrock but were still unmistakable. One bright, two fainter neighbors. We slowed to pick our way farther north. The nut orchards around us had given way to drier land, the plants themselves were sparse, scattered, oddly misshapen. When I saw the right one, my eyes almost slid over it before noticing the plug. Only that one had a plug cut.

We thundered toward it, dismounted at the run, and hammered at the side of the plug until I thought myself of pombi claws and Shifted some for the job. Then the plug fell to the ground, and I leaned into the dank, nut-smelling dark to call, "Jinian! Jinian!"

There was an answering cry, faint as a breath and hoarse. We began to climb in, but I heard the gnawing of the groles. They cared not what they ate. They loved the taste of bone. I thrust Chance to one side, muttering fiercely at him. "Stay out of here. Do not come in! But, keep calling. I need to hear her to lead me to her." Then I had crawled into the place, all tunneled through with grole holes like the inside of a great cheese, and Shifted.

Do you care to know what it is to be a sausage grole? It is an insatiable hunger coupled to an unending supply of food. It is a happy gnawing which has the same satisfaction as scratching a not unpleasant itch. I began as a rather generalized grole-thing. Within moments, I encountered a real nut grole, and my long, pulsating body slid over and around that of my fellow in a sensuous, delightful embrace, half dance, half play. After that, I was more sausage grole than before. I heard a shouting noise somewhere, another one somewhere else. Neither mattered. Nothing mattered except the food, the dance.

I suppose it was some remnant of Peter which brought me out of this contented state, some artifice or other he had learned to use in Schlaizy Noithn, perhaps, or the touch of the Gamesmen from within. At any rate, after a little time of this glorious existence, the grole-I-was began to make purposeful munching toward the screaming inside the nut. Groles have no eyes. I remedied this lack. There was no light. I remedied this as well, creating a kind of phosphorescence on my skin. I saw her at last, high on an isolated pillar of nutmeat, crouched beneath the curve of the shell, three groles gnawing away at her support. In light, she might have been able to avoid them. In the dark? I doubted it.

So there was Jinian atop the pillar; there was Peter in shining splendor below. What did one do now? She solved the problem by half falling, half scrambling over the intervening bodies and onto my back where I grew a couple of handholds and a bit of shielding for her. It was no trouble, and I was pleased to think of it. We got out in a writhing, tumbling kind of way, over and under, and I was still not quite full of nutmeat when we slithered out of the shell and I gave up all that bulk to become Peter once more. It lay behind me, steaming in the night air, and I wondered what the grole growers might make of it when they returned at dawn.

Only then did I realize she was crying. I put my arms around her and let her shake against my nakedness, gradually growing quiet as I grew clothes. I did not release her, merely stood there in a kind of unconscious, not un-grolelike content, stroking her hair and murmuring sounds such as people make to small animals and babies.

"I was frightened," she said. "It was dark, and I was afraid you would not come. I was afraid you would not come in time."

I gave Chance a look which should have fried him into his boots, and he had the grace to mumble that it had been his fault. I told her I had used Sorah.

"I knew you would do something," she said. "I knew you would find me because you are clever, Peter, though you often do not seem to know it. But so much time went by, and I became terribly afraid." After which we murmured nonsense things at one another and did not move very much until Chance harumphed at us.

"All well and nice, lad, lass. I'm sure it's gratifying in all its parts, but we don't know who put you there, do we? Or why? What's next? Will they be coming back to find out whether you're sausage or what?"

She stepped away from me to leave a cold place where warm content had been. "It would be better if they think I'm dead, Chance. We must find some place to hide me. Queynt's wagon, I think. The ones who took me must think they succeeded, at least until we find out what's going on!" And she directed us to replace the plug as it was when we found it, turning the pombi-scarred place to the bottom.

She told us what had happened as we rode back. "I saw King Kelver leaving the camp. I thought there was something odd about it, about the way he looked, or the men with him—something. Well, perhaps foolishly, I decided to follow him. After all, it is Kelver I am promised to—if, indeed, he still cares about that promise, which I have doubts over. I followed for a time, then lost them. I searched, quartering about, and was probably seen doing it. I gave up and returned to camp.

"Then in an hour or so, came a fellow saying he came from Armiger Mendost with words I should hear about King Kelver. I knew that was a lie. Mendost sends messengers, but never yet sent any except Heralds or Ambassadors or others in full panoply. Mendost is too proud to do else.

"But I thought even lies lead to the truth, somewhere, if one knows them for what they are, and a lie announces a Game as

well as many a truth. So I left word with Chance and went
with the fellow. He had another hid nearby, and the two of
them bagged me and would have fed me to the groles surely
had you not found me in time. As it is, I never saw what
Gamesmen they were.''

"And all that merely because you followed King Kelver?" I
asked, thinking it did not seem like much.

"For no other reason," she said. "Something is toward
there, Peter, and whoever Games wants no one to know of it.
So I must hide and you must find out what goes on.''

She thought to hide in Queynt's wagon. I didn't trust the
man. We argued. She won. She thought she could hide even
from Silkhands, though Silkhands rode upon the wagon seat
all day. Well. What could I do. We hid her away in some
brush near the camp, and I returned with Chance. At first
light I sought out Queynt and took him aside as quietly as the
man would allow me to do so.

"Consult with me, young sir? Ah, but I am flattered that
such a proud young Gamesman—for surely pride goes with
honor and ability, isn't that so?—would have use for such an
old and traveled body as myself. Advise, I often do. Consult,
indeed, I often do. Though when advice and consulting are
done, who takes any serious regard for the one or puts any
faith in the other—why, it would surprise you to learn how
seldom words are given even the weight of a fluff-seed. Still, I
am flattered to be asked, and would lie did I pretend a false
and oleaginous humility . . . ''

"Queynt," I said in a firm voice. "Hush this nonsense and
listen." His jaw dropped, but I saw a humorous glitter in his
eyes. It went away when I told him someone had tried to kill
Jinian, that we wanted to find out who, that she needed to
hide in his wagon. "No one must know," I said. "Not even
Silkhands. And, Queynt, it is Jinian's thought to trust you. I
don't. So, if no one knows but you, and anyone finds out or
harms her, I will consider my suspicions justified.''

He coughed. I thought he did it to hide laughter which was
inappropriate for there was no matter of laughter between us.
"I will guarantee to hold her beyond all possibility of
discovery, young sir. The word of Vitior Vulpas Queynt is as
highly valued as are the jewels of Bantipoora of miraculous

legend. Say no more. Wait only a bit and then bring her to the camp. I will have sent all eyes to seek another sight that she may come unobserved.''

"Queynt," I replied, "I will do so, but I tell you that you talk too much.''

"But on what topics, Gamesman? Ask yourself that? On what subjects do I talk not at all?'' He smiled at me and went away. In a little time Kelver and Silkhands and the Dragons rode away toward Leamer. Queynt opened the wagon door at the back of the vehicle, and we brought Jinian to be lifted in. It was a well fitted place, almost a small house, with arrangements for food and sanitation. "A technish toilet," said Queynt. "Something I obtained from the magicians long ago, when I used to trade with them." He greeted my incredulous stare with equanimity. Jinian took his words at face value.

"Thank you, Queynt," she said. "I will treat your property with respect. If I may lie up within for a few days, we can perhaps discover who means us ill." She gave him her hand, and he bowed over it, eyes fixed sardonically on me. I left them, hoping she would have sense to shut the door in time. I need not have worried. When Silkhands and the others rode back from their expedition to the orchards, the wagon was shut tight. Silkhands, however, was in a fury. She came to visit me and Chance.

"That little fool Jinian. The King tells me she has left us! Without a word to me! Mendost may Game against me, or against the House in Xammer because of this. She did not even tell me goodbye.''

Chance blinked at me like an owl and went on stirring as I feigned surprise. "King Kelver told you this? When was that?''

"This morning. Queynt suggested we might like to see the grole sausage made, so we rode over to the orchards. We had gone no distance at all when the King told me she had gone. Gone! It seems she told him she did not like the bargain she had assented to and intended to return to her brother's Demesne.''

"The King must be mightily disappointed," I said carefully. "He looks very ill over it.''

"I know." She dabbed at her eyes where tears leaked out.

"He does look ill. I reached out to help him, Heal him, and he struck my hand away as though I had been a beggar. He is very angry."

"Ah, the King did not want you to help him." I cast another long look at Chance who returned it with a slow, meaningful wink. "I will tell the King we share his distress," I said, rising and walking off to the other fire.

Once there, I bowed to the King where he sat over his breakfast, the bowl largely untouched before him. I murmured condolences in a courteous manner, all the time looking him over carefully beneath my lashes. Oh, he did indeed look very unwell. The crisp curl of his beard was gone, the hard, masculine edges of his countenance were blurred, the lip did not curl, the sparkling eyes were dim. The man who sat there might have been Kelver's elder and dissolute brother.

I returned to our fire, comforted Silkhands as best I could, and waited until she rejoined Queynt upon the wagon seat before saying to Chance, "It isn't Kelver."

"Shifter?" he asked.

"No, I think not. Few Shifters can take the form of other Gamesmen. Mavin can, of course. I can. Most of Mavin's kindred probably can. It isn't easy, but those of us who can do it at all can do it better than it has been done here."

"Perhaps someone less Talented than Mavin's kindred, but more Talented than most Shifters?"

"I think not," I said. "Instinct tells me not. Is there not some other answer?"

Chance nodded, chewing on his cheeks as he did when greatly troubled. "Oh, yes, lad, there's another way it could be done right enough. I like it less than Shifters, though, I'll tell you that."

"Well? Don't make me beg for answers like some child, Chance. What is it?"

"Mirrormen," he said. "Never was a Mirrorman did anything for honorable reason, either. When you find Mirrormen, you find nastiness afoot, evil doings, covert Game, rule breaking. That's always the way with Mirrormen."

I cast frantically back to my Schooldays for what I could remember about Mirrormen. It was little enough. Something . . .

"They will need to keep Kelver close by, and unharmed," I said. "They will need to take his reflection every day or so, so they cannot harm him or keep him at any great distance."

"Oh, that's true enough, so far as it goes," said Chance. 'If by 'harmed' you mean maimed or ruined permanent. They'll have done something to him, though, to prevent his using Beguilement on them. He's a King, after all. He can be pretty discomforted, let me tell you, and still give a good reflection."

"There must be two Mirrormen," I said, remembering more from my Schooldays.

"Two," he said. "That's right. One takes the reflection, which is backwards, like seeing your own face in a mirror. Then the second takes the reflection of the first, which makes it come out right. That's what makes it a bit blurry, too. They can't usually get it very crisp. Well, wherever Kelver is, he isn't far from here."

So we made it up between us to find King Kelver as soon as dark came once more. Meantime, since we had been up through the whole long night, we slept in the saddle throughout the whole long day, nodding in and out of wakefulness as the day wore on. Leamer vanished behind us, the road went on north, and at last we came to the fork where we could look back to the southwest to see the huge notch in the highlands and feel the warm wind rushing out of it into our faces. "Wind's Gate," said Chance.

"Wind's Gate," called Queynt from the wagon seat. "A great and marvelous sight, gentlemen, Healer, where the highlands slope into the lowlands and the wind travels that same road. Oh, many a traveler's tale could be told of the Wind's Gate, many a marvelous story woven. See how Yittleby and Yattleby stride forth, eager to see their kindred upon the heights. Oh, you will be amazed, sirs, Healer, at the wonders which await you there."

There was no real reason for King Kelver to accompany us, now that Jinian was gone. Some spirit of devilment in me called him to account for his presence.

"It was courteous of you, King, to accompany us thus far in our journey. We understand that it was courtesy offered to young Jinian, promised to you as she was, and that you might feel reluctant to withdraw that courtesy now that she is gone.

However, may I express all our thanks and willingness that you feel no obligation to continue. Indeed, sir, you have done enough and more than one might expect." There, I thought. That's out-Queynting Queynt himself, and find an answer to that, Mirrorman.

He hemmed and hawed, reminding me of the way Riddle had fumed and fussed when I had called him to account similarly. "Not at all, Gamesman," he finally managed to say. "I am led by curiosity now. Having come so far, I will not go home again without having seen the heights." And he smiled a sick, false smile at me which I returned as falsely. Devil take him.

When we started into the notch, Chance told me to watch to the rear with my Shifter's eyes. "They have to bring the real King along near," he said. "They couldn't try to bring him anyway but by this road—there is no way save this road unless they fly. So you look back there for dust. That'll tell us how far they are behind."

We had gone on for several hours before I saw it, far behind, just then turning at the fork. I could not have seen it had the land not sloped down behind us so that we looked upon the road already traveled. Even then, no eyes but a Shifter's would have seen it. I did not make any great matter out of peering and spying. It was well enough to know that the true King was probably behind us several hours upon the road, which distance would likely be decreased under cover of dark.

So when evening came we built our separate fire once more, and Chance and I made much noise about weariness, how we had not slept the night before out of worry over Jinian and how we must now go early into our blankets. I made up a convincing bundle and slipped away into the dark. Behind me Chance conversed with my blankets. Once away from the light I Shifted into fustigar shape and ate the leagues with my feet, carrying with me only one thing I thought I might need.

I found them without any trouble at all. There were two of them and a closed wagon, not unlike that which Queynt drove. One of the men was an Elator, a cloak thrown over his close leathers against the night's chill. The other was Mirrorman, right enough, got up in King's robes and a feathered hat like Kelver's.

The wagon was shut tight. I had no doubt Kelver was in it. I would learn all I needed by waiting for the other Mirrorman, the false Kelver, to return to his allies. I lay behind a rock and watched the two as they ate and drank, belched and scratched themselves. Finally the false Kelver arrived, riding in out of the darkness, and they unlocked the wagon. I saw where the key was kept, crept close behind them to peer through the crack of the door. The true King was bound and gagged, lying upon a cot. When they took the gag from his mouth, he swayed, obviously drugged. He could not bestir himself to anger, mumbling only.

"You are dishonorable, Gamesmen. Your Game is dishonored. Who Games against me?"

One of the Mirrormen struck him sharply upon the legs with a stick he carried. "Silence, King. Our master cares not for your honor or dishonor, for rules and forbiddings. You may keep your life, perhaps, if you cause us no trouble. Or you may lose your life, certainly, in Hell's Maw."

I had heard Hell's Maw mentioned a time or two, by Mertyn, by Mavin, both with deep distaste and horror. I knelt close to the door crack, not to miss a word.

"Hell's Maw," the King mumbled. "What has Hell's Maw to do with me?"

"Hell's Maw has to do with the world," said the Elator. "Our Master, Huld, moves from the mastery of Hell's Maw to the mastery of the world. You are in the world. Therefore, you are in his Game. Now be silent."

The first Mirrorman took up his position before the true King, stared at him long and long. I saw his flesh ripple and change. When he turned, his was the King's face, but reversed and strange. Now the second Mirrorman, the false King, stared at the first in his turn, the flesh shifting slightly along the jaw, around the eyes. What had been a blurred, sick looking image became slightly better, not unlike King Kelver. Still, while all who knew the King would have accepted this face, they would have thought the King very ill, for it was not the face of health and character which friends who knew the King knew well. They gagged Kelver once more and left him there. I saw where they put the key.

They talked, then, of Hell's Maw. I learned much I would

rather not have known, of Laggy Nap and Prionde, of many powerful Princes from the north. I heard of the bone pits and the cellars, the dungeons and bottomless holes. These three talked of all this with weary relish, as though they had been promised some great reward when the ultimate day arrived. Finally the Elator flicked away, was gone a short time, then returned. There were a few further instructions for the false King. He was to signal the Elator if Peter left the others, signal if anything was discovered. The Mirrorman mounted and rode away toward the camp he had left some hours before. Only then did I move after him to take him unaware in the darkness. When a Mirrorman meets a pombi there is no contest between them. The pombi always wins.

I returned then to the Mirrormen's camp, the false King trailing behind me, obedient to the little cap I had brought with me. I had said to him, "*You* are King Kelver, the true King Kelver. You will hear no other voice but mine. You will lie quiet in the wagon, drugged and quiet. You will say nothing at all. You are the true King Kelver, you will hear no voice but mine." Then I laid him behind a stone to wait while the other two drank themselves to sleep.

Then it was only quiet sneaking to get the key, to open the wagon, untie the King, hush his mumbling. "You must be silent! Hush, now, or I'll leave you here tied like a zeller for the spit!" At which he subsided, still drooling impotent anger into his beard. I put the false Kelver in his place, cap fastened tight under the feathered hat the King wore. Before we left, I reinforced his orders once more. I intended to come back the following night, perhaps, to take the cap from him before he lapsed into emptiness as the Invigilator had done in Xammer.

When we had come the weary way back to camp, the night was past its depth and swimming up to morning. I took him straight to Silkhands and told her all the story, after which it was only a little time until she had the poison out of him and he sputtering by the fire, angry as a muzzled grole.

"The Elator will probably spy on us," I said. "We must decide how to keep them from knowing."

"They will know in any case," said the King. "When I do not return tomorrow for my reflection."

I snapped at him. "Nonsense. Of course you will return.

They will expect to see a Mirrorman come in the likeness of the King, and you will come in the likeness of the King. If you do not, I must, and that is too many Kelvers entirely even for this group." He seemed to be chewing on this, so I gave him reason. "The false Kelver will simply lie there, thinking he is you. The other Mirrorman will do what Mirrormen do, no different. Surely you have guile enough for this? To keep them unsuspecting? To feed information back to Hell's Maw which may be to our liking? If for no other reason, to work vengeance upon them for what they would have done to Jinian."

I was angered that he did not seem as concerned as I about what they had almost done to Jinian.

10

Wind's Eye

He may not have been concerned enough about Jinian, but his concern knew no bounds for Silkhands. When I quoted to all of them the words I had heard from the mouth of the Elator concerning Huld and his desire to master the world, Silkhands turned away retching. Kelver went to her, held her, and she cried between saying that Huld had come to her often while she was captive in Bannerwell, had threatened her, invaded her mind, set such fear in her that she had not dared think of it again. Now she was drowning in that same terror. King Kelver began to burn, hot as fire, swearing vengeance against those who had hurt her, mirrored him, Gamed against any of us. "Your enemy is mine," he swore, putting his hand on mine. "We stand allies against those foul beasts."

I had heard more of the Elator's talk than he had, more than I had repeated to any of them. I was glad of any who would stand against terrors I was uncertain I could face myself. We put Silkhands in the wagon with Jinian to let them comfort one another as to what had been misunderstood between them. I needed no further proof that Kelver was no longer interested in Jinian or that Silkhands would never be more than my friend. So I drank with the King and shared objurgations of all enemies with him until we slept at last from inability to do anything else.

On the morning we climbed farther to the endless chattering of the krylobos. Queynt clucked at them indulgently. I asked if he feared to return to the place he had found them, and he shook his head. "It is impossible to say. It was all so very long ago."

"How long ago?" I asked.

"Ummm." He grimaced. "A very long time ago. I was searching for a place. There had been a great catastrophe, and my maps proved useless. You have heard of the cataclysm, flood and wind, storm and ruin? It caused great destruction the length of the River Reave."

"The same catastrophe which destroyed Dindindaroo," I said. "I have been told that was flood and windstorm. Do you know what caused it?"

"Most certainly. When we come to the top, you will see for yourself. A moonlet fell from the heavens, blazing with the light of a little sun. It thrust into the top of this tableland like a flaming spear, causing the ground to shatter for a hundred leagues in all directions, breaking natural dams and letting loose the pent floods of a thousand thousand years, sending forth a hot, dry wind which spread from this center to blow forests into kindling. You may see the destruction in Leamer yet, in certain places.

"Many ancient things were uncovered. And perhaps many other ancient things were covered past discovery." He was quiet then for a little time, loquacity forgotten, before he said, "Perhaps it is only that the signs were lost, the trails thinned. . . ."

If he had been attempting to astonish me, he succeeded. "I have heard a song sung to that effect," I managed to choke.

"Ah, young sir, so have I. It was that song brought me all the way south almost to the Phoenix Demesne searching for a Healer and a Gamesman to whom that song might mean something."

"Our meeting was no accident then," said Silkhands, entering the conversation from her wagon seat. "No accident at all!"

He flushed a little, only a touch of rose at the lobes of his ears. "No, my dear. Not totally accident. But intended for no evil purpose for all that."

It was too much. I was not assured of his honesty and could not fence with him further. I waited until Chance came up to me, then spent a league of our journey complaining about mysteries, Gamesmen in general, an education which had ill fitted me for the present circumstances, and other assorted miseries including a case of saddle chafe.

Chance ignored me, cutting to the heart of my discomfort. "He's a one, that Queynt," he said. "Says more than he cares about and knows more than he says."

"Spare me the epigrams," I begged him. "Can I trust the man? That's all that matters now. He has not seemed to hurt us in any respect, but he has been far from honest with us. . . ."

"As we have been with him," said Chance. "I suppose he's wondering if he can trust us. I would if I was him."

My own honor and trustworthiness was not a topic I chose to think upon. Not then. I could only go on with the journey by not thinking of it, and so I whipped my horse up and rode ahead of all the rest to the top of the notch, seeing the monstrous bone forms edging the rimrock on every side so that I dismounted to stand in amazement while the others caught up to me.

Queynt jumped from the wagon seat to stretch and bend himself, puffing a little in the high air. "They were not here," he said, "these bone forms were not here before the cataclysm. They were buried deep, buried well, buried for a thousand thousand years. When the moonlet fell, the soil which covered them was blown outward to fall upon the orchards of Nutland or was carried by the wild winds to the edges of the world."

The huge shapes were all around us, north, south, west as far as we could see. They were indeed like the skeletons of unimaginably prodigious beasts, pombis or fustigars perhaps. Here and there the shapes were pentagonal, star shaped, like the skeleton of any of our tailless animals, so like a pombi's that I could not believe them wind carved. They felt and sounded, when struck, like stone. Jinian came out of the wagon to lay her small square hands beside my own. The spies were far behind. She could risk this brief escape from the wagon. We remained there, staring, for a long time before turning away.

The King came to us with the Dragons. I had seen them conferring together as they rode, and now he came to ask my advice. "I have two Dragons here who can be sent as messengers. Would you have any thoughts about that?"

I had been worrying the thought of taking Hafnor in my hand and Porting to the Bright Demesne to ask for help. I had not done because I was not sure I could return, not sure I could visualize clearly enough the surroundings where we traveled. This offer was welcome, and I thanked him for it, suddenly wishing most heartily for Mavin and Himaggery, but most of all for Himaggery's host.

"If and when word reaches Huld that we have found what he is seeking," I said, "he will come. We could give up the search and go away. But Huld would move against the world and us, sooner or later. We may find what we may find and keep it secret. But Huld will come, sooner or later. The Elator who follows us says that there are bone pits outside Hell's Maw piled so deep that no man knows where the bottom of them lies. Huld will come with Bonedancers and Ghouls and Princes of the North who share his ambitions. He will come in might with a horrible host. If that host could be met and conquered in this wasteland . . ."

"Or even delayed," whispered Jinian. "Fewer would suffer."

"Except ourselves," said the King.

"Except ourselves," I agreed. "So while we hope for powerful allies before us, let us call upon whatever others we may."

King Kelver examined me narrowly. "What allies before us, Gamesman? I have not been told of any . . . formally."

I flushed and turned from him. Had Silkhands hinted to him? Hoped with him? Well, probably. Behind me, Jinian said, "There may be none, King Kelver. We hope, that is all."

He laughed, not with any great humor, and made some

remark about fools living on hope. Well, that was true. Fools did. My hope was in Mavin.

So it was that one scarlet Dragon sped northeast, trailing fire and pennants of smoke to make himself even more conspicuous while another, slate gray with wings of jet, fled south close upon the mountain top, unseen, to the far off mists of the Bright Demesne. He carried a message from me which said, without any circumlocution, "Help!" Meantime Jinian dressed herself in the Dragon's cloak and brave plumed helm to ride alongside the wagon. If the Elator got a look at us, we were precisely as we should have been: one King, one Queynt, one Chance; one Silkhands, one Dragon, one Peter. One Jinian, gone, eaten by groles. One Dragon gone, flown back to the Dragon's Fire Purlieu with much noise and fire.

Having thus done what we could against the certainty of Huld's coming, we rode forward once more, to the north where Yggery's charts identified the Wastes of Bleer though it was difficult to imagine a place more waste-like than that we traveled already.

We crossed long lines of scattered ash which led away to the south. "There's a hole there that would hold a battle Demesne," said Queynt. "Where the moonlet fell, spewing this ash in trails across the stone. In time the thorn will hide it. . . ."

Little thorn grew on the flat, though the canyons were choked with it and devil's spear grew thickly under shelter of the stones. Else was only flat, gray and drear. The farther north we went, the more fantastic the twisted stone, convoluted, bizarre, no longer looking like isolated bones or joints but like whole skeletons of dream monsters. It was like moving in a nightmare, dreamy and echoing. Had it not been for the wide sky stretching above us to an endless horizon, it would have felt like a prison beyond hope of release.

It was almost dusk when we came to the chasm, knife edged and sheer. At either end of it a mountain had sprawled into an impenetrable tumble of stone. "Abyss opens, mountains fall," sang Queynt under his breath. I knew it was not the first time he had seen it. "It opened at the time of the cataclysm," he said. "Before that time, one could have ridden on into the wastes."

"Tomorrow," I said wearily. "There is no sense worrying at it now. We have other things to do."

And, indeed, there was enough to do for the evening. King Kelver and I would make his obligatory visit to the Mirrormen, he ostentatiously, I secretly to guard him. With many pricked fingers and scratched arms, we hacked enough thorn for a fire. The King had speared two ground-running birds which we roasted and ate with hard bread and dried fruit. The abyss had stopped us early, so that we had finished our meal before dark, the light falling red behind the line of mountains beyond Graywater. We were gazing at the sky thinking our own gloomy thoughts when the giant strode into our view against the bleeding light.

He was coming toward us. As we had seen him from the gentle valley of the Boneview River, so we saw him again, this time from a frontal view. He strode toward us, towering against the sky, shredding and fraying at his edges as though blown by a great wind, ever renewing his outline, his gigantic integrity of shape and purpose. The sun sank behind him; stars showed through him as he stalked toward the place where we sat wordless and awed. There was something so familiar about him, something so close to recognition. I strained at the thought, but it would not come.

At last the giant came so close the shape of him was lost. We felt the cold, ill wind blow around us, heard that agonized voice, "Kinsman, kinsman, find the wind . . . " and then it had gone on past. We turned to follow its progress over the abyss and beyond where it changed, tumbled, seethed into another shape, a tall, whirling funnel of darkness which poured down into some hidden pocket of the world.

In that instant I saw what I had not seen before, how the shredding edges of the great form resembled a furry pelt, ends flying, how the great shape shifted, Shifted . . .

"Thandbar," said two voices at once. Mine, and Queynt's.

There was a long silence full of waiting and strain. Then Queynt said, "It is fitting I should recognize him, Peter. I knew him. Now, how it is that you would know him?"

I was not sure that I should answer. Silkhands gave me no help, merely staring at me owl-like across the fire. It was Jinian who finally said, "Tell him, Peter. If you cannot trust

Queynt, you cannot trust any in this world and we may as well give up."

It was there, then, in the dusk of the Waeneye, beside a dying fire that I set the Gamesmen of Barish upon a flat stone, reserving only the blue of Windlow to my secret self. They stood under the eyes of all, but it was only Vitior Vulpas Queynt who leaned above them with tears flowing down his face as he touched them one by one. I wanted to strike him, wanted to seize the Gamesmen and flee into the dark. I could feel the serpent within, knotting and writhing. Only Jinian's eyes upon me, her hand upon my knee, kept me quiet as the man picked them up, turned them, called them by name.

Oh, Gamelords, but they were mine. Mine. Not his.

In a little time, the worst of the feeling faded, and I was able to speak and think again. I had to tell him I could speak with them, Read them, and he looked at me then with such awe I felt uncomfortable.

I tried to explain. "It is my brain they use to think with, Queynt. Otherwise they are as when they were made. I have been under the mountain of the magicians. I have seen how they are made. Have you?"

"Oh, yes, Gamesman," he affirmed, no longer joking or voluble. "I have been beneath the mountain. I went there last some decades ago to search for Barish."

We waited. He seemed to debate with himself whether we should be enlightened or not. At last it was Jinian again who spoke, as she had to me. "Queynt, we've trusted you. You've hinted to us and hinted to us a hundred times asking if we know what you hope we know. Now is time to set all mystery aside. There may have been reasons to stay hidden, but they are in the past. Now we must trust one another."

"Barish and I," he said, "were brothers."

He stood to walk to the side of the abyss, stood there peering northward as he talked, seeming not to like the sight of our faces. "We came to this world together. You know that story. If you do not, it is not important now. . . .

"Well, let it be said. We came, Barish and I, and a host of others. We came to serve a lie. There were wives who were loved and children who were loved and a world approaching war with another world which neither would win—well. Some powerful persons of that world sought to send certain loved ones away to safety. They needed an excuse. A fiction. A lie . . .

"There was a woman, a girl. Didir. Some thought she could read minds. Others thought not. The people of her home place were afraid of her, true, naming her Demon and Devil. The powerful men of the place said they would send researchers away to another place to find out about this strange Talent she had. 'In later time it may prove useful. However, the research may be long, so it will be necessary to send support staff and agriculturists and bio-engineers and technologists and so on and so on.' Their wives were the agriculturists and their children the bio-engineers. Among them were a few, a very few, who really knew something about such matters."

"You," said Jinian. "And Barish."

"I," he admitted, "and Barish. And a few others, though most of the so called scientists were second rate academics caught in a strange web of vanity and ambition. They stayed under the mountain, caught up in their dreams of research—research on 'monsters.' When we would not let them have Didir, they created monsters of their own. And we, the rest of us, came out from the mountain into this new, supposedly uninhabited world. . . ."

"Supposedly," prompted Jinian.

"Well, supposedly. There were living things here. There were intelligent creatures here. There was material the bio-engineers could use, mixes, crosses, deliberate and inadvertent. Children began to be born with many Talents. The Talent of Didir proved to be real. Barish said it was simply evolution, a natural evolution of the race. I said no, it was this world, this place."

He was silent for so long after that that Jinian had to prompt him again. The rest of us were silent, afraid if we spoke we might stop him, interrupt his disclosure and never learn what he would tell us.

"Well, the poor fools stayed under the mountain. The Talents began to be born, and to grow, and feed on one another. Some were good people. Others were truly monsters.

Barish was always an activist. He decided to intervene, to make plans. . . .

"He stole one of the transport machines, disassembled it, brought it here to the wastes. Then he sought out the best of the emerging Talents, seduced them with hope and high promises, and brought them here. There were twelve with Barish, the Council. They made plans. They would accumulate those among the Gamesmen who had notions of justice, accumulate them like seed grain, and when the time came, they would plant that crop for a mighty harvest."

He returned to us by the fire, shivering, though the night was not yet that cold. "It was not enough to plan a great future if one might not be alive to see it. So he asked me to work with him to develop a strain of people who would be immune to the Talents of Gamesmen and immutable through time. Well, we had longevity drugs and maintenance machines as well as the transport machines themselves. It gave us centuries to work. When there were enough of the Immutables, Barish made a contract with them. They were to find the good seed among the Gamesmen and communicate those names to those under the mountain. Those under the mountain would have them picked up, blued, and stored in the ice caverns. He got their agreement very simply, by playing on their fears. He told the 'magicians' that those identified were a danger to them, a danger to be removed but preserved as a later source of power. They believed Barish. Everyone believed Barish.

"And so, the Immutables became the 'Council.' Up until the death of Riddle's grandfather, some eighty years ago. The chain was broken then. We may never know why."

"And Barish himself," prompted Jinian as I was about to do so.

"And Barish himself lay down beside the eleven others he had brought up here to Barish's Keep. Once every hundred years the Immutables were to come and wake him, bringing with them some brain-dead body which he might occupy in order that his own not age, for he wished to save his lifespan for the great utopian time which was to come. And once every hundred years I met him in Leamer, he in one guise or another, I always as Queynt, to talk of this world and its future.

Once a century we would argue about the methods he had chosen, I urging him to waken his stored multitudes and learn from those who had been here before he came; he saying that there were not yet enough, to give him just another hundred years. . . ."

"Until?" I asked, knowing the story was almost at an end.

"Until some eighty years ago I came to Leamer to meet him only to find it in ruins. No Barish. Until I came up here to find his Keep, where I had been only once before, to find tumbled stone and Wind's Bones, abysses and fallen mountains. I went to Dindindaroo to ask Riddle—the current Riddle of that time—where Barish was. Dindindaroo was in ruins, Riddle dead, the new Riddle ignorant of the very name of Barish.

"I grieved. I went against my judgment and kept up his work. I became the new Council as Riddle had been before me. I sent my hundreds into the icy caverns. I waited for Barish. He did not return. And then, at last, a year ago the mountain of magicians went up in fire and I knew Barish would not come again of himself.

"He lies upon this mountain, or he is gone. I seek him. You seek him. And we must find him because where he lies is the only machine which can restore Barish's multitude to life once more. If this thing is not done, he will have lived and died to no purpose, and I will have been party to a very grave miscalculation. . . ."

I believed him. We all did. There was no fantastic pretense in him now, no egregious eccentricism. He was only one, like us, driven by old loyalties and a sense of what could be good and right. If Windlow had been there, he would have taken the man by the hand and reassured him, so I did it, wordlessly, hoping he would understand. It seems he did, for he said, "Your purpose is like mine. If you have been guided here by songs, by Seers, by a giant form striding to the north, well—if there is anything of Barish remaining, he will be trying to reach me."

"As Thandbar tries to reach his kindred," I said. "His is the only Gamesman I have never touched. His was my own Talent, so I never called upon him."

"I never knew that any living thing or any known device

could reach what lies preserved within the blues," said Queynt. "Though some once said that travelers between the stars sometimes wakened with a memory of dreams. Who knows? I don't. I know very little."

"Do you know how you have lived this thousand years?" asked Jinian. "While I am much inclined to trust you, Vitior Queynt, this is one thing about you I find unbelievable."

"I have lived this long by learning," he said, "from shadowpeople and gnarlibars and krylobos and eestnies. You have not seen eestnies, but they were here before we came and would teach you, too, if you asked. Barish had not the patience for it, so he said. Then, too, he kept thinking I would die. He will be offended I have not."

Well, we had enough to chew on for one night. King Kelver went back along our trail to appear as a Mirrorman. He retrieved the cap at the same time, and my help was not needed. It seemed that the Elator or the Mirrorman suspected nothing.

When morning came, Queynt suggested that Jinian and I take Yittleby and Yattleby and continue the search across the chasm. "The birds can leap the abyss," he said. "If the rest of us stay here or spend some time seeking a trail, it will delay those behind us a bit more. Perhaps we will spend a day or two searching off in different directions while you and Jinian go in the direction we believe correct." It seemed as good an idea as any other, so I Dragoned across, carrying Jinian, then showed myself high in the air to let the followers know that the abyss had been crossed by Dragon. The others were scattered among the rocks, seeming to seek a way through the maze. From my height, I could see several, and I knew they could follow us whenever they felt it wise to do so. Delay, obfuscation, Game and more Game. I was as weary of it as possible to be.

Yittleby and Yattleby had leaped the chasm, galloping to the very edge to launch themselves up and out with ecstatic cries, long legs extended before them, for all the world like boys vying with one another in the long jump. They were saddled, which surprised me, and they knelt at our approach to let us mount. Then it was only necessary to hang on while they lurched upright and began their matched, unvarying stride toward the north. They would bear no bit or bridle. One or two attempts to guide them taught me merely to point in the direction I wanted to go.

Late in the day I saw a fallen stone with a waysign painted upon it. By matching the stone to its broken pedestal, I could see which way the arrow had originally pointed, and I indicated that direction to Yittleby. She ignored me. I tapped her on the neck, sat back in startlement as the huge beak swung around to face me. "Krerk," she said, stamping one taloned foot. "Krerk."

At that moment I heard a harsh, rumbling roar as of a great rockslide. As it went on, rumbling and roaring, I realized it was not the sound of stone. "Gnarlibar?" I whispered.

"Krerk," both birds agreed, turning away from the line I had indicated. When the sound changed in intensity, the birds again changed direction, ascending a pile of rough stones. Halfway up they knelt and shook us off, gesturing with their beaks in an unmistakable communication. "Go on and see," they were saying. "Take a good look." They crouched where they were as we crawled to the top of the pile.

Below us was a kind of natural amphitheatre, broken at each compass point by a road entering the flat. Assembled on the slopes of the place were some hundreds of the shadow-people, their chatter and bell sounds almost inaudible beneath the ceaseless roaring. In the center of the place a single, gigantic krylobos danced, one twice the height of Yittleby or Yattleby, feet kicking high, feather topknot flying, wing-arms extended in a fever of wild leaping and finger snapping. The roaring grew even louder, and through the four road entrances of the place came four beasts.

Jinian clutched at me. My only thought was that this was what Chance had wanted me to Shift to and he had been quite mad. They were like badgers, low, short-legged, very wide. They were furry, had no tails, had a wide head split from side to side by a mouth so enormous either Yittleby or Yattleby would have fit within it as one bite. They came *leat*, that is to say, from the four directions at once, each uttering that mountain-shattering roar. The giant krylobos went on dancing. Queynt's two birds came to crouch beside us, conversing in low krerks of approval, whether at the dance, the dancer, or the attack, I could not tell.

As the gnarlibars reached the center, the krylobos leapt upward, high, wing-fingers snapping, long legs drawn up tight to his body, neck whipping in a circular motion. Yittleby said to Yattleby, "Kerawh," in a tone indicating approval. "Whit kerch," Yattleby agreed, settling himself more comfortably.

The gnarlibars whirled, spinning outward, each counterclockwise, in an incredible dance as uniform in motion as though they had been four bodies with one mind. The krylobos dropped into the circle they had left among them, spun, cried a long, complicated call, and then launched upward once more as the four completed their turn and collided at the center in a whirling frenzy of fur.

"Krylobos, bos, bos," cried the shadowmen over an ecstasy of flute and bell sounds. "Gnarlibar, bar, bar," called another faction, cheering the beasts as they spun once more and retreated. In the center the enormous bird continued his dance, her dance, wing-fingers snapping like whip cracks, taloned feet spinning and turning. "Bos, bos, bos," said Yittleby, conversationally. I had raised up to get a better view, and she brought her beak down sharply upon my head. "Whit kerch," she instructed. I understood. I was to keep low.

The circus went on. I did not understand the rules, but it was evidently a very fine contest of its kind. When the gnarlibars withdrew after an hour or so, roaring still in a way to shake the stones, Yittleby and Yattleby rose to lead us down into the amphitheatre. Almost at once I heard familiar voices crying, "Peter, eater, ter, ter," and my legs were seized in a tight embrace. Flute sound trilled, there was much shrieking and singing in which I caught a few familiar words of the shadow language. One small figure pounded itself proudly upon its chest and said, "Proom. Proom." I remembered him and introduced Jinian with much ceremony. She was immediately surrounded by her own coterie all crying "Jinian, ian, an an," to her evident discomfort.

"What is it?" she asked. "What's going on?"

"It looks rather like a festival," I suggested. "I was told once that the shadowpeople are fond of such things. Some here have traveled a long way from the place I met them."

I felt a hard tug at one leg and looked down into another familiar little face, fangs glistening in the light. They had never come out into the light when I had traveled with them before. Was it that they felt safe among the krylobos and the gnarlibars? Or that a time of festival was somehow different for them? Whatever the answer, my wide eared friend was busy communicating in the way he knew, acting it out. He was going walky, walky, pointing to the north, patting me and pointing. I nodded, turned, walky walked myself toward the north, going nowhere. He opened his hands, so human a gesture that Jinian laughed. "What for?" he was saying. "Why?"

Inspiration struck me. I held out a hand, "Wait," then peered into the south, hand over eyes. The shadowpeople turned, peered with me. At first there was nothing as the sun dropped lower. Then, just as I was beginning to think it would not come, there was the giant striding upon the wind toward us once more. I pointed, cried out. Jinian pointed, exclaimed. All the shadowpeople chattered and jumped up and down.

"Andibar, bar, bar," they chanted. "Andibar!"

Jinian and I were astonished. "The sound is so very close," she said. "They mean Thandbar!"

"Andibar," they agreed, nodding their heads. We waited while the giant approached, dissolved into wind and mist around us, then went on to the north. I cried out to the shadowpeople, pointed, made walky, walky. Aha, they cried, louder than words. Aha. They were around me, pushing, running off to the north and returning, indicating by every action that they knew the way well. We went among them, propelled by their eagerness.

Ahead of us we could see the giant twist and change, flowing onto the stony mountain like smoke sucked into a chimney. Yittleby and Yattleby followed us, conversing. We half ran, half walked among the mazes of stone and Wind's Bone to come, starlit at last, to a pocket of darkness into which the shadowpeople poured like water. Jinian and I dropped onto the stone, panting. We could not see well enough to follow them.

They returned, calling my name and Jinian's, querulously demanding why we did not come. Yittleby said something to them, and they darted away to return in moments with branches of dried thorn. One burrowed into my pocket to find the firestarter, emerging triumphantly in a bright shower of sparks. Then we had fire, and from the fire torches, and from the torches light to take us down into the earth.

We needed the fire for only a little time. The clambering among tumbled stone was for only a short distance before we emerged into corridors as smooth as those I had seen beneath the mountains of the magicians. There was light there, cool, green light, and a way which wound deep into a constant flow of clean, dry air. At the end of the way was an open door. . . .

11

The Gamesmen of Barish

The shadowpeople opened the door wider as we approached it. The place was not new to them, and I had a moment's horrible suspicion that we might find only ruin and bones within. Such was not the case.

The pawns have places called variously temples or churches in which there are images of Didir or Tamor or of other beings from an earlier time than ours. I had been in one or two of these places on my travels, and they were alike in having a solemn atmosphere, a kind of dusty reverence, and a smell of smoky sweetness lingering upon the air. This place was very like that. There were low pedestals within, clean and polished by the flowing air, on each of which one of my Gamesmen lay.

The shadowpeople had surrounded one pedestal and waited there, beckoning, calling "Andibar, bar, bar," in their high, sweet voices. When Jinian and I came near, they sat down in rows around the recumbent figure and began to sing. The words were in their own language, but the music. . . .

"The wind song," whispered Jinian. "The same melody."

Though the singer in Xammer had played it upon a harp and these little people upon flutes and bells, the song was the same. I knew then where the frail singer in Leamer had heard

it first. How she had translated it into our language, I might
never know. They sang it through several times, with different
words each time, and I had no doubt what they sang and what
I had heard differed very little in meaning. When they finished, one very tiny one leaned forward to chew on Thandbar's toe, was plucked up and spanked by another to the
accompaniment of scolding words. It did not seem to have
damaged Thandbar. He was fully dressed, helm lying beside
him, fur cloak drawn about him under a light coverlet. Jinian
laid her hand upon him and shivered. "Cold." I already knew
that. Except for the ceremonial setting, the careful dignity of
his clothing, his body was as cold and hard as those in the ice
caverns. And yet, something had left this body to pour into
the evening sky, to wander the world and beg his kinsmen for
release from this silent cold.

I walked among the others. Tamor and Didir, looking
exactly as I had known them; Dorn, piercing eyes closed in
endless slumber; stocky Wafnor, half turned on his side as
though his great energy had moved him even in that chill
sleep. Hafnor bore a mocking smile as though he dreamed;
and Trandilar dreamed, likewise, older than I would have expected, but no less lovely for that. Could she Beguile me, even
through this sleep?

Shattnir lay rigid, hands at her sides, crown in place, as
though she had decided to be her own monument. Dealpas
was huddled under her blanket, legs and arms twisted into
positions of fret and anxiety. Buinel's mouth was half open.
The machine had caught him in mid-word. And, finally,
Sorah, the light gauze of her mask hiding her face. I drew it
aside to see her there, calm, kindly looking, eyes sunken as
though in some inward gaze.

And lastly . . .

Lastly. I gasped, understanding for the first time the implications of what Queynt had told me. "Barish," I said. He
lay before me, wrapped in a Wizard's robe embroidered with
all the signs and portents, two little lines between his eyes to
show his concentration even in this place.

"Barish," Jinian agreed. "He has a good face."

He did have a good face, rather long and bony, with dark

bushy brows and a knobby nose over wide, petulant lips.

"I did not expect to find him here," I said.

"Only his body," she replied. "Queynt said he was awakened into different bodies each time."

"Perhaps he wasn't awakened. Perhaps the blue is here, somewhere."

"If it had been," she said soberly, "Riddle's grandfather would have taken it to Dindindaroo with all the rest."

Still, we looked. There were cabinets on the walls, doors leading into other rooms. We found books, machines. In a room we identified as Barish's own there was a glass case which still showed the imprint of a Gameboard which was not there. I fit the Onomasticon into a gap in a bookshelf. This was the place from which Riddle's grandfather had removed the treasures he had sworn to preserve.

We returned to the outer room. The machine was there, behind a low partition, a tiny light blinking slowly upon its control panel.

"There is still power here," I said.

Then I said nothing for a while.

Then, "Let us go out of here. I have to think."

She gave me a long, level look, but did not say anything until we had climbed upward through the tumble to the open air. The little people came with us, chattering among themselves. When we took food from the saddlebags, they clustered around, and I realized there were more of them than we could feed. "I must go hunting," I said. "They will be happy to stay here. Their word for fire is 'thruf.' If you can keep one going, with their help, I'll bring back some kind of meat."

Then she did try to say something to me, but I did not wait to hear. Instead, I Shifted into fustigar shape and loped off into the stones. I did not want to think, and it is perfectly possible not to think at all, if one Shifts. I did not think, merely hunted. There were large, ground-running birds abroad in the night, perhaps some smaller kin of the great krylobos. They were swift, but not swift enough. I caught several of them, snapping their necks with swift, upward tosses of my fustigar head. What was it brought me up, out of mere fustigar to something else?

Perhaps it was the awareness of my bones, the long link bones between my rear legs and forelegs, the shorter link bone between the rear legs, the flat rear space where a tail might have been but was not, the curved link bones between shoulders and head, the arching, flexible ribs which domed this structure and anchored all its muscles. . . .

The starshaped skeleton of this world. Unlike the back-boned structure of our world, whatever world it might have been. This world, into which we came, uninvited, surely, to spread ruin and wreck. And yet into which we were welcomed. The shadowpeople waited beside the fire with Jinian for the feast their friend would bring them. They would call Peter, eater, ter, ter into the darkness, play their silver flutes, ring their bells, sniff the bones twice when they had done, and sleep beneath the stones. And they might gnaw a bit on Thandbar and be spanked for it.

And in Hell's Maw they were meat for Huld. So had said the Elator, laughing, as he ate other meat at his campfire.

Some acid burned in my fustigar throat, some pain afflicted my fustigar heart. Ah, well, I could not leave them behind me to flee into a darkness forever.

The animal turned itself about and ran back the way it had come, to stand upon its hind legs and Shift once more. Into Peter once more. Into the same confusion I had left.

They welcomed me with cries of pleasure, assisted in cleaning the birds and spitting them over the fire while others foraged for more thorn and devil's spear. We ate together, bird juice greasing our chins and hands, and sang together in the echoing dark. I saw Jinian's eyes upon me but ignored her as if I did not understand. Tomorrow was time enough for decision.

"I sent Yattleby with a message for Queynt," she said.

"Ah," I replied. "A message for Queynt."

"Written," she said. "I gave it to Yattleby, pointed back the way we had come and said 'Queynt.' He seemed to understand."

"I'm sure he did," I said, fighting down anger. I did not need more pressure on me. Through the thin fabric of my Shifted hide I could feel the pouch I had carried for two years.

Inside it were Didir and Tamor. Mine. Shattnir. Mine. Even Dealpas. Mine. "When I give them up," I said in a carefully conversational tone, "I will be powerless to confront Huld. If I had not had them, you would have been meat for groles instead of sitting here beside me, eating roast bird."

"When you saved us from the bones in Three Knob," she said, "it was by your own Talent. If you had not had Sorah to call upon outside Leamer, you would have found another way. You need nothing but yourself, Peter."

"I *do*," I shouted at her, making wild echoes flee from the place. "Without them, I am nothing. Nothing at all . . ."

She wiped her hands fastidiously, poured water from her flask to wash her face, turned that face to me at last, quiet, unsmiling, unfrowning, quiet. "I have told you I am a Wizard, Peter. I will give you Wizardly advice. Think on yourself, Peter. Think on Mavin, and Himaggery and Mertyn. Think on Windlow. Carefully, slowly, on each. Then think on Mandor and Huld. And when you have done, decide with whom you will stand."

Gamelords, I said to myself. Save me from the eloquence of Wizards. She sounded like Himaggery, or rather more like Windlow, though Windlow had been a Seer, not a Wizard. This abstraction called justice was all very well, but when it meant that one had to give up one's own power. . . . One considered being Huld-like.

"Jinian," I cried. "Do you know what it is you ask?"

"Of course," she said. "Wizards always know what they ask. And they ask everything."

I held out my arms and she came into them to hold me as a mother might hold a child or a Sorceress her crown. When we slept, it was thus twined together, and for a time I did not think of her being a Wizard. The shadowpeople let us sleep. They faded away in the morning light, into the deep caverns of the rock, to return at dusk, I was sure, expecting another feast, another song fest. Well. Perhaps by then we would have more guests to feed. So saying, I took Jinian by the hand and we went back into Barish's Keep.

"Which of them first, Wizard?" I asked. "Shall it be Shattnir or Dealpas? Buinel or Hafnor? I think not Buinel. He would ask us to prove our authority before raising the rest.''

"Thandbar," she said. "It is he who has searched for his kinsmen, Peter. Is it not fitting he should be raised first?"

I should have thought of it myself. We lifted the rigid body of Thandbar off the pedestal on which it rested, tugged it around the partition to the machine, and spent both our strengths in heaving it onto the metal plate which was precisely like those I had seen on similar machines under the mountain of the magicians. There was even the small, circular receptacle for the blue. I set it in place, stepped back, and thrust down the lever as I had seen Mavin do it.

Nothing happened. There was no hum, no scream, no nothing. No sound. No movement. Jinian looked at me with quick suspicion. I protested: "This is how Mavin did it! There is power here. The light is on. Perhaps it must be set in some way." She helped me wrestle Thandbar to the floor before I began a twisting, pushing, turning circumambulation of the device, moving everything movable upon it. I tried the lever again. Nothing.

I turned to her to expostulate, explain, only to meet her level regard, no longer suspicious. "This is why he never returned. Why Barish never returned."

Seeing my confusion, she drew me away to Thandbar's pedestal where we sat while she puzzled it out. "They would wake Barish every hundred years. They would bring some brain-dead but living body for him, some poor fellow brain-burned by a Demon perhaps, and would put the body in that machine with Barish's blue. Then he, Barish, in a different body each time, would go into the world to meet Queynt, assess the progress of his plan. He would return here after some years—how many? Ten perhaps? Twenty? Give up the blue again, and the attendant Immutables would take the body away to be buried.

"But the last time he was awakened, the machine malfunctioned? Yes. I think so. Something went wrong. Either during the process or right after? Yes. Otherwise his blue would be with the rest. That red light you see upon the device is probably a warning light, something to tell the operator that things are awry within. So Barish was no tech. Or if he was, he had no part or lacked some contrivance. The fact that he did

not fix it means that he could not. And whoever or whatever
Barish was, it went forth from this place knowing it would do
no good to return.''

I went back to Thandbar's body, lying on the cold floor of
the place. Such is the contrary nature of mankind, or perhaps
only of the Peters among mankind, that I now wished most
heartily to do what I had fought before against doing. Now
that it was impossible, I was determined to do it.

"Since you are so reasonable, Wizard," I said. "Reason us
a way out of this dilemma."

"I will wait for Queynt," she said. "Since he may have
some knowledge of the device. If he does not, then we will
think again."

She went up out of the place. I heard her talking to Yittleby,
who had remained behind when Yattleby went away, saying
something about patience. I took some confidence from the
impatience of the krylobos. It was better than fear. I walked
around and around the machine. Surely there was some way it
could be understood? Surely some way that a Shifter could
understand it.

In Schlaizy Noithn, I had become a film upon a wall in a
place where my very presence was a danger. I reached a tenta-
tive finger to the machine, flowed across its metal surface like
oil, a thin film, an almost invisible tentacle. This filament
poured into a crack, down through the interstices of the mechanism. Here were wires and crystals, hard linkages, soft pads,
rollers, some kind of screen which scattered light, a device for
casting a narrow beam and manipulating it. I went deeper.
This is what Dealpas had done to Izia upon the heights of
Mavin's place. Here were strangenesses which I entered and
surrounded, tasting, smelling, creating temporary likenesses
of. Where was the failure? Where the malfunction? No part of
it ached, throbbed, was fevered. Should this dark crystal be
alight? This cold wire, should it be warm? Who could tell? No
network of nerve enlightened me. I flowed deeper yet.

Who were the voices crying to me? Why did Dorn cry so
loud? Why did Didir sting me with her voice? Out? Out of
where? Of what? The mysteries which lay around me were tan-
talizing. Why come out?

Was that Jinian? Silkhands? I felt hands upon me, pulling

me, some inner person walking my veins and my nerves, hauling upon my bones. I wanted to tell them to let be, but it would take a mouth and lungs to do that. A mouth. Lungs.

Panic. So does one who is more than half drowned struggle to the surface of water, gasping for breath, unable to breathe. Someone helped me from within. Silkhands.

And I lay upon the floor of the place while Silkhands and Queynt hovered over me and screamed and cried on me.

"Fool, fool," said Silkhands. "Even Mavin would not have tried such a thing."

"Fool, fool," wept Jinian. "Oh, Peter, but you are hopeless and I love you."

I was not afraid until I knew what I had done, which was to spend the better part of two days trying to become a machine. Silkhands was worn and exhausted. She had spent the time since her arrival trying to extricate me. If there had been no other reason for her to come to the Wastes of Bleer than to save my life, I was grateful for Windlow's vision and the musician's song. It was she who had come into my inside out body and followed it down into madness, calling it out of its strange preoccupation. When I learned of her effort and my foolishness, I wept tears of weary frustration.

"I don't know what's the matter with it," I confessed.

"And nor do I, my boy," said Queynt. "I had little knowledge of maintenance. We had techs who were specially trained to do that work. It may be that the books are here, somewhere, and even the parts we may need, but I find Jinian's reasoning persuasive. If Barish could have fixed it, he would have done."

"I find it odd," said King Kelver, "that the plans of a thousand years would be allowed to go awry on the failure of one mechanism."

I could not have agreed with him more. However, I had no time for such fine philosophical points because of the news they brought. "The Elator told me last night that Huld is coming," said the King. "I am to betray your location to him when he arrives. He grew impatient and left Hell's Maw last night."

Jinian had my map upon the floor, measuring the distance

with her fingers. "Three days," she whispered. "They will be upon us within three days. Four at most!"

In a few moments I built and discarded a hundred notions. I could take Wafnor and make a mountain fall. Buinel would burn the bones as they came toward us. Hafnor would flick me to the Bright Demesne where I would repeat my call for help. Didir would Read Huld's mind. All these wild thoughts tumbled one upon another until Jinian took my hand, and I knew she had followed them almost as though she could have Read them.

"Peter. You can manage two or three of the Gamesmen of Barish at a time. If worst comes to worst, you will do it and we will all pray your success. But oh, how much better it would be if all of them fought at our side."

She was right, of course. I leaned upon her shoulder and gave a great sigh, half weakness and half weariness, thinking the whole time of roast fowl. My weakness was simple hunger, and I said so. She remedied the lack as soon as I expressed it by putting a mug of hot soup into my hand and crumbling hard bread into it. As I ate it with a tired greediness, she went on.

"There is something we are not thinking of," she said. "Something simple and obvious. The song we heard in Xammer was learned at the Minchery in Leamer from a young songsmith who dreamed it. It is the same music we heard when the giant strode across us in the hills behind Three Knob. It came from Thandbar, somehow, and Thandbar's blue is in your pocket. Somehow, Peter, the separation of body and blue is not as complete as we thought, for something sensible of Thandbar escaped, rose up from his body lying here in the cold wastes of Bleer to stride across the world crying for our help. There is a clue there we are not seeing, Peter. Help me think."

"It probably has something to do with cold," I mumbled around a mouthful of bread. "In the School Houses, we always kept the blues cold. They have not been cold in my pocket. Perhaps that has something to do with it. Perhaps it is natural for them to recombine, and the machine only aids that process. . . ."

"What does the machine do, Peter?"

"Ahh," I said, remembering chill wire and hostile casing, the infinite lattices of crystal in which I had lost myself. "It warms the body, warms the blue, scans the blue and Reads it into the mind of the body. Having seen the innards of the machine, I can do part of what the machine does. I can Read the blue, I think, with Didir's help. And Shattnir can help me warm the place. But I don't know how to Read the thing back into a body. It seems all a puzzle. . . ."

"I can Read the body," said Silkhands. "If you will link with me, as they linked in the Bright Demesne when they searched for you. As Tragamors sometimes link to increase their strength."

I shuddered, remembering that such a linkage was precisely what Mandor and Huld had demanded of me in Bannerwell—of me, or of Mavin. Still, this was to no evil purpose. It took me a while to work myself up to it, but once we were started it seemed to flow along of its own movement. It was not as simple as that sounds, and yet it was simpler than I would have expected.

First was Shattnir, gathering all the warmth she could from the sun to bring it below and warm the chamber of the Gamesmen. Then was Didir, to set her pattern firmly in my head, telling her what we intended, begging her to stay within and help me, show me the way.

Then I took the blue of Thandbar in my hand and put my arms tight around Silkhands as she laid her hands upon Thandbar's head. He came into my mind and greeted me with such joy that it burst through me in a wave, a wordless, riotous joy, the rapture of a prisoner released, a caged thing set free. "Only free," I heard him murmur in my head. "Only free." I remembered it as one of his names and knew in that instant what innate quality it was had enabled him to escape the cold room and move out across the world. His Shifter's soul could not have been held, had not been held. I had no time to think of it, for with Didir's pattern tight in my mind I began to Read him, spark by spark, shivering lattice by lattice, sending my warmth down the chill circuits of his being, following those circuits as Silkhands Read them from me and impressed them once again into the body before her.

Time went, seeming hours of it, days of it. Pictures fled through my head. I saw Schlaizy Noithn, bright in the noon light, where Thandbar walked with a loved one. I saw far mountains as seen from above by the eyes of a mist giant. I heard music, not only the wind song I had heard before but generations of bell and flute in the high, wild lands of the shadowpeople. I became tree, mountain, road, a whole legion of beasts I had never seen and knew nothing of. In Thandbar's day, they had lived closer to mankind. In the intervening centuries they had fled away.

I saw memories of Barish: Barish lecturing; Barish pounding a table; Barish laughing; Barish cajoling. I felt horror at the things being done by some Gamesmen, revulsion, anger, and felt Barish play upon that horror and revulsion. In Thandbar's mind, I heard Barish's voice. "We will accumulate the best, like seed grain. We will plant them in the ground of today, for a mighty harvest in the future," his voice ringing, passionate. In Thandbar's mind, I Read belief, then doubt (centuries of doubt), then terror at a conviction of eternal imprisonment. Out of that terror he had fled like mist, to walk the wide world calling for help from his kinsmen.

So the pictures fled across my mind as the blue melted away in my hand, becoming a featureless lump, a sliver, a nothing at all. The body before us stirred, stirred again, until at last its eyes opened, its mouth moved. "I dreamed you, Healer," it whispered in a voice whiskery with dust and age. "I dreamed you." The eyes blinked, blinked, tried to focus. I knew they saw only blurs of light, mute shadows. At last they fastened upon me, and the dusty voice said, "Kinsman. Thanks."

And after that was a long, cloudy time in which Silkhands lay upon the floor exhausted and I trembled in my place like a wind gong perpetually struck, and the others had to take us up, we two and Thandbar, to wrap us up warmly and feed us to the wild piping and cheers of the shadowpeople. It was night. "How long?" I whispered to Queynt.

"You were both exhausted when you began," he said. "You must not try any more tonight. Silkhands could not, in any case. On the morrow, raise up Dealpas. She must help you. Then Didir, for she can do what you have done if I understand it aright." So I slept. Bones marched against us from over the edge of the world, and I slept. Horror collected itself and thundered toward us with drums and trumpets, and I slept. If I had been condemned and upon the scaffold ready to be hanged, I would have slept. There was no more strength in me to stay awake, and morning came and moved itself toward noon before I wakened again to find Silkhands sitting beside me, looking a little wan but determined.

"Come," she said. "Let us waken Dealpas."

Which we did, though Barish's Healer did not wish to be wakened. She fought us the whole way, moaning and weeping, carrying on as though she were the only creature in the world ever to have felt pain. Her whining sickened us, and I was ready to give up and let her lie there forever, but Silkhands was not. I felt her do something I had never known of before: she administered a mental spanking—a lashing along the nerves like a snake striking—and we had Dealpas' attention at last. When we had her awake, she began to moan, half-heartedly, and Jinian came forward to shake her into full wakefulness.

"I have no patience with this Broken Leaf nonsense," she cried into Dealpas' pouting face. "I know not why Barish chose you as a worthy one of his Eleven, why he chose you from among all Healers, unless perhaps there were no others in your time. Well, you are not the best, by any rule, not fit to wear Silkhands' smalls, but you will do what you will do or by the Giant of Thandbar I will teach you what pain is!"

Dealpas was stung, furious, her pain forgotten. I linked with her, somewhat reluctantly, to raise Didir, and in that linkage I learned what had set Dealpas upon her course of whines and plaints. Barish had thought her pretty, had babied her, had petted her—the more she whined, the more petting. So it was I began to doubt that Barish was what I had thought him to be. Wizard, perhaps, but not all wise to have spoiled her so.

We did not work together as well as Silkhands and I had done, but Didir was helping from within to raise up her own body, so all went well and expeditiously in the end. She came up off the stone slab in one fluid movement, not at all grand-motherly, but lithe and still young. "Peter," she said to me, looking full into my eyes, "there will be a better time than now for thanks. Be sure that time will not be forgotten." She hugged me then, and kissed me as a mother might (as Mavin never had in my memory) and went off above to gather some power and settle some ancient matter between herself and Dealpas. When they returned, they were ready for work, and I did not hear Dealpas whine again.

The two of them began with Shattnir, who rose as she had slept, straight, all at once, rising as if she had lain down the night before. I saw her keen eye upon me, recognizing me, and was not surprised. There had been much more life in the blues than I had known. They had changed while with me, while within me. They had used me as I had used them, and I prayed as I saw her glance that she would consider the bargain good. Then she gave me a quick, mocking smile—nothing about Shattnir was ever wholly human—and went about her way.

Meantime Silkhands and I awakened Dorn. Having done this once before, I did not need Didir's help again but was able to Read out the blue of Dorn as though I read a familiar book. Oh, there were surprises, particularly in his youthful mem-ories; and there were terrors as he gained his Talent and learned to use it, but still, what I had known of him was the greater part of him, and he rose at last to greet me by name.

"You do know me," I mumbled.

"How should I not, Peter? Have I not walked in your head as a farmer walks his fields? Have we not raised up ghosts together?"

"I wasn't sure you would remember," I said weakly, remembering myself thinking things I had rather he not know of.

"Why shouldn't I remember a friend?" he asked me, draw-ing me into an embrace. I had never felt for Mertyn or for Himaggery what I felt in that instant for Dorn. I had never known Mertyn or Himaggery as I knew Dorn. Perhaps he had shaped some essential growing in me, as a father might shape it in a pawnish boy or a loving thalan who knew his sister's child from infancy. What he said was true. I remembered him as a friend. He had never had to do me any hurt, not even for my own good, and so there was no taint between us.

Then Dealpas and I awakened Buinel while Silkhands rested and Didir took time to learn all that was happening. I felt her searching mind go forth, seeking Huld, I thought. It was not difficult to raise up Buinel, only boring. In my whole life I was never to meet anyone so relentless in putting down any spontaneous thought or evanescent desire as was Buinel. He wanted rules for everything, and he wanted them graven in bronze or cut into stone so that he could see they were no temporary things. Well, we persevered, Dealpas and I, she with her mouth all twisted up in distaste and some anger still. When we had him fairly roused he became deeply suspicious of us for having wakened him, so we turned him over to Queynt and Dorn. If they could not settle him I cared not whether we got him settled, though I did owe him much for having saved our lives from the Ghoul. Then Silkhands and Didir returned to wake Hafnor, Wafnor, and Tamor, one after another, each time quicker. It was true, with practice the thing became much easier. Wafnor gave me a glad hug, from a distance, his sturdy body creaking as he bent and twisted, trying to free himself in a few short minutes of the stiffness of centuries. Hafnor gave me a teasing wink. If he had had more power, he would have done something silly and boyish, I knew it, but he had to go above to warm himself in the sun. There was no power below except what Shattnir brought down to us from time to time for the work.

Then Silkhands and I were alone once more, only Sorah and Trandilar upon their pedestals. And Barish. I stood there looking down at him, fingering the lone blue in my pocket. Now that I had given up the others, it seemed an evil thing to keep Windlow by me, an evil thing to keep him so imprisoned. He had no body of his own. It had been burned and destroyed in the place of the magicians. Barish had no blue. It had gone into some other body, perhaps, or been destroyed by the machine. Why not put the two together? Then Windlow might at least live again, live long, and be no worse off than he was now. The body would be strange, but surely it was better to visit a strange place than not to live at all. Silkhands and I were alone in the place. The others had all gone above to seek for Huld or plot their strategy or discuss ways in which we might leave the mountain top without condemning the rest of the world to Huld's fury.

I called her over and showed her Windlow's blue in my hand, letting my eyes rove over the body of Barish.

She did as I had done, looking back and forth from one to the other. "Why not," she said. "Let us do it now before someone comes down and makes some objection."

"He may only live a little while, to be killed in that battle which is coming," I warned her.

"He will at least die in reality then," she said bitterly, "not be lost in some rock crevasse forever, caught in neither living nor death, perhaps in that same terror Thandbar felt."

I nodded, took Windlow's blue into my hand and put my arms around her as she laid her hands upon Barish's head.

Then was maelstrom. Nothing which had gone before had prepared me for it. There was Windlow, surging in my mind like a flood, like a mighty stream pouring over a precipice. There was something else, surging to meet it as the tide meets the outflow of a river, battering waves which meet in foam-flecked flood to crash upon one another, flow around one another, mix together in an inextricable rush and tug and wash. Cities toppled in my head; rivers burst mighty barricades; millennia-old trees fell and splintered. Faces passed as in an endless parade. The sun made a single glittering arc across the sky, flickering between darkness and light as day and night sped past. Then the struggle eased, slowly, and I felt things rise in the flood to heave above the waves, to rock and stabilize themselves upon the flow like boats until all within was liquid and quiet above the steady roll of whatever lay below. Windlow's blue was gone. Silkhands leaned back within the circle of my arms, exhausted. I heard someone come into the room behind us, recognized Queynt's step but was too strained to turn to him as he gasped.

The figure before me on the pedestal opened its eyes. Someone behind those eyes smiled into my face and said, "Peter?"

Then that same someone—or another—looked across my shoulder and spoke to Queynt. "Vulpas?" I felt myself thrust aside as Vitior Vulpas Queynt moved to his brother's side.

His brother.

My friend.

Windlow.

Barish.

The same.

12

The Bonedancers of Huld

"You had him all the time!" Queynt advancing as though to strike me.

A voice from the pedestal, laughing weakly, not Windlow's voice. Not entirely Windlow's voice. Pattern and intonation different. Not so peaceful, not so kindly. "Oh, Vulpas. He didn't know he had me. Poor lad. And he didn't have much of me, at that, or all of me, depending upon how you look at it. He didn't know; Windlow didn't know."

So that Queynt turned again to that voice which seemed more familiar to him than it did to me. "Windlow?"

A long silence. I looked at the body on the pedestal, close wrapped in its Wizardly robes. It had not moved yet, seemed uncertain whether it could. One hand made a little abortive gesture; a foot twitched. The eyes were puzzled, then clearing, then puzzled once more. When he spoke it was tentatively, slowly, as though he had to consider each word and was even then not certain of it.

"The body they brought for me, Vulpas. The bodies were always supposed to be brain-burned. Plenty of those around. Every Game always left them littered about, weeping women, mothers crying, pathetic bodies, able to walk, breathe, eat—

nothing else. They were supposed to bring one like that. So
they did; body of a Seer named Windlow. Only it wasn't
brain-dead—maybe half, maybe only stunned, sent deep. . . .

"The machine. It had been acting strangely. Meant to go to
the base and get some tech to come back with me and fix it. I
didn't go. Why? Forget why. The time before, the last time
I was in this body—the machine didn't separate me. Not all
of me. Most of me was still here, in the body, cold. I
dreamed. . . .

"Dreamed I saw Thandbar go out of this place like a wind,
like a mist, singing. Dreamed little people came in here, singing. Wanted to say 'Help,' wanted to ask them to find Vulpas,
find Riddle. Imprisoned. No movement. No voice . . ."

"Who was it then, who went out of here?" demanded
Queynt. "Who was it Riddle put the blue into? That last time.
When you were supposed to meet me?"

The figure on the slab moved, a supine shrug, a testing of
long unused muscles. "Windlow, mostly. Partly me. The machine broke that time, once for all, finally. Screamed like a
wounded pombi, like a fustigar in heat, screamed and shrieked
and grated itself silent. The light went on. I saw it when I
departed, and Riddle said something about not bothering to
come back, there was nothing anyone could do. . . ."

"But if you knew all that," I said stupidly, "then why
didn't you tell me, Windlow? Why all the mystery? The hiding
and hunting and not seeming to know everything there was to
know about the Gamesmen and the book? Why all that?"

"Ah, lad." Whoever it was began to sit up, struggling more
than any of the others had had to do, achingly. I moved forward to help him, and he patted me on the arm in a familiar
way. "I didn't remember. *Windlow* didn't remember. It was
all so dreamlike, so strange. How would Windlow tell the difference, Vision or reality? And it was then that the moonlet
fell, the world shook and tumbled and fell apart. Then it was
run and run and try to stay alive, partly Windlow, partly
Barish, the memories all mixed and tumbled with the world,
all the people and all the landscape. I forgot Vulpas, forgot
the Gamesmen almost, forgot the book almost. Then later
some memories came back. Were they memories? Visions of a

Seer? How would Windlow-Barish know? And then the memories began to tease, began to make mysteries. Then Windlow-Barish began to search for the book, search for the Gamesmen, remember odd things. Did he ever come back here? Why would he? If he did, the way was lost I suppose. . . .''

"What do you mean, did he?" I shrieked at him. "If Windlow is in you at all, he knows whether he did or not! *Think* him. *Ask* him." I was grieving. I had not meant to trade Windlow, whom I loved, for this stranger.

There was long silence from the pedestal, then the rustle of his cloak, the harsh scratch of the embroideries rubbing upon one another. His voice, when it came, was more as I remembered it. "Right, my boy. Of course. I did not come here. I did not remember this place. I did remember the book, the Gamesmen, but did not remember why they were important. Well, why would Windlow remember any such thing?"

I turned to him desperately. "Are you in there, Windlow? Have I killed you?"

He laughed, almost as Windlow would have done. "No, Peter. No. See. All of Windlow is here when I reach for him. I remember the garden of Windlow's House, the meadow you chased the fire bugs through. I remember the tower in which Prionde had us imprisoned, the way we escaped by creeping through the sewer. . . ."

"You did not creep," I said. "We carried you."

"You carried me. Yes. And I came to Himaggery's place, to the Bright Demesne. It's all there, my boy, all the memories of Windlow's life. They may not be exactly as they were in Windlow's head before, but they are there."

I felt as though someone had told me I was not quite guilty of some grave crime. The face was not Windlow's face, the body not Windlow's body, but in those memories Windlow still lived. Except—he lived alloyed with another. Silver melted with tin is still silver, and yet it appears in a new guise. One cannot call pewter silver with honesty, and yet all the silver one started with is contained therein. Unless, I thought, the mix was rather more like oil and wine, in which case the oil would rise to the top and the wine lie below, seething to be so covered. Was he silver, Windlow, or oil? Or was he wine? Did it matter, so long as he lived? For a time.

For it would be only for a time. Until what he knew and thought became no longer relevant or necessary and was forgotten. But that was the same with all of us. We were only what we were for a time, at that time. Then our own silver began to mix with the tin of our future to change us. I knew this to be so and grieved for Windlow while I grieved for me. In time I would not be this Peter, even as now I was not the Peter of two years ago who had grieved for Tossa on the road to the Bright Demesne. Yet that Peter was not lost. So Windlow was not lost, and yet he was not Windlow, either.

Silkhands took me by the hand and led me away, shaking her head and murmuring to herself and me. She had loved him, too, perhaps more than I had done, and I wondered if she felt as oddly torn as I did. We did not speak of it just then. Instead, we sat beside the fire, drinking tea and looking into the flames as though to see our futures there, my head feeling like a vacant hall, all echoing space and dust in the corners. We heard Queynt and Barish-Windlow come up out of the place, so we went below to raise up Trandilar and Sorah. If what was to come was wreck and ruin upon us all I did not want them lying helpless under the stones.

There was some milling about when they were all raised up, with much talk, before Hafnor flicked himself away to the north, hoptoad, to see what moved against us. Night was coming, the second night since we had raised up Thandbar. I had spent two days and a night below, and the morrow would be the third day since Huld's host had left Hell's Maw. I warmed my hands at the fire while hoping Himaggery and Mavin would reach us before Huld did, even though I feared it unlikely. There was nothing much we could do in the dark. I told Thandbar of my meeting with the Bonedancer outside Three Knob, and he chuckled without humor. "Grole, eh? Well, I've done that, or something like. It'll take time to grow big, though, so I'll go back among those rocks when we have eaten. I relish the taste of these birds more than the flavor of stone." He had been hunting, as I had done a few days before, in the guise of a fustigar.

So we sat eating and warming ourselves, thinking small thoughts of old comforts and joys. I kept remembering the kitchens in Mertyn's House and the warm pools at the Bright Desmesne. In the hot seasons, one does not often remember how delicious it is to be warm, but beside this fire in the high, windswept wastes, I thought of warm things. Jinian sat down beside me to take my cold hand in her own and rub it into liveliness. I used it to stroke her cheek, feeling I had not seen her for days. Across the fire, Kelver did something similar with Silkhands and smiled across the coals at me in shared sympathy. Queynt was talking to the krylobos, freeing them from their harness so that they could leave us. They stalked away over the wasteland, into the darkness, making a harsh, bugling cry. "They do not like those who feed upon the shadowpeople," Queynt said. "They will bring some help for us from among the krylobos and gnarlibars. I do not expect it will amount to much, but they will feel better for its having been tried. I wish there were some of the eesty here, though they would probably refuse to interfere. . . ."

Dorn talked of laying bones down again which another had raised, telling stories of the long past and the far away. Some, I am sure, were not meant to be believed, but only to cheer us. Some were funny enough to laugh at, despite the plight we found ourselves in. Then Trandilar took up the storytelling, stories of glamour and romance and undying love, turning the fullness of her Beguilement on us so that we forgot the bones of Hell's Maw, forgot Huld, forgot the cold and the high wastes to live for a time in such lands and cities as we had never dreamed of. And all this time Sorah and Wafnor passed the food among us, saving nothing for the morrow, thinking, I suppose, that we would be too busy to eat then and glad of anything we had eaten tonight. So it was we were all replete, and so Beguiled by Trandilar that danger had vanished from our minds, and we were calm and still as a day in summer, lying close together in our blankets, to drift into sleep. I think Trandilar probably walked among us all night long, softly speaking words which led us into pleasant dreams, for when we woke in the morning, it was with a sense of happy fulfillment and courage for the day. Now it was Barish passed the cups among us, but I saw him gathering the herbs he put into them from the rock crevasses, and the way he searched them out and bent above them, the way he crushed them and brought them to his nose, all that was Windlow. The brew was hot and bitter, but it brought alertness of an almost supernatural kind. We had just finished it when Hafnor returned to tell us our fears were less than the truth.

"This Demon Huld, whom you have made so effectively your enemy, must have been recruiting Necromantic Talents for a generation or more. He has Sorcerers as well, aplenty, and such a host of bones and liches as the world may collapse under. They stretch from horizon to horizon, across the neck of the wastes from the gorge of the Graywater to the valley of the Reave."

"What of the Gamesmen within that host of bones?" asked Jinian. "Talents which are useless against bones may be used against the Gamesmen."

"If one can get at them through the host of bones," replied Hafnor. "You will have to see it for yourself. The Gamesmen are within the bones as a zeller stands in the midst of a field of grain. You cannot get to them without scything what stands in between."

"I have found chasms full of brush," offered Buinel. He was not quite so odd in person as I had pictured him, still fussy and inclined to procedural questions, but he seemed to have grasped the danger we faced and be trying to make sensible suggestions. "When the bones cross them, they will cross a river of fire."

"And I will seek out Huld among the hosts of bones," said Tamor. "He comes from the north, which means I can come at him from out of the sun. If my hands have not utterly lost their cunning in these long centuries." He bent his bow experimentally, heard the string snap, and bit back a curse. "Well, I have others. Lords, what a time and place to awaken to." A little later I saw him go out with his bow strung.

Didir had spent some time with Barish. I saw her holding his hand, leaning her head against his, face puzzled and remote. She had loved him, I had heard. Now he was no longer the Barish she had known. I pitied her; Windlow was her stranger

as Barish was mine. Neither of us quite knew our old compan-
ions. She stood up beside him at last, laid her cheek against
his, then moved away. "I will do what I can to let you know
what is in Huld's mind," she said. "Though it is probable that
we know exactly what is in his mind now. He will overrun us in
order to demonstrate his strength to those allied with him. He
says he seeks Barish, but that is probably only pretense. He
seeks to overrun the world, and this will be his first trial." She
moved off to some high place, striding with great dignity but,
I thought, a little sadness. Barish looked after her, the expression on his face one of remote sorrow. I turned from them
both, for it hurt to see them.

Trandilar announced her intention of going down into the
cavern, with Sorah and Dealpas, and staying there until
needed or wanted by someone. "We will be out of the way,"
she said. "You need no Beguilement. If Visions will help, we
will bring them to you. If a Healer is wanted, call down to
Dealpas."

Hafnor had gone back to spying on the host. Wafnor had
placed himself near a pile of great boulders. Shattnir was
standing in the sun, arms wide, soaking up all the power she
could to help us all. This left me, Peter, among the Wizards
—Barish, Vulpas, Jinian. King Kelver stayed with them also,
but I thought I would emulate Thandbar and become a grole
once again.

I had barely time to engrole myself and gain size before I
felt the tickle in my head which said Huld was seeking his
prey. Long and long I had leaned upon Didir's protection in
such cases, and strangely enough it did not forsake me. I
remembered the pattern of her cover and dipped beneath it as I
went on chewing at the stone. He could not find me. With
Didir on watch, I thought it unlikely he could find any of us.

I had set myself in a high notch between the flat plateau he
marched across and the tumbled stone we were hidden in.
Stone lay above me as well as below and to either side. I made
eyes for myself for, though groles were blind, I chose not to
be. I needed to watch for Himaggery. I needed to see Huld's
approach. It was not far to see, not far at all, for he came
upon us like a monstrous wave, a creeping rot, a fungus upon

that land, white and rotten gray with the brilliance of banners like blood in the midst of it. I could not see individual skeletons, only the angular mass of it, as though a heap of white straw blew toward me in a mighty wind, all joints and angles, scattered all over with white beads which were the skulls of those which marched. I could not see the Gamesmen. I only knew where they were by the shimmering of the banners, for the bones carried nothing but themselves. Within that mass somewhere were drummers, for we could all hear the brum, brum, brum which set the pace of the bones. Perhaps the Bonedancers marched near the drums, to keep their time from the far west of the great horde to the far east of it, coming in an unwavering line. Brum, brum, brum. It sent shivers through the stone I rested upon, louder and louder as they came nearer.

First into the fray was old Tamor, though he had not been so old as to warrant that name when he laid down to sleep. He was younger than Himaggery by a good bit. I saw him come toward the host out of the sun, saw his arrows darting silver, then a retreating streak as he fled away before the spears which came after him. Huld's Tragamors were alert. I did not see him again for a time, then caught a glimpse of him, glittering and high, just before another flight of spears. This time the spears arched higher, and I thought I saw him lurch and fall, but he did not come to the ground. I felt Demon tickle, then Didir's voice in my head. Evidently she knew me so well she could speak to me easily even now. "We see him, Peter. Kelver and Silkhands are working their way around to the west where he came to the ground. There are birds here who will carry them. . . ."

So. Yittleby and Yattleby had returned, their recruitment done, to help us as best they could. Well, at least Silkhands would be out of the battle. At least she and Kelver would have some time to themselves, to share what had been growing between them all this long way from Reavebridge. If Tamor were not seriously injured, perhaps all three would survive. For a time. Looking at the army marching toward us, I thought there was little hope for any survival longer than a season or two. Huld would not stop with overrunning us. As Didir said we were only an excuse to try his strength. If he had truly wanted Barish, he would have come with fewer and cleverer than he had brought. No, this was to be warning to the world, a flexing of his muscle. I hated him in that moment, hated him for all he cared nothing about—for love and honor and truth and a word he had never heard: justice.

The bones had come closer. They were approaching a great chasm now, a canyon brimmed with thorn. The bones leapt across it, light as insects, not even brushing the branches. They came in dozens and hundreds and thousands, then the Games-men behind them, Bonedancers lifted over the tearing thorn in Armiger arms.

The chasm went up in flame, all at once, a sheet of fire leagues long and tower high. I was too far away to hear the Bonedancers screaming, but I saw them fall in fiery arcs into that towering pyre. The bones kept coming, piling in and burning, falling as the thorn burned away to make room for more. They never stopped, not even for an instant, but went on scrambling across like spiders. Somewhere inside my great grole shape Peter puzzled at what he had seen. Why had the bones kept coming when the Bonedancers died? Other Bone-dancers back in the host? Or simply one of those special cases in which things once raised went on of themselves? If that were so, then whatever we might do against the Gamesmen themselves would not help us.

"Some are gone, Buinel," I whispered to myself. "But there are more coming than all the thorn in the world can burn."

The rock beneath me throbbed; boulders began to heave themselves up from the hillside to launch away in long curves toward the center of the host. They were aimed at Huld, surely, but his Tragamors deflected them. They flew aside, bowled through acres of bones, crushing a hundred skulls or more to leave the fragments dancing, a shower of discon-nected white, like a flurry of coarse snow. The first great stone was followed by others, and the center of the host milled about, slowed for a moment. What did Huld intend? Would he merely overrun us, smother us under that weight of bones? Or were some among that host seeking us, seeking Barish, making an excuse for this Game, Great Game, the Greatest this world had ever seen?

Still they came on. We had done nothing to slow them, not with Tamor's arrows or Wafnor's great stones. I had seen no evidence that Dorn had tried to put this host down, and having seen the size of it, I did not blame him. It would have been like calming the sea with a spoonful of oil. Far to my right I saw the first files of bones entering the defile where Thandbar waited. "Good appetite, kinsman," I wished him. He was not far from me. Even as I made my wish for him, the first of the horde poured onto the flat before me, threading between the mighty Wind's Bones, the huge star-shaped skeletons of this world, bones arranged like my own grole bones. I settled myself, scrunching into the rock, mouth open.

Didir called in my head. "Peter! Sorah has Seen . . . Seen . . ."

Gamelords, I said to myself. What matter what she has Seen. They are about to overrun us, bury us, sift us out with bony fingers and take us away to the horrors of Hell's Maw. Far our on the field I saw the rush and flutter of krylobos attacking the fringes where some Gamesmen stood. Run, kick, and run away. A few bones fell, a few liches stumbled, nothing more. Big as they were, the big birds were not large enough to afflict this host.

And now a circlet of banners came toward me, Huld in the midst of his Gamesmen, Prionde at his side, borne on the shoulders of his minions, Ghouls posturing in tattered finery around him. Was that Dazzle among them? Oh, surely not. And yet, given Huld's purposes of terror, why not.

And, as I had done for two years, over and over, I reached for the Gamesmen of Barish, for comfort, for kindness, for safety, for reassurance—and found them. All. All with me in my great grole body with its star-shaped skeleton, all with me in my great this-world shape, looking out at the threatening horde where it poured like water among the Wind's Bones. . . .

Between me and the marching skeletons a leg bone loomed, half buried, stone heavy, not stone, so obviously not stone I gasped to have thought it stone so long. These were not Wind's Bones. These were not carvings done by wind and water. These were old bones, real bones, true bones, this-world bones of some ancient and incredible time. I cried to Dorn and Shattnir in my head, screamed at them to help me raise that bone up, to feed me the power to raise that bone up, screamed to Wafnor to break the soil at its base, to all of them to look, see, join, move, fight. I saw the mighty bone heave, the rock around it cracking and breaking to spatter away in dry particles. It came out of the ground like a tree, growing taller and taller, lunging upward from its hidden root, one great shape, and then another linking to it, then another and another yet, the five link bones and then the arching ribs, the neck, the monstrous skull armed with teeth as long as my legs, the whole standing ten man heights tall at the shoulder, moving toward the skeleton host who came on, unseeing, into fury.

The Wind's Bones went to war, to war, and not alone. Others sprouted from the soil of the place, a harvest so great and horrible no Seer would have believed it. They came out of the rock in their dozens and hundreds, sky tall, huge as towers, flailing, trampling down with feet like hammers of steel, the pitiful human skeletons falling before them like scythed grain to be trampled and winnowed by prodigious feet and by the wind. Particles of bone went flying on that wind, west and north, away and away in an endless, billowing, powdery cloud.

Before me the first monster had overstepped Huld to leave him behind with a few of his Gamesmen, a Bonedancer or two thrown into panic, a Ghoul, and yes—Dazzle. They looked about them wildly. I heard Huld screaming at them, threatening them for having raised up these giants. Were they to retreat? Of course. Away, away from the horrors they thought they had raised, away from the creatures who had owned this world before they came, away from this justice they had not sought, into the defile where they might find a way out, but did not.

You must believe me when I tell you that I shut the grole maw upon them and merely held them there in that rock hard prison of myself while I thought long about justice and goodness and all those things Windlow had often told me of. I

did not grind at once. I waited. I waited, and thought, and
listened to them within, for they could speak and pound upon
my walls and threaten one another still, though they did it in
the dark. I tried to remember any good thing Huld might have
done. He had played a part in Bannerwell, pretending shock
and remorse at his thalan's terrible plans and as terrible deeds,
but that had all been pretense. It had been his way of doing
what he pleased while pretending not to be responsible for it;
thus he could continue for a time in the respect and honor of
the world. His true self had been seen in the cavern beneath
the mountains of the magicians, and in Hell's Maw, for
though I had not seen him there, I had heard enough to make
me sure of him. What was he, the real Huld, the true man?

And after a time, I answered my own question.

He was not true man at all. He was only aberration, beast,
hate and hunger, without a soul. If the Midwives had delivered
him, he would not have lived past his birth. As it was, he did
not deserve to live further. So. Then the grole bore down and
gained out of him what good there was in him. In return for
the terror you brought Silkhands, and the pain you brought
me, and the horror you brought the world, I bring you peace,
Huld. So I thought.

And after a long time there, watching what it was the great
bones of this world did upon the wastes of Bleer, I gave up
bulk and went up onto the stones to find my friends. Then we
sat there together in wonder until the thing was done. Dorn
was not moving them, nor was I, nor Wafnor. They drew no
power from us. They warred because the world desired that
they do so.

I saw in them giants which could have been pombis, or
fustigars; things long and curled which might have been groles
of some ancient and mightier time. Things with great scimitar
teeth raged among the Gamesmen while the trampling of the
bones continued. It went on well into the night. Long, long
after the last of Huld's Gamesmen were dead or had fled
away, the great beasts of the heights continued their battle.
Only toward dawn did they begin to collapse and fall, to lie as
we had seen them first upon the high plateau, like wind carved
things, dead, gone these hundred thousand years. Among

them ranged the shadowpeople, singing lustily, piping upon their flutes and calling my name and Jinian's. When we went down to them, they clustered about us and begged earnestly for something roasted and juicy. Not for them any lasting awe, thus not for me. We fed them, and sang with them, and in the dawn we saw Himaggery and Mavin falling toward us out of the sky.

13

Talent Thirteen

They came, Dragon and Dragon-back, Mavin and Himaggery.
Behind them came a small host of Armigers, flown not from
the Bright Demesne but from some place north of Schooltown. One of Himaggery's Seers had told him help would be
needed long before my message reached them. I began to be a
little acid about this until Mavin hushed me.

"The Seer said we would not be needed *during* the conflict, but afterward. Indeed, look around you. Where are any
Gamesmen standing against you? There are none. Not against
one of *my* tricksy line."

She was right, of course. Somehow the battle had been not
merely turned but decisively won. Chance was jogging about
saying "Ob*lit*erated" over and over. He had observed the battle through his glass from a safe distance. "Ob*lit*erated." The
word, I thought, could be applied to a number of things with
equal pertinence. There was no time to consider it. Himaggery
had to be introduced to Barish and to the Wizard's Eleven, he
so overcome by awe and respect during this process as to lose
all his crafty volubility for the space of several hours. When
Mertyn arrived, the introductions were repeated, and again at
the arrival of Riddle and Quench.

178

I was very stiff with Riddle. He flushed bright red and almost sank to his knees begging my forgiveness. "My only thought was to learn what I could, Peter. I did not want you to know about it, as it was a matter secret to the Immutables. Quench assured me the cap was perfectly safe, that it could not harm you in any way. . . ." He fell silent beneath my glare.

Jinian, who stood beside me during all this ceremony, saved the situation. "Peter knows that you meant him no harm, Riddle. But a Pursuivant is dead in the forests near Xammer, and whether you meant Peter harm or not, the result was harm to someone."

"My fault," asserted Quench. "You must forgive Riddle, young man. I did not understand the complexity of all this Gaming. I did not realize that death often results. I was too many years in that pest hole beneath the mountains. Nothing was real there. All was ritual and repetitions and hierarchy and concern about relative positions in the order of things. Nothing was real. You must forgive him. Hold me responsible, for I am."

The end result of which was that I offered Riddle my hand, though not smilingly, and accepted his explanation for what it was worth.

"It was a year ago, Peter, that I found some old papers of my grandfather's. They told of an ancient contract, a promise of honor between our people and Barish. I had never heard of it. My father was only a child when his father died. I was only a child when my father died. So if there had been a contract, this sacred and secret indebtedness, the chain of it had been broken at Dindindaroo. The papers spoke of a certain place in the north. You recall traveling with me a year ago. I left you below Betand to go on to Kiquo and over the high bridge into these wastes. It was all futile. There was no guide, no map, nothing.

"Then, not a season gone, came this fellow Vitior Vulpas Queynt to tell me of this same contract. He was full of hints, full of words and winks and nods. And at that same time, some of our people found Quench here wandering among the mountains to the west. Well, Quench and I put our heads together, and it seemed the only way we would know anything surely was to raise up my grandfather. As I said, we meant no harm."

"So that is why you were burrowing about in Dindindaroo," I said. "You had only recently learned of this ancient agreement."

"Learned of it," rumbled Quench, "for all the good it did us. I wanted proof the Gamesman Huld was a villain. I wanted to know where Barish had gone, and what this Council business was all about. Our own history spoke of Barish, mind you, and Vulpas too. I wanted to know everything, real things, but you sent us scurrying off to the south on an idiot's quest. Well. I suppose we deserved being ill led for having led you ill. Let it be past and forgotten."

"When we returned," said Riddle, "with empty hands, we went to Himaggery as we should have done in the first place. I knew him to be honorable. We should have gone there first."

"It would have saved us much thrashing about," said Himaggery, who had come up to us in the midst of all these revelations and confessions. "We were hunting Quench all over the western reaches from Hawsport south, and we were hunting Huld everywhere but Hell's Maw. We knew it for a den of horrors, a Ghoul's nest, but we did not envision Huld as master of the place. He had seemed too proud for such dishonor."

"I believe," said Jinian, "that we will find it necessary soon to revise our notions of dishonor." She squeezed my hand and left me to ruminate upon that while the others continued their explorations into history in a mood of such profound veneration that it almost immobilized them.

Dorn was not among the group. I went off looking for him. He was with Silkhands, Tamor, and King Kelver upon a bit of high ground near Barish's Keep. Tamor had been healed of his wound, though not of the wound to his pride, for he had been the only one of us to be wounded at all. He bowed himself away after a wink at me, as did Kelver and Silkhands, hand in hand, oblivious of much else in the world. I think I sighed. Dorn gave me a sharp look which I well recognized, though I had not seen it with physical eyes before.

"You had plans concerning her?" he asked.

"No. And yes," I confessed. "Yes, some time ago. But no, not since Kelver came along."

"And Jinian came along?"

That was rather more difficult. True, she had said she loved me at some confused point during the last day or two. True, she had told me I was clever and that had proved to be marginally accurate, if the outcome of the battle was any test. True, parts of me stirred at the thought of her, at times. But . . .

"She says she is a Wizard," I said.

"Ah," said Dorn. "That is difficult."

"I think it is hard to love a Wizard," I said. "Though it is very good to make alliances with them."

"Who else knows of this Wizardry?"

"No one. I was not supposed to tell anyone, but you and Didir—well, you are part of me. It is like talking to myself. Oh, Chance knows, for he was there when she told me. But she doesn't trifle with the truth, Necromancer. If she says she is, she is."

"Oh, I have no doubt of it. I wonder if you've thought what else she is?"

"Another Talent than Wizardry! I didn't know such was possible."

He laughed. "Peter, the young are truly amazing. In each of the young, the world is reborn. No, I do not mean that Jinian has any other Talent. What she is, other than a Wizard, is a human person, female, about seventeen years old. In my experience, human persons of that age—and those considerably older also—are much alike. Most of them love, hate, weep, lust, tremble with fear. Most of them fight and forgive and resolve with high courage. May I suggest, if you are resolved upon friendship with Jinian, that it be with the person rather than with the Wizard. Likely the Wizard needs no one—not even Jinian herself. Likely Jinian needs someone during those times that the Wizard is not in residence." And he patted me very kindly as though I had been some half trained fustigar.

This so gained my attention that I wandered off for several hours and did not talk to anyone during that time.

Chance caught me when I returned. He wanted to talk

about the battle, about the great bones, the mightiness of them. "And they went on and on, long after you'd all given up raising them. So Dorn and Queynt say."

I was truly puzzled by that, but I told him it was true, so far as I knew. "The forces of the world," he said, "according to Queynt. Oh, there's things here we know nothing of, according to Queynt." He spoke proudly, not at all awed or envious, possibly the only person in all that company save Jinian who accepted Vitior Vulpas Queynt as mere man. I knew Queynt had found a follower, a companion, a true friend. Well, part of me said, I no longer need a child minder. Well, part of me said, you will miss him dreadfully if he goes off with anyone else.

So.

What may I tell you?

Of Mavin and Thandbar? She approached him warily, ready to become a worshipper if he proved to be an idol, holding reverence in readiness. When I passed them an hour later, Mavin was telling him some story about Schlaizy Noithn, and he was bent double with laughter. I sniffed. I had not thought it that amusing when it had happened to me.

Of Barish-Windlow and Himaggery, circling one another in mixed antagonism and love, Himaggery full of protest and fury at the fate of the hundred thousand in the ice caverns, Windlow equally distraught, Barish trying to fight them on two fronts, justifying his experiment on the grounds of human progress. Himaggery wondered what it was a hundred thousand master Gamesmen were to do, how they were to live when released from age old bondage; Barish overrode Windlow's concern to shout that he expected people to use their heads about it. I pitied Barish and envied him. He had too much Windlow in him to be what he had once been. But then, what he had once been had needed a lot of Windlow in it.

Later I saw him bend down to pluck the leaves from a tiny gray herb growing in a crack of the stone. He crushed the leaves beneath his nostrils and touched them to his tongue as I had seen Windlow do a thousand times. I went to him then and hugged him, looking up to see the stranger looking at me out of Barish's eyes. But it was Windlow's voice which called me by name and returned my embrace.

Of Quench and the techs, gathered around the machine in Barish's Keep, talking in an impenetrable language while some of their group scavenged among the bookshelves. "Fixable!" Quench crowed at last. "The machine can be fixed! There are spare parts in the case. We can take the thing apart and reassemble it in the caverns. . . . " So he had been set on a proper track by Himaggery and Mavin, and I was glad to have him among the people I liked and trusted. I decided to forgive him for that business with the cap. He had not meant it ill.

Of Mavin and Himaggery and Mertyn when they heard that the machine could be fixed? Of their plans to raise up the hundred thousand from their long sleep and bring them all to the purlieus of Lake Yost and the Bright Demesne? They were determined to raise them all in one place and build a better world from them.

Windlow-Barish, hearing this, was puzzled and torn once more. He started to say, "Now wait just a minute. That's not the way I had planned. . . ." But then he fell silent, and I could sense the intense inner colloquy going on. Then the argument started all over again, and this time Windlow-Barish had things to say which Himaggery listened to with respect.

Later, of Jinian and Himaggery.

"Will you have Rules?" she asked. "In your new world?"

"There will be no irrevocable rules," he said ponderously.

"How will you live?"

"We are going to try to do what Windlow would have wanted," he said. "He told us that nations of men fell into disorder, so nations of law were set up instead. He told us that nations of law then forgot justice and let the law become a Game, a Game in which the moves and the winning were more important than truth. He told us to seek justice rather than the Game. It was the laws, the rules which made Gaming. It was Gaming made injustice. We can only try something new and hope that it is better."

She left it at that. I left it at that, thankful that the thing Windlow had cared most about had a chance to survive.

Of Barish and Didir, standing close together and so engaged in conversation that they did not see me at all.

"Well, my love," he said. "And are you satisfied?"

"How satisfied? You told me to lie down for a few hundred years so that we might wake to build a new world out of time and hope and good intentions. So I wake to find others building that world, others in possession of your seed grain, others planning the harvest, another inhabiting you, my love. Perhaps I should think of something else. Have a child, perhaps. Raise goats. . . ."

"There are no goats on this world, Didir. Zeller. You can raise zeller."

"Zeller, then. I will domesticate some krylobos, become an eccentric, learn weaving."

"Will you stay with me, Didir?"

"I don't know you. This you. Perhaps I will. But then I would like to know what it is that Vulpas knows. How has he lived all this time while we slept?"

"Will you stay with *me*, Didir?"

"Perhaps."

Of Buinel and Shattnir, drinking wine in Barish's Keep.

"And my thought was, Shattnir, that he should have written it down very plainly, not in that personal shorthand of his, and have made at least a hundred copies. They could have been filed in all the temples, and certainly it was a mistake to confide in only one line of the Immutables."

"It doesn't matter now, does it?" Shattnir, cold, impersonal.

"It's not a question of it mattering. It's a question of correct *procedure*! If he'd only asked me, I could have told him. . . ."

Of Trandilar.

To me. "Well, my love, and what does your future hold of great interest and excitement?"

I blushed. "I haven't had a chance to think of it yet, Great Queen."

"Ah, Peter. Peter. Great Queen? Gracious. So formal. Do we not know one another well enough to let this formality go? Do you need to think about it, really? I should have thought your future would have raced to meet you, leapt into your heart all at once like the clutch of fate."

She was laughing at me, with me. She stroked my face, making the blush a shade deeper, and then went on.

"You do not want to be part of Himaggery's experiment, do you? There is scarce room in it for Himaggery and Barish, let alone any others. You would not live under their eyes and Mavin's? No. I thought not." She beckoned over my shoulder to someone, and then rose to hold out a hand to Sorah who sat beside us, laying her mask to one side.

"Sister," said Trandilar, "you see before you one who is quite young and confused. It would help him to know where his future lies."

Solemnly, but with a twinkle, Sorah put on the mask, smoothed it with long, delicate fingers, held out her hand in that hierarchic gesture the Seers sometimes make when they want to impress a multitude.

"I See, I See," she chanted, "jungles and cities, the lands of the eesties, the far shores of the Glistening Sea, and you, Peter, with a Wizard—a girl, yes, Jinian." Her voice was mocking only a little, kindly and laughing, and I readied myself to laugh with her. Then, suddenly, her voice deepened and began to toll like a mighty bell. "Shadowmaster. Holder of the Key. Storm Grower. The Wizard holds the book, the light, the bell. . . ." And she fell silent.

Trandilar shook her head. "Peter, learn from me. Mock Talent at your peril. It is no joke." And she helped Sorah away to find a place to lie down.

Of Peter and Jinian.

"It is probably difficult to live in close association with a Wizard," she said to me. "I believe Mavin found it so, which is why she and Himaggery have this coming and going thing between them. But then, it is not easy to know a Shifter, either."

"A Shifter is usually the same inside," I objected.

"Usually, though not always. Do we not learn from our shapes what we are? You have told me of Mandor. Did he not learn from his beauty what he became? Oh, I do not mean that there is goodness in some shapes and evil in others, but simply that we learn from them to our own good or ill. So might you change, Peter?"

"Don't Wizards change?" I wanted to ask her, desperately, what the Talent of Wizards might be, but I was too wary of the answer I might get. "Are they always the same?"

She grinned at me. "Oh, we change. I was quite content, so I thought, to become an alliance for my brother with King Kelver, until I met you, Peter."

"Kelver is better looking," I said.

"True, but then he is older. He has had a chance to grow up to his face. You may do the same, in time."

"You do not think me too young for alliancing?"

She sighed. "I think we are not too young to decide what we will do when we leave this place. Himaggery will expect you back at the Bright Demesne. I could return to Xammer. Neither of us wants to do that. I said a silly thing when I said we would do what Barish would have done. Barish will do it. Himaggery will do it. It is their plan, not mine."

I shifted from foot to foot, bit my lip, wondered what to say next. Then I thought of Sorah's words, not the bell tolling ones, but the earlier, laughing ones.

"Jinian, would you like to see the jungles and cities, the eesties, the shores of the Glistening Sea? Queynt is going there, so he says. He would let us go with him."

"Oh, Peter, I would like that more than anything."

So what is left?

Hell's Maw.

We went there, Dorn, Himaggery, Mertyn, Mavin, and a host. There were bones there wandering free, moving on their own, talking to an old, blind man who wandered among them with a key, trying to find the lock he had lost. Dorn put them to rest, large and small, in such form as they may not ever be raised again. There is nothing left of the place now. Every stone of it has been tumbled and spread by a hundred Traga-mors as far away as the Western Sea. There I linked the Gamesmen once again, realizing for the first time that I had what Himaggery called Talent Thirteen. Jinian was right. I do not need anyone but me—and a hundred or so Gamesmen with large Talents.

So you may picture us now as we ride to the very highest point of the road across the Dorbor Range, that place where he road bends down toward the jungles of the north. Queynt and Chance are upon the wagon; Yittleby and Yattleby are pulling them along with that measured, effortless stride. Jinian and I are looking back to the south where all the lands of the True Game are spread, town and demesne, land and stream, tower and field, far and veiled by distance in the light of the westering sun. There is no mist giant now to walk the edges of the world. We may walk it ourselves, in time, in chance, in hope.

Who knows?

BEST-SELLING
Science Fiction
and
Fantasy

] 47809-3	**THE LEFT HAND OF DARKNESS,** Ursula K. LeGuin	$2.95
] 16012-3	**DORSAI!,** Gordon R. Dickson	$2.75
] 80581-7	**THIEVES' WORLD,** Robert Lynn Asprin, editor	$2.95
] 11577-2	**CONAN #1,** Robert E.Howard, L. Sprague de Camp, Lin Carter	$2.50
] 49142-1	**LORD DARCY INVESTIGATES,** Randell Garrett	$2.75
] 21889-X	**EXPANDED UNIVERSE,** Robert A. Heinlein	$3.95
] 87328-6	**THE WARLOCK UNLOCKED,** Christopher Stasheff	$2.95
] 26187-6	**FUZZY SAPIENS,** H. Beam Piper	$2.75
] 05469-2	**BERSERKER,** Fred Saberhagen	$2.75
] 10253-0	**CHANGELING,** Roger Zelazny	$2.95
] 51552-5	**THE MAGIC GOES AWAY,** Larry Niven	$2.75

Available at your local bookstore or return this form to:

ACE SCIENCE FICTION
Book Mailing Service
P.O. Box 690, Rockville Centre, NY 11571

Please send me the titles checked above. I enclose _____ Include 75¢ for postage and handling if one book is ordered; 25¢ per book for two or more not to exceed $1.75. California, Illinois, New York and Tennessee residents please add sales tax.

NAME_____

ADDRESS_____

CITY_____STATE/ZIP_____

(allow six weeks for delivery)   **SF 9**

COLLECTIONS OF FANTASY AND SCIENCE FICTION